"SAY YOU LOVE ME."

Ren shook his head, not knowing what to do. "I . . . I love you, Annie." And as he spoke the words, he knew he'd said them a thousand times before. It was as if one of the thousand veils between Ren and his past had been removed. The words were warm and real and familiar. And . . . they even felt . . . true.

"Again," she whispered.

"I love you." He ached inside. For her. For himself. For what they must have had, what they'd lost.

He kissed her, then. Because he wanted to kiss her. He wanted to know just a hint of what he'd left behind. And though he wasn't supposed to feel anything. He wasn't prepared to feel anything.

He did.

Other Contemporary Romances by
Maggie Shayne
from Avon Books

FAIRYTALE
FOREVER ENCHANTED

MAGGIE SHAYNE

Annie's Hero

AVON BOOKS ⬥ NEW YORK

AVON BOOKS
A division of
The Hearst Corporation
1350 Avenue of the Americas
New York, New York 10019

Copyright © 1997 by Margaret Benson
Inside cover author photo by Karen Bergamo
Published by arrangement with the author
Visit our website at http://AvonBooks.com
Library of Congress Catalog Card Number: 97-93169
ISBN: 0-380-78747-4

First Avon Books Printing: October 1997

AVON TRADEMARK REG. U.S. PAT. OFF. AND IN OTHER COUNTRIES, MARCA REGISTRADA, HECHO EN U.S.A.

Printed in the U.S.A.

WCD   10   9   8   7   6   5   4   3   2   1

Dedicated to my very own hero, Rick,
and to his fellow Knights of the Highway,
wherever they may be

Part One

❧

The Journey Begins

The Dying of the Light

❧ Annie had no idea when she woke that morning that the world as she knew it was about to end. When Richard wrapped his arms around her in bed and kissed her until he elicited a sleepy response, when he whispered in her ear that he loved her, his stubbly face grazing her cheek, she had no idea that these moments together might be their last.

Richard rolled away and started to get up, and that was when Annie felt the first stirrings of nausea. She sat up, slid her hands over his arms, and planted her lips on the birthmark right between his shoulder blades. "You can't just kiss a girl like that and then go off to work and leave her all alone, you know."

"Have to."

He looked at her over his shoulder, and she saw the dark embers flaring in his deep blue eyes. Then he shifted his gaze to the clock on the bedside stand, and his lips thinned. "Have to," he repeated, but more firmly this time.

"Sorry, Annie. Much as I regret it, we both knew the honeymoon couldn't last forever."

"It was great while it did last, though." She kissed his neck and let him get up. Then she curled her legs under her on the bed and watched him moving, naked and glorious and wonderful, around the bedroom. He took jeans out of the dresser, giving her a perfect view of his tanned backside and reviving pleasant memories of the last two weeks. "I'm glad we spent it at Mystic Lake. Aren't you?"

"I enjoyed every minute of it." This he delivered with an over-the-shoulder glance and wiggling eyebrows. Golden blond eyebrows that perfectly matched the hair framing his face. He took the rest of his clothes with him and strolled into the bathroom.

Annie jumped out of bed, snatched her robe off the chair beside it, and followed him. "You sure about that? I know you wanted to travel."

He twisted the shower knobs and tested the water with his hands. He had terrific hands, her Richard.

"What better place to celebrate our marriage, Annie, than the place where we met? Hmm? You were right about that. I admit it."

She smiled, and when he stepped into the shower and closed the curtain, she hopped onto the counter beside the sink and waited for him. She wasn't eager to let him out of her sight just yet.

She *had* been right about Mystic Lake, though. She'd been just a little girl when her parents had learned that the parcel of state land in the hills bordering their own property, including the lake, was going to be put up for auction. They'd been determined to buy it, but couldn't swing it on their own. When they'd run into Richard's parents exploring the same property with the same intentions and the same limitations, a partnership had been born. Together they'd bought the lake and the surrounding forests.

No one wanted to see the natural beauty of Mystic Lake spoiled, but practicality had reared its ugly head. In the end, they'd compromised, putting up rental cottages along the easily accessible southern and western shores, and preserving the natural beauty of the harder-to-reach north and east shores of the lake. The only thing on that side was one gloriously rustic log cabin. And the only people to set foot there were Richard's and Annie's families.

Annie had met Richard there when they were small children. He'd teased her mercilessly because she'd been insisting she'd spotted a fairy in the woods. She sometimes thought she'd fallen in love with him right then, at the tender age of four.

Her stomachache got a little worse while she waited for him to finish his shower, and continued as he dressed. She was nearly green when she stood by the door and kissed him good-bye.

He was just straightening away from her when the thunder rumbled in the distance, and she clung to him a little tighter. "It's going to storm, Richard. Maybe you shouldn't go."

"Honey, I've driven a truck in the rain before. You forget, you're talking to an expert." He gave her a wink and bent to kiss her again. "You're the one who ought to stay home today. You don't look so good."

His concern was genuine, she knew. No one had ever loved her the way Richard did. Her parents loved her, but not like this. Richard's love was all-consuming. It exceeded every emotion. It enveloped her and hugged her in its warm embrace, even when he was away. And she loved him just as much. Sometimes it amazed her, the strength of the bond between them. But it was so much a part of her, and had been for so very long—all their lives, really—that she couldn't imagine *not* feeling this way.

The nausea rose in waves through her belly, and a curious and inexplicable chill rippled up her spine.

"Are you okay?" he asked, bending closer

and laying his broad, warm palm across her forehead.

"Fine." She forced a bright smile for him, closed her hand around his, and pulled it lower to press it to her lips instead of her head. God, how she loved this man.

He nodded but was still frowning at her. "I'll call and check in on you later. And I should be home early. You take it easy today, okay?" She nodded. "I love you, honey," he told her.

"I love you back," she told him. She stood in the doorway until he was out of sight, and then she ran into the bathroom without a moment to spare.

Annie called in sick that day. All queasy and dizzy and weak, she was sure she must be coming down with that bug that had been plaguing her students. It got worse, even as the storm did. Thunder rolled incessantly. Flashes of lightning were the only relief from a murky gray sky. The wind raged and rain came in torrents.

The storm went on all day, but her symptoms disappeared by noon. By then the day was pretty much shot, and Principal Hayes had already called in a sub, so there would have been little sense in going to school.

Besides, she was tired, really wrung out. She decided to pamper herself just a bit this afternoon so that when her energy returned, she'd have time to plan something special for dinner. Buy some wine. Maybe light those vanilla-scented taper candles in the crystal holders. Put some music on, soft and low. She'd greet Richard at the door in something sexy and pay him back for the lingering kiss he'd given her that morning.

Smiling, she imagined the expression on his face when he came home to her planned seduction. She sank onto the sofa with a cup of herbal tea, kicked off her shoes, and tuned in to *Oprah*. She planned to relax for just a few minutes before she got busy. Today's theme, life after death, had always fascinated Annie, and she was forever interested in hearing a new or different take on the subject.

She sipped her tea and was only mildly irritated when the words "Special Report" flashed across the bottom of the screen, and a newsman replaced her favorite talk-show hostess.

And then he seemed to look her right in the eyes, and everything changed. The strange part was that she felt the blackness creeping over her soul before he even opened his mouth. The tea sloshed over the sides of the cup, and she realized it was because her hand was shaking. She stared at the man on the screen as his lips parted in exaggerated slow motion, and some small voice inside warned her to turn the set off. Now. Hurry. Thumb the remote before he says it.

But she didn't. She couldn't move or even blink.

"There was a powerful explosion just off Eighty-One North, when a tractor-trailer, reportedly carrying over eight thousand gallons of gasoline, plunged through the guard rails and down a one-hundred-foot embankment. Details are sketchy, but one eyewitness claims a school bus had skidded out of control and was sliding into the path of the truck. The driver, apparently in a deliberate act to avoid hitting the bus, veered sharply to the right and through the rails. No injuries reported among the forty-five elementary school students on board the bus. The truck driver is assumed dead, though his body has not been recovered, and experts claim it may never be retrieved due to the extreme heat generated by the blast and the burning gasoline. The driver's name is being withheld pending notification of his family."

Annie didn't need the notification. She knew. It was as if some dark moon had eclipsed her heart, blocking out every bit of light. She knew.

She sank slowly to her knees on the floor and waited there in a state of borderline sanity. She couldn't speak or move or cry. Couldn't think. She only stared at the telephone, hating it with everything in her.

And then the phone rang.

Came the Hero

ℂ Richard had a split second to make a decision. His brakes were useless. He tried anyway, and his wheels locked up, but the truck with its deadly cargo kept moving, all eighteen tires hydroplaning, riding the water-covered surface of the bridge the way a hockey player rides the ice. The yellow bus skidded sideways and came sliding toward him. He couldn't stop in time. The bus was out of control and showed no signs of slowing. There was nowhere to go. Beyond the rails on the sides of the bridge was nothing but a hundred feet of rain-slashed sky, ending abruptly with the narrow, shallow river and its rocky banks below.

So much went through his mind in that slow-motion instant he was given to make the choice. He thought of his mother, and he thought of Annie. *Annie.* He couldn't do it. He couldn't leave her.

Then he saw them. The kids. Wide, innocent, terror-filled eyes beyond the rain-spattered side windows of the bus. Beautiful babies sliding toward the nose of his semi. And when they collided and his truck split that bus in two, those who weren't killed instantly would probably die when the gas he was hauling flared up.

Richard looked at the rails to his right, the misty storm beyond. "Hell, I'm dead either way," he muttered, and he released the brakes, caught a gear, jerked the wheel, and pressed the accelerator to the floor.

As the truck smashed through the guard rails and sailed out into the sky, Richard thought it hung there for just an instant. Just that brief moment while its momentum altered from forward to downward. He turned his head to glance back and saw the bus sliding, right past where he would have hit it and on to the relative safety of the barren stretch of road beyond.

And then the descent began and he braced himself and whispered, "I'm sorry, Annie. Damn, I hope you know how much I love you." He closed his eyes when the ground came rushing up toward his windshield.

He felt no impact. No explosion. No pain. Only darkness. Timeless night.

When Richard opened his eyes again, he had no idea how long he'd been in that darkness. He blinked several times to clear his vision because this wasn't right, what he was seeing. The rain was gone, and he was sitting, not in the air seat of his crumpled rig but on a spongy patch of moss. Around him were trees and plants. Birds were singing. The sun blazed down from an electric-blue sky.

Richard gave his head a shake. He must be dead. Or comatose or hallucinating. He was sitting in a forest. Where was the truck? The bridge? The river? Where was the damned storm? Hell, what about all those little kids on the bus?

"The children are fine, Richard. Oh, a little shaken and perhaps bumped and bruised a bit. But they'll be all right. Thanks to you."

Richard swung his head around at a deep, ancient-sounding voice that was like dark water chuckling over stones, and met a pair of eyes that might have belonged to time itself. Instinctively, he rose, though he was amazed that he was able.

The man smiled gently and came forward. He looked like . . . like some medieval sage come to life. Hose and pointed boots of thin, soft leather. A tunic of red, with a rampant lion on its front in gleaming gold. Delicate-looking chain mail encased his arms beneath the tunic, as if he wore a shirt of the stuff underneath. And a sword was belted around his waist.

Richard released a breath and whispered, "What's happening to me? Who . . . who *are* you?"

The old man's painfully pale cornflower eyes met his. His was the craggy face of a granite mountain. His hair, snowy white, hung over his shoulders. And before Richard's eyes, his garments changed as if by magic. He now wore a dark-colored suit beneath a long gray coat. The sword, Richard suspected, remained at his side.

"I have many names, Richard. Some call me Sir George, the slayer of dragons. Others knew me as Perseus, destroyer of Medusa. Still others—"

Richard held up a hand; then his eyes fell closed and he lowered his head. "Am I . . . am I dead?"

"I plucked you from the truck before you could experience physical death."

Meeting the old man's eyes again, Richard set his jaw. "So I'm not dead?"

"You're supposed to be. I was a bit eager to bring you over."

Richard's brows rose. "Over?" He looked around, but the forest that surrounded him seemed perfectly normal. Certainly not heavenlike. "I don't want to be here," he said, facing the man again, his voice firm. "I want to go back to my wife."

The old man nodded slowly. "Yes, you love Annie very much, don't you? I'll admit, I've rarely seen any mortal love as powerful. Never that I can recall, in fact."

"We belong together," Richard whispered. "We've always known that." Tears tried to blind him as the thought that he might be dead and that this might be some form of afterlife assailed him. Would he ever see Annie again? His knees threatened to buckle.

The man placed a gnarled hand on Richard's shoulder, easing him lower until he sat on that mossy stump once more.

"I'll ask you again," Richard muttered, "who are you?"

"I am a servant of the Light," the old man said. "I'm older than you could comprehend, my friend. The eldest White Knight in the army. First Knight of Goodness, in fact." The hand on Richard's shoulder tightened. "And I need you to join us."

Richard gave his head a shake, barely reacting to the man's odd words. He felt dazed, as if none of this were real. "I don't want to be in anyone's army," he said. "I just want to go home to Annie."

"Yes, well, that can be easily resolved."

He did react this time, sending the man a

steady gaze. "Nothing could change how I feel for her. Nothing."

The ancient eyes narrowed a bit. The old man drew a breath. "I've watched you all your life, Richard. I know when a mortal man has the makings of a Hero. A White Knight. And from the time you were very young, I've sensed you could be one of my finest. Perhaps the best knight ever to wield the golden sword."

Richard shook his head. "I'm no hero."

"You gave your life to save those children just now."

Shrugging, Richard looked up at him, emptiness filling his heart. "I can't go back to her, can I?"

"How much do you truly love your Annie, Richard?"

He lifted his chin. "I'd die for her."

The old man nodded, expelling his breath in a knowing sigh. "That, my friend, is precisely what you have done."

"I don't understand."

"She's going to need help, Richard. She'll need defending against a power so evil that even my army is challenged by the prospect of defeating it. And I've seen enough of men and of knights and of valor to know that no knight in my service can help her. In fact, I know of only one man with enough love, courage, and strength of will to save your Annie. And that man, Richard, is you."

Richard frowned, shaking his head slowly. "Then you have to send me back."

"No, Richard. I have to keep you here. For only from this realm, only as a White Knight, can you save Annie. Not as her mortal husband. Richard, if you love her as you say you do—"

"I do," Richard said. "I don't understand any of this, but I'd do anything for her. I swear it."

"Even give her up?"

Richard, feeling the slow crushing sensation in his chest, lowered his head, battling the tears that choked him, and whispered, "if . . . there's no other way."

The man placed his gnarled hand on top of Richard's head this time. "Kneel, then, valiant one."

Richard knelt, head still bowed.

"The sorrow will go now. It will go along with every remnant of the life before. Only your soul will remain. The memories, the mortal life—all of those things are going now. Drifting away from your mind like sand before a strong wind. You begin again, here, like a slate that has been wiped clean. Prepared to learn the ways of the White Knights."

There was a black mist swirling in his mind.

He felt light-headed, and then suddenly empty. Just empty. He felt tears on his cheeks, and the heartache, the emptiness inside him, remained, but he couldn't remember what put it there. Why he'd been crying. Why he *still* felt like crying.

"Arise, Ren, White Knight of the Light."

Ren. Yes. He was Ren, a White Knight. He knew that. Odd—for a moment he hadn't been able to remember his own name. But it was there now, firmly implanted in his mind where it belonged.

He rose slowly, felt an odd weight pulling at him, and blinked down to see the gleaming white-gold hilt protruding from a sheath at his side. His hand trembling, he touched the cool metal guard, closed his fingers around the handle, and drew the weapon slowly. It fit his hand as if made for him, and seemed to warm to his touch as he turned the blade, watching it gleam. And for a moment he struggled to remember the old man's name, because he felt strongly that he should, and yet it had fled his mind like everything else.

"Are you ready, Ren, to swear your vows to me? And to do so knowing that to break those vows would mean facing the second death?" the ancient one asked.

A trill of foreboding tiptoed through Ren's heart, and a feeling that he should be mourning some terrible loss. But another sense raced through him, too. One telling him that he had to do as this man asked. That it was vital somehow. That something more important than life itself depended upon it. "I'm ready," he whispered.

He still held the sword. Initially its weight had seemed alien, its hilt strange to him. But now it felt as if he'd held this gleaming weapon all his life, and he knew he could wield it as if it were an extension of his own arm. Lowering his head, Ren laid the sword across his heart and repeated his vows of service in a voice that shook every once in a while with a sorrow that he could not name.

The Embrace of Darkness

℗ The memorial service was attended by the parents of every child on that bus. Annie didn't know them. They were not from her own district, these children who owed their lives to her dead husband. All the teachers from that district showed up, as well as everyone from her own little school. And there were dignitaries in droves. The governor came. And the press. Richard had become a celebrity. The entire nation was calling him a hero. His photo had been on the cover of *Newsweek*. He'd been the lead story on all the network news shows.

Annie stood beside an empty coffin and hated all of it. It was because of his death that they were all here. She didn't want a damn hero, she wanted her husband. Alive and beside her, holding her.

Her mother and father, Georgette and Ira, with their laughable names—known by their friends as the Gershwins instead of the Schroeders—stayed close to her while the others ran the show. They were worried about her. They watched her, waiting for her to fall apart. And beautiful, broken María sat limply in a chair near the bier. Richard's mother wasn't the same since his death. She would probably never be the same again. She'd gone into total denial, and Annie didn't think she was going to come out of it. And it struck her as odd that the strongest woman she'd ever known should suddenly seem so fragile. María had lost her vision years ago and handled it. Then she lost her husband and dealt with it. Now she'd lost her only son, and all she could do was deny it. "He isn't really gone," she'd been muttering since the accident. "It's some kind of mistake. Richard isn't dead."

A group of elementary school students sang a song they'd rehearsed for the occasion. The governor said a few words. Then the preacher took the podium, his voice level and sad. Annie didn't hear any of them. She didn't want to hear them. She was glad when, in her mind everything got quiet, aside from the comforting buzzing sound in her head.

"Annie?" her mom whispered to her, squeezing her hand. "Hon?"

Her mother's voice drew her away from that comforting buzz she'd been homing in on, drawing closer, pulling up around her like a big, dark blanket. Irritated, Annie looked up and blinked at the brightness. Had it been this bright before?

People were starting to parade past her, each one saying something they thought was comforting, or leaning down to kiss her cheek. Annie hadn't even noticed them. Now that she did, an odd sort of panic fluttered to life in her chest. They were leaving. Stopping to offer condolences and hugs, and then leaving. As if it were over.

It couldn't be over.

María's soft hand patted hers. "It's all right, child. Our Richard isn't gone. He's coming back, you know."

Annie looked at the coffin. A ridiculous symbol. Richard wasn't in there. There hadn't been anything left of him. And once this day ended, there wouldn't even be that.

She turned toward the door, saw people heading toward it and cried "No! No, wait. It isn't over. It . . . it isn't over. It . . . can't . . . be . . . over. . . ."

Stunned silence. Eyes, wide with worry, turning on her, all of them on her. And Annie felt nothing but a gaping hole in her chest where her heart should be. "I'm sorry," she whispered, glancing at her mother. "I can't . . . I can't do this."

"Annie?"

Annie closed her eyes.

"She's fainted!" someone yelled.

"Get a doctor!"

But she didn't want a doctor. She wanted this darkness, and the soothing buzz that was growing louder now, but not loud enough. Not yet. She could still hear past it. Here, in the darkness, she could find solace. If only she'd never have to open her eyes again. If only she could stop hearing them all as well as seeing them. If only she could sink a little deeper into the darkness.

"It was the stress." The doctor's soft monotone floated through Annie's head. "She's been through a lot, Mrs. Schroeder."

"She fainted over an hour ago. She should be awake by now," Georgette insisted.

"Her body is just giving her mind a break from the pain," the doctor explained. "It got to be too much, and so she just shut down. She'll come around as soon as she's able to deal with all of this again."

"And what if she doesn't?" Georgette asked. "What if she just decides she *can't* deal with it? What then?"

The doctor sighed softly. "Mrs. Schroeder, the chances of that are very slim."

"But it's not impossible."

"It's not impossible," the doctor conceded.

"But in all my years of practice, I've never seen it happen."

"You've never seen anyone as much in love as Annie and Richard were," Georgette whispered. Annie could hear the tears in her mother's voice.

"Don't think the worst, Mrs. Schroeder. There's no indication this is anything more than a stress-induced fainting spell, and until there is, there's no reason to borrow trouble. Frankly, in Annie's condition, it's a wonder she didn't have a spell like this much sooner."

"My daughter's *condition* is just fine, Dr. Grossman. Physically as well as mentally."

Her mother's voice dared the doctor to suggest her daughter was anything less than perfect. But Annie wasn't perfect. She was aching inside, and nothing could make it stop. Even in the darkness where she'd briefly retreated, there had been pain. And the thought had occurred to her that maybe she could sink a little deeper. But there was something inside her that wouldn't let her do that. A kernel of awareness that hadn't even made its way to her conscious mind just yet.

"She's coming around, Doctor," a soft voice said.

Someone leaned over Annie. She sensed them there. Ignored the presence. Damn, she wished she didn't have to wake up.

The presence receded, and the voice came again. "I didn't mean to imply there was anything wrong with your daughter's health, Mrs. Schroeder, physically or emotionally. However, you should be aware that depression is a risk here. I'll get you some pamphlets. You'll need to watch her for a while."

"She'll be fine," Annie heard her mother insist, as if she could will it to be the truth. "If I can just get her to snap out of this, she'll be just fine." But Annie wondered how she'd ever be fine again. Without Richard. Without love.

"Yes, well, I hope so. At any rate," the doctor went on, "the *condition* I was referring to before was her pregnancy."

Annie felt a jolt zap her from head to toe.

"Her . . . my daughter is . . . she's pregnant?"

"Oh, my," Annie's father muttered. "My poor girl. Lord, all alone and expecting a baby!"

"Annie?" The bed moved. Damn, her mother was going to order her to wake up now. Annie knew she'd have to face reality soon, but not yet. It was difficult to remain in the blackness of oblivion, though, when Mom was on the edge of the bed, stroking her face and giving orders.

Annie tried anyway. She'd been having the

sweetest dream. Someone had just told her she was going to have a baby, and she'd been planning how she'd tell Richard, envisioning the rapturous expression on his face.

"You listen to me, young lady. Enough is enough. I'm not standing for any more of this, do you hear me?"

Sorry, mother, Annie thought. *Sorry to put you through all this worry. But I don't want to wake up yet. It hurts too much.*

"It was one thing when it was just you. But there's more at stake now, Annie." Hands clasped Annie's shoulders, firm hands that gripped and even shook her. "You have to wake up now, Annie," her mother all but shouted in her face.

"Really, Mrs. Schroeder, I don't think—"

"You're pregnant," her mother said. "Are you listening to me, Annie Nelson? You are carrying Richard's baby, and I'm not going to let you lie around feeling sorry for yourself when my grandchild needs you."

Annie's descent into darkness slowed. What was this her mother was saying? But . . . it had only been a part of her dream. It wasn't true. It wasn't—

"Richard would want you to be here for his baby, Annie. He'd expect you to be strong and take care of it and love it and tell his son or daughter about him one day. He'd never let you down the way you're letting him down now. Dammit, daughter, you wake up and take care of your baby! Do you hear me, Annie? Do you?''

Then the doctor's hands were there, prying her mother's away. "Enough, Mrs. Schroeder. This isn't doing anyone any good. She probably can't even hear you. She's exhausted, emotionally as well as physically. She'll wake up when she's ready.''

But Annie *had* heard her. And she heard the soft sobbing and the shuffling footsteps as her mother moved away from the bed. Annie turned her vision inward, feeling inside herself, wondering if there was any truth to what her mother had just told her. There was a stirring of warmth from deep in her abdomen. A sensation that something . . . that something made of pure love was there, alive and growing inside her. She *felt* it.

She moved her hands to her belly to touch that warmth, that life. Struggling, fighting, she reached for consciousness, strained toward the surface, pushing aside the murky depths where the pain was so much less. She didn't want to go back to the real world. Because the closer she got to lucidity, the closer she got to the hurt. The loss. The knowledge that Richard was gone. It was blinding, that pain. But she reached for it, all the same.

And somehow she managed to open her eyes.

Her vision was blurry, but she made out the two shapes moving away from her, toward the door. And she tried to speak, but what came out sounded more like a hoarse bark than the words she'd intended.

Her mother's back went rigid. Slowly Georgette turned around. Her eyes met Annie's, and her trembling hands rose to her cheeks. "Honey?" she whispered. "Annie, sweetheart?"

Annie cleared her throat, tried again. "Is . . . it true?" The pain was closing in on her again. The heartbreak. Losing Richard. The weight of it crushed her. She began to tremble beneath the force of the pain. God, if what her mother said had been a delusion or . . .

"Yes, baby. Yes, it's true." Her mother was back at the bedside instantly, running her hands through Annie's hair, stroking her cheeks while the doctor simply stood where he was, staring at the two of them with his mouth slightly agape. "They ran tests when they brought you in, just to be sure you were okay, you know? And, honey, you're pregnant."

Annie felt her lips pull into a grimace of agony. She felt tears burning in her eyes. She couldn't just fade away into darkness, could she? No. Not now. Oh, but it would have been so much easier if she could. "It hurts, Mom. God, it hurts so much."

"You're strong, Annie. You've always been so . . . so *incredibly* strong."

"That was . . . before. . . ."

"No. You just have to find it again. You have to be strong; you know that, right? For Richard. And for your baby."

Oh, yes, she knew it. She just didn't know if she had it in her. Nothing could hurt this much and not kill her, could it?

Between Two Worlds

∽ Ren battled until battle became second nature. The art of wielding a broadsword against forces darker than midnight had become as much a part of who he was as the color of his hair or his eyes. More so, on occasion. And other things faded as the desire to fight for the cause of goodness grew stronger. Mortality was left behind and with it, mortal things. Emotions, aside from zeal for his cause and fury in battle, all but vanished. Physical sensations, such as hunger or desire or sensitivity to heat and to cold, faded as well. He ate when he sensed his body needed sustenance. Drank when his throat felt dry. But taking pleasure in the taste of food didn't exist for Ren. Eating was done of necessity, and for no other reason. Sexual desire had been forgotten, shelved in a dark corner of his mind where it lay dormant. He had no use for such cravings. He lived to fight. Pain he felt at the blow of an enemy's sword. Pleasure, when he won the day. And beside them, an inexplicable sorrow that ate at his soul. It had no place there, Ren knew. It made no sense and did nothing to help him or the army of good, and so served no purpose. But ridding himself of it seemed impossible.

He'd gone wherever Sir George had sent him. Back in time, centuries back. Or forward to times he might never have dreamed of. Or anyplace in between. Sometimes a battle would take years, other times only hours, but always he'd return to learn that very little time had truly passed while he'd been away. It boggled the mind, really.

He'd never understood it, until once when Sir George, who had become many things to him—father, comrade, commander, teacher, and friend—had asked, "How long have you been a White Knight, Ren?"

The question had thrown him. And in silence he'd begun adding up the years he'd spent fighting for goodness in this time or that until the numbers had muddled in his mind. He shrugged and whispered, "I've no way of knowing, Sir George. Centuries?"

Sir George had smiled. "But time doesn't pass for you when you're out of it, Ren. For you, the time passes only when you're here, resting between assignments."

"But I spend so little time here."

Sir George nodded. "True. Because you're the best, as I always knew you would be, Ren. Of all of my knights, you're the only one ever to defeat Blackheart."

Ren sat down in the wooded paradise that was the place for resting between missions. A time that is not a time in a place that is not a place, was Sir George's answer when Ren had asked about the location. He pondered what his friend had told him about the opponent he'd encountered so often, one of those dark heroes who fought for the army of evil.

"Blackheart seems to show up often when I'm sent to right the mortal world's wrongs or prevent those wrongs from occurring," he observed.

"And astute fellow that you are, you're thinking there's a reason for that," Sir George said, studying Ren's face.

Ren simply nodded. "You told me once that there is a reason for everything, and I've found it to be very close to the truth."

"*Close* to the truth?" Sir George's white brows lifted, one slightly higher than the other.

"So far," Ren said softly, "I've found no reason for this endless sorrow I feel in my heart," he whispered, and automatically cast his eyes toward the ground. "You say I have become your finest knight. I rarely lose a skirmish. My skills are honed to precision, and yet . . ."

"And yet?"

Ren closed his eyes and brought his fisted hand to his chest. "I *ache* inside."

Sir George cleared his throat. "I'm sorry for that." He got up from his seat and paced a bit. "Perhaps you're not ready for this after all."

The whisper of a doubt about Ren's abilities brought his head up fast. "Ready for what?"

Sir George shrugged. "No doubt, Ren, you've guessed that these *centuries* of skipping through time to do battle with the dark forces have been more than simple missions for the cause of good. That they've also been a form of training for you."

Ren tilted his head to the side. "Training?"

"I've sent you back to any mission where Blackheart was likely to be involved. He is, you see, the Darkness's finest warrior."

"And you wished to see which of us was the better?" Ren shook his head in disgust. "I guess it was time wasted, then. He defeated me as often as I did him."

"True, Ren. But you are the only White Knight ever to defeat him at all."

Ren frowned and searched Sir George's face.

"It's true. I suspected you would be equal to Blackheart, and you are. And now it's time for you to accomplish the mission you were brought here for, Ren. A mission of dire importance to all of humanity. If you think you're ready to take it on."

"I am," Ren said with confidence.

"Good," said Sir George. "That's very good."

"To what time will I be going?" Ren asked, eager to be busy again. Because only when he was busy could he ignore the nameless pain that ate constantly at his soul.

"To the time from whence you were taken, Ren. Or nearly there. It will be eight months later. That's truly the length of time you've been away."

"Eight months?"

Sir George nodded.

"But it seems like ages. Aeons, at least."

"You have no memory of that other life, Ren. And that is for the best. Because you must return to my service when this battle ends. It's of utmost importance you remember that. You swore a vow—"

"I haven't forgotten my vows, Sir George. How could you doubt that?"

Sir George sighed and nodded. "Just remember, your mortal life ended before your immortal one began. If you give up this one, all that remains is the second death—the permanent one."

"I know."

Sir George studied Ren for a while. "All

right, then. You know. Now, because this is
the time that was once your own, Ren, I will
use my powers to cast a glamour over you—
a cloak of disguise. No mortals must recognize
this man they believe to be dead."

"I'll be . . ." Ren swallowed hard as something seemed to squeeze tight in his throat.
"I'll be among people I knew in the other
life?"

Sir George shook his head from side to side
and said, "Of course not!" a bit more loudly
than was necessary. Then he cleared his throat.
"This is just a precaution, just to cover the *very*
slim possibility that someone who knew you
might glimpse you in passing. That's all."

Ren nodded, seeing clearly the wisdom in
that. Then he knelt and waited while Sir
George moved his hands around and about
Ren's face. After a few moments of this,
George told him to rise, and Ren did. Immediately he drew his gleaming white-gold
broadsword from its sheath, lifting the blade
before him to stare down at his reflection in
its face.

"Sir George, I don't look any different!
Look," he said, and opened his hands before
his own face. "My hair is just as blond, my
eyes just as blue as they were before!"

Sir George smiled. "The cloak of magic, Ren,
cannot hide a man from himself. You know

yourself far too well to be fooled by a mere disguise. So naturally, when you look at your own reflection, you see right through the magic."

Ren tilted his head, rubbing his chin. "Suppose someone in the mortal world knew the man I was just that well?" he asked.

"No one can know a man as he knows himself, Ren. To anyone who looks on you—why, even to my eyes—you are a man of your own size and shape, but with dark hair and ebon eyes. Your lips are a bit thinner than before, and your nose a bit more Roman in shape. Your brows and lashes are darker as well. No, I daresay even someone who knew you well would not recognize you now."

Ren ran his fingers over his face in response to Sir George's words, but nothing felt any different to him. "And you're certain it will work?"

"Certain," the old man said. "Now, come. It's time for you to go."

"You haven't told me my mission yet."

"Ah, yes. The mission," Sir George said softly, taking Ren by the arm. "It involves a young woman named Annie, and the child she is about to bear."

A strange tingling sensation spread up

Ren's nape, tickling into his scalp. "The woman is in danger?"

"The child is," Sir George said. "And Ren, this is a child of great importance. It will grow to become one of the greatest leaders the free world will ever know. It will pave the way to world peace, stomping out ignorance, poverty, bigotry, and war. This child will change the world, Ren."

"And so the forces of darkness will try to kill it," he said, and his heart clenched with fear for the innnocent baby.

"You know the rules as well as I," Sir George said, his voice low, grim. "They cannot take a mortal life. If they could, they'd have simply murdered the mother and been done with it."

"Annie," Richard said.

Sir George looked at him, one brow crooked. "Yes. The child, however, is another matter. Once it is born, it will be safe from the dark assasins. But you can bet the forces of evil will do everything in their power to see that the child dies *before* it is born. It's fair game to them, right up until it draws its first breath."

"Hard to believe even those bastards would sink so low," Ren whispered.

"You're the only hope that child has, Ren,"

Sir George told him. "Will you accept this challenge?"

Ren met the old man's eyes with a feeling of determination filling him like none he'd ever known before. "I'll do more than accept the challenge, Sir George. I'll succeed."

Part Two

‍

The Tale Continues . . .

Chapter One

❀ Rain pummeled the windows and stampeded over the roof. Annie hated nights like this. *Hated* them.

She scooted across the braided rug to sit a little closer to the framed photograph of her husband. If he'd been there, she'd have been scooting closer to him, instead of a cold photo in a silver frame. But he wasn't. And this was the best she could do. Poor substitute. She took the eight-page instruction manual with her, settled down closer to Richard's face, and glanced at the pages. "Easy to assemble, my eye," she muttered, holding up various-sized bolts, trying to match one to the figure on the page that read "actual size." None of them matched. Ugh.

She ought to be grading test papers. She ought to be preparing tomorrow's lessons. Or maybe thinking about the new girl, Sara Dawson, and maybe planning some way to draw her out of her shell.

She shivered a little as she thought of Sara, with her straight sable hair and her huge dark eyes. That strange birthmark on her neck. A burgundy-hued crescent moon that looked more like a tattoo than a random bit of pigment. What a strange girl she was. So pensive and so intense. Her expression seemed knowing, wise beyond her years, as if she saw things no one else did. She stood out among the other sophomores at Otselic Valley High, and that had to be tough to deal with at sixteen.

Annie liked the girl, though, and wanted to help her adjust. So she felt guilty about not reading her essay right away.

But the incessant rain wouldn't let her concentrate on anything that involved too much brainpower. She got distracted every time the wind howled around the eaves, moaning like some disembodied spirit. Every time that damned tree limb outside brushed its soggy branches against the window upstairs. Or every time a gust sent twigs and debris clattering down on the roof.

Lightning flashed. A split second later a clap of thunder split her composure as surely as a gunshot fired next to her ear would have, and she stiffened, dropping the bolts to the floor.

God, she couldn't even concentrate on putting the crib together. Richard would have had it done in twenty minutes flat. And nothing as mundane as a thunderstorm would have distracted *him*.

Never used to distract her either, though. Until that day. Annie looked at his photo again, reaching out to caress his face with her fingertip. "Honey, I wish you were here." Tears formed in her eyes, and she rapidly blinked them away. It had been eight months. It shouldn't hurt this badly after eight months, should it?

She shook her head slowly, knowing full well it would hurt just this badly after eight years. Maybe even after eighty. But it didn't matter how much she hurt. She couldn't give in to it. She wouldn't. Not now. She tried to draw strength from the familiar shape of Richard's face in the photo, the boyish grin he'd saved just for her. But it wasn't easy. The blond hair he'd inherited from his father contrasted madly with his bronzed skin, a gift of heredity from his Spanish mother.

Annie had thought she might lose her mind when he'd died. But she hadn't. She couldn't. Richard would have expected more of her. He used to say she had a special strength down deep inside. Annie always thought he was the only one who could see it there. But maybe he'd been right after all. She'd survived losing him with her grip on reality still intact. She didn't think she'd ever go through anything worse. Maybe she was stronger than she thought.

Not so Richard's mother. Sweet María with her leathery skin and beautiful, sightless Spanish eyes. She was still delusional, and there didn't seem to be anything anyone could do to help her.

It would have been so much easier on her if Richard's body had been found. But with the force of the explosion, the intense flames, and the river so nearby . . .

There'd been nothing left to find. It was as if Richard had never been.

No, Annie thought, running her hands over her swollen middle. It wasn't like that at all. He had been, right here, real and warm and incredible. And she held the proof of that in her womb. Richard's baby. Their child. And maybe this child was part of the strength she was beginning to discover inside her. She had to be strong, take the pain, deal with it, and go on living. Because of the baby. A baby that must have been conceived at Mystic Lake, on their honeymoon, when life was perfect.

She'd forced herself back into the present, back into a convincing mimicry of life. Back into teaching. She walked around wearing a persona she'd created for her sake as well as her child's, but it was as shallow as the make-believe grave where Richard's headstone rested and his body did not. It was as fake as the old adage that time heals all wounds. It was a daily game of pretending that everything was just fine, that she was adjusting to life without Richard. And she was getting very, very good at it.

But she'd never stop hurting. She'd never stop missing her husband, much less stop loving him. And nights like this were the hardest of all.

Nights like this, when she used to curl into his strong arms and feel safe and cherished and protected. And oh-so-loved.

Annie's little secret was that she existed in the grip of a black depression, one she hid deep inside herself. But storms brought back the anger, the rage. The stupid storm that day had been to blame for Richard's death. The wicked rain had made the damned roads wet, and that's why that godforsaken bus had skidded into the path of his truck.

Richard had loved kids. No way in hell would he have hit a busload of them. No way. He'd adored kids. He'd wanted kids. Now he was going to have one, but he wouldn't be here to see it.

Thunder cracked and she grated her teeth. These were the times when she realized how hard it was to stand tall on her own. It was exhausting being strong, keeping her chin high and her spine straight. Showing up in her classroom every day with a smile so sweet it turned her stomach and pretending everything was fine. Knowing that if she wavered in the least, everyone in this small town would be wondering about her, fussing over her, worrying and checking in and poking around in her own private pain. Whispering that maybe poor little Annie Nelson was slipping the way she did at that memorial service. Wondering how she'd ever manage to raise a child all by herself. So she faked it. But she was getting tired.

It would be awfully nice to lean on someone else once in a while.

Thunder exploded, louder this time, rattling the old house, vibrating through the windows, and jarring her out of her self-analysis. This was the way it was, and it wasn't going to change. There would be no one else to lean on. There'd been one man in her life. Just one, and there'd never be another. Richard had been one of a kind. Special. A hero. Annie had always known that, but in the end, the whole country had known it as well. And Annie vowed to make sure Richard's child knew what kind of man his or her father had been.

Annie dabbed at her eyes with the backs of her hands and gripped the arm of the couch to pull herself, belly first, up off the floor. The crib was a lost cause. Tonight, at least. She pressed a hand to the small of her back, rubbed tiny circles there with her fingertips, and decided to go to bed. There was no use staying up when she wasn't getting a thing accomplished anyway.

She started for the stairs, but lightning flashed again, and there was a distinct *pop!* that seemed to come from very near. The lights flashed brighter and died, leaving Annie in absolute darkness.

Damn. Was it just her place, or was the power out all over the neighborhood? The thought of braving the cellar stairs alone in the dark in order to check the breaker box gave her the creeps, so she almost hoped for the latter.

Carefully she made her way to the nearest window, feeling her way and taking her time. She didn't want to risk tripping over something and hurting the baby. She pushed the curtains apart and tried to see if any lights shone from her neighbors' houses. Through the deluge, though, no lights glimmered. It was difficult to see even the houses through the rain. They were only dim outlines, utterly dark. The power must be out all over.

A brilliant streak illuminated the night for just an instant, and Annie caught her breath.

Frowning, she peered through the rain-streaked glass, but it was too dark. For a second she could have sworn she'd seen a man standing in the rain at the roadside, looking toward her house. Maybe even looking right at her.

But that was impossible.

A little chill raced up the back of her neck, and she told herself to stop imagining things and go to bed. But instead she waited, gaze glued to the spot where she'd seen him. There'd been something about him . . . his stance, or . . . She shook herself and stared harder, straining her eyes. Sooner or later the sky would light up again, and then she could be sure. The idea of some stranger standing in a rainstorm staring at her house gave her a serious case of the shakes, even though she was sure she'd imagined it. She must have. Who'd stand outside on a night like this?

Suddenly she was acutely aware of her solitude. Utterly alone in the house. No one else there, or even within screaming distance. Were the phones working? If she saw him again, should she call the police? Could she?

One hand reached down to check the lock on the front door. It was fastened. Good. The other hand slid protectively to her swollen abdomen.

She pressed closer to the glass in the front

door, squinting in the darkness, searching for that dark silhouette in the night. Lightning flashed again and the man was on the other side of the glass, his face inches from hers. Annie jumped away from the window when the blinding glow illuminated him standing there on her porch, with only a thin pane of glass between them, staring right at her from huge, haunted eyes. His rain-plastered hair and wet face were perfectly visible this time.

Richard!

The last thing Annie heard was her own anguished scream.

Ren saw her face go white with fear, saw her green eyes widen as she took a faltering step backward, her screams shattering the night. And then he saw her go limp—and crumple to the floor.

The child!

Without hesitation, Ren forced the door open and lunged into the house. He fell to his knees beside the small woman, water running from his clothes to make puddles on the floor and dripping from his brow to hers.

One of his hands touched her belly, fear clutching at his heart as he realized the child he'd been sent here to protect could very well have been harmed when she'd fallen. And if it had, he'd have only himself to blame for startling the woman.

His chilled palm flattened upon the woman's belly. And a vigorous kick came from within, thudding against his hand. An odd sensation spread through Ren, like melted butter filling his veins, and he smiled.

Then he shifted his gaze upward, over the woman's face once again, and caught his breath. She was . . . she was beautiful. Tiny and delicate. And the sight of her sent the strangest sensations through him. Disturbing feelings. Distracting ones. He blinked and gave his head a stern shake. Best to focus on the task at hand.

Moving carefully, he gathered the woman into his arms and carried her to the sofa. She was light, considering the burden she carried. Very warm in his arms, and that warmth seemed to seep through his cold, damp clothing to permeate his skin, heating him and taking the night's chill away. Her warmth was more than physical. It was a warmth of the soul flowing into him. He felt . . . odd. As if he'd entered a cozy place where he fully belonged, after wandering in an endless blizzard. As if he'd found a snapping hearth fire awaiting him with its welcoming light and heat.

For a moment he didn't want to put the woman down.

Ren swallowed hard, once again shaking himself free of the unfamiliar sensations, and lowered her to the sofa. Then he grabbed the blanket lying nearby and spread it carefully over her. He scanned her face once more. Very strange how much he liked looking at her. How it felt. It wasn't physical desire. Couldn't be that. Such urges didn't exist in White Knights. They were erased along with their mortal memories.

Ren tucked the blanket around her and straightened, but before he could take his hand away, hers closed around it.

And he felt sorrow. A sorrow so familiar to him it was frightening. That same ache that had been with him, inexplicably, for as long as he could remember. The one he couldn't explain. It intensified at the desperation he felt in her touch. The way she clung. The force of her grip, and the way her hand trembled slightly.

His gaze shot from their clasped hands to her face. And from beneath her tightly closed eyes, he saw the sparkle of a tear as it rolled free.

"Richard," she murmured, her lips barely parting but shaking so delicately he wanted to touch them, smooth them with his fingers until they steadied again. Her pain was vivid, so real that he could see it like a dark aura ringing her very soul.

Richard?

Ren blinked because the sound of that name on her shuddering breath sent a shiver through the core of his brain. Like a blinding light, but it was brief. A flash or a feeling too brilliant to bear, and then gone.

He shook with the effect of it and wondered why. What could it mean? Who was this Richard she cried for? And as her hand went limp again, he pulled his free, slowly backing away from her and yet unable to drag his gaze from her face.

And then there was a sound. Footsteps on the front porch, and Ren's hand reached automatically for the sword concealed beneath the folds of his dark coat. But then there was a voice, a man's voice, calling her name. Her man, perhaps? George had said the woman was alone and without protection, that her husband was dead. But maybe she'd found someone, this Richard whose name she whispered with such longing.

The idea shouldn't be so disturbing. The doorknob rattled and the concerned voice called out again. Ren was out of place here. And it would do his cause no good to be discovered standing over the unconscious woman in the dead of night by her lover. He might end up having to kill the man.

And that thought shouldn't be so pleasing.

Ren turned and moved quickly through the house, unerringly heading into the kitchen and out the back door without even taking the time to get his bearings or find his way. He retreated into the rainstorm, shaken to the marrow.

Her screams, he told himself, were all that was making him shiver like this. Her blood-curdling shrieks, splitting through the storm's fury and stabbing straight into his heart. Or the way she'd fallen. The danger to the child he'd been sent here to protect.

But no. No, it was more than that and he knew it. There was something gnawing at him. The same something that had been niggling in his brain every once in a while for so long he couldn't even remember its cause. It was an odd feeling, like an itch he couldn't quite scratch, and it came to life at seemingly random moments. He'd felt it often, as if he were craving something, something he needed as much as he needed air to breathe and water to drink. Something he couldn't identify. And it always left him feeling empty and incredibly alone.

The feeling seemed to occur with a new and surprising frequency since he'd arrived in this small town. Like when he crossed the little bridge and looked down into the shallow, fast-running waters passing beneath it. Or when he caught a whiff of the corn being cut in a nearby field. Most of all, when he stood outside that old house on the corner.

The feeling had taken on a new, powerful intensity just now, when he'd looked on that woman's delicate face, and even more when he'd held her in his arms. And try as he might, he couldn't identify it. Maybe it was the impact of those eyes of hers, staring out into the rain at him. So big and filled with so much emotion, it was nearly spilling from them. So green that when lightning flashed, they seemed to glow.

Or maybe it was the sensation of that tiny hand closing around his and holding on so tight. As if she was clinging to him with everything in her. As if she didn't want him to leave.

Ren shook himself. He had things to see to. He needed to get warm and dry. He could take sick as easily as any other man, and though it wouldn't kill him, carrying out this mission while weak and battling illness would be foolish.

He took shelter in a barn a few hundred yards down the road. The smell of hay and cattle permeated the place, instigating a return of that itchy sensation in his mind. He stripped down to his shorts and hung his wet coat and his dampened black jeans and shirt on a nail in the wall, hoping they'd dry a bit by morning. The hay scratched at his thighs, but it was warm and dry, and that outweighed any discomfort. His sword lay, as always, close to his side, within quick and easy reach.

Ren was worried. He hadn't failed in a mission yet. Not in all this time. But he had a feeling his abilities were going to be more severely tested than ever before. And a mission that had at first seemed simple was becoming more complicated with every passing moment.

Especially since he'd seen her, looked into her eyes. Hell, a Hero—especially one as well trained as Ren—felt very few emotions, and even fewer baser urges. A Hero possessed an innate sense of goodness and fair play. Loyalty to the point of death. Courage, even fearlessness.

He was not, however, supposed to feel the urge to gather a frightened woman into his arms, and to hold her there until her fears melted away. He'd *never* felt anything like that before.

And yet he suspected that maybe he had.

"Annie? Come, now, Annie, do wake up."
The deep voice with its almost charming but

unidentifiable accent reached into the depths of her mind to bring her back to consciousness. Then she remembered what she'd seen, and her eyes flew wide open.

But there was nothing out of the ordinary here now, no ghostly image of her husband staring back at her. The lights had come back on. She scanned the room, half expecting—for just an instant—to see Richard standing in a corner, dripping wet, with that achingly sad look in his eyes.

Instead she saw the enigmatic dark-haired man who'd recently moved into Octagon House, a short walk from her own. He had a whipcord build, not overly muscular but far from skinny, and his impeccably groomed hair, with a few silver streaks, framed his face, clashing with the jet-black mustache. He was striking. Even more arresting when you heard him speak in that dulcet, almost hypnotic voice with its mysterious accent. And when you factored in the intense black eyes, well, the man seemed more likely a sorcerer than a retired psychiatrist.

She'd noticed all of that about him when he'd first stopped by to introduce himself, and she noticed it all over again now. Dr. Bartholomew Cassius was a charmer.

"Ah, that's better," he said, offering a relieved smile. "How are you feeling, Annie?"

She tried to smile back at him. She was lying on the sofa, head resting on its arm. An afghan kept her snug and warm, and Bartholomew sat beside her like a worried lover. His hand touched her forehead in search of a fever.

"I'm fine. Really, I . . ." Richard's face reappeared in her mind. She closed her eyes, but still it lingered there. She could not have possibly seen him outside last night.

"I got worried when the lights went out," Bartholomew explained. "I had flashlights and candles within easy reach, but I was concerned for you. Could just picture you tripping over something in the darkness and lying injured all night. I tried to call. There was no answer, so of course I had to check in."

She frowned, studying his narrow face and those winged brows that couldn't seem to decide whether to be black or silver. They had strips of both. "You came out in that storm just to check on me?"

He seemed a bit sheepish as he looked away. "Of course I did, Annie. Any *good* neighbor would have done the same." His eyes said what he thought of those who lived in the houses on either side of hers, much closer than he was, none of whom had braved the storm to check on her safety.

She wasn't so sure about his point of view. Probably the closer neighbors just stayed away because they knew her better than he did. Knew she guarded her independence with vigor. In fact, she detested anyone giving her special treatment just because she was: *(a)* a woman, *(b)* a pregnant woman, *(c)* a pregnant woman on her own, or, worst of all, *(d)* a pregnant woman on her own who needed constant looking after because of the recent death of her husband. But she let it slide. Bartholomew seemed to her like a decent man with good intentions.

"Is that what happened, then? You tripped in the darkness?"

She frowned and shook her head. "I'm not sure exactly what happened. Where was I when you—"

"Lying here on the sofa," he said. "But I couldn't wake you up. I'd have called an ambulance if the phone lines hadn't been knocked out."

She felt a prickle of unease and searched his fathomless eyes. "Bartholomew, how did you get in?"

As always, there wasn't a flicker in the black depths.

"The door was open, Annie. That's what worried me."

"But I thought I checked the lock, just before . . ." She bit her lip. She'd also thought she'd seen Richard standing on her front

porch, dripping wet. Just went to show what
kinds of games the subconscious mind was ca-
pable of playing. She'd probably tripped, as
Bartholomew suggested. Maybe hit her head.
She'd come to the sofa to lie down, and she
had probably dreamed all the rest.

Funny, though. She didn't feel any bumps
on her head now.

She glanced toward the front door, shuddering at the memory of seeing her husband
there last night. The storm seemed to have
passed, leaving only darkness and a light rain
in its wake.

"Bartholomew, when you arrived here . . ."

"Yes?"

She drew a deep breath. "Did you see anyone else? Outside, I mean?"

Bartholomew's black eyes glittered and narrowed. "No, Annie. Why? Did you?"

His voice had altered just a little, taken on
the tone of a psychiatrist speaking to a troubled patient. He could just as well have been
saying, "No, Annie, I didn't see any pin-
striped elephants dancing in your driveway.
Did you?"

She knew that tone. She'd talked to a handful of therapists in the days and weeks following Richard's funeral, mostly at her mother's
insistence. They were concerned about her
mental state. About depression. About a hun-

dred other things. Of course they'd pronounced her perfectly sane, though that hadn't stopped the local tongues from wagging. Simply *seeing* a therapist was enough to generate gossip in a small town like Otselic. Even the school board had voiced concern over her "emotional state." As if grieving were somehow abnormal. As if fragile Annie Nelson couldn't possibly withstand such a blow without sustaining mortal damage.

She bit her lip and sighed. She'd resented those therapists back then for their concern, and it hadn't been warranted. Now she was projecting that feeling onto Bartholomew, just because he was a psychiatrist like them.

She thought about simply telling him what she'd thought she'd seen last night. Just for an instant she thought maybe she needed to tell someone. But then she shook herself and reasoned the whole incident away. She *had* been thinking about Richard all evening. And the damned storm had been stirring up memories. It was no wonder she'd conjured his image in her imagination. That's all it was. All it could possibly have been.

"No," she answered at last. "No, I guess I didn't see anyone either."

Bartholomew smiled at her. Perfect white teeth. "Would you like me to stay, Annie? I'd be glad to sit up with you until morning."

His concern was touching. But her natural aversion to appearing weak or dependent came to life just enough to make it a bit irritating as well. "No, Bartholomew. But it's kind of you to offer." At least she thought it was kindness. It was hard to be sure. She saw no hint of lascivious intent in his jet eyes. Then again, it was tough to detect anything in those eyes. They were as emotionless as marbles. So if he was coming on to her, she was blind to it.

She glanced down at her belly and almost laughed out loud that the notion he might be interested had even occurred to her.

He nodded. "Well, then, can I get you anything before I go? Tea? Warm milk, perhaps?"

She shook her head. "I'll be fine."

His eyes seemed to probe hers, and for a moment she was certain he'd question her further about what had happened tonight. But he didn't. Instead, he reached for his jacket, which was slung over the back of the sofa, and as he pulled it on, he dipped a hand into a pocket. He withdrew a small velvet box and pressed it into her hand.

"What—"

"I'd like you to have it. It's just a token, really."

Frowning, and growing more uneasy with the situation by the second, she opened the box. It held a necklace, a silver chain with an odd-looking stone suspended from it. About two inches long and tubular, as thin as a piece of straw, and translucent if you looked at it right.

She turned the stone in her hand, studying it.

"It's pink tourmaline," Bartholomew explained. "And it's said to bring friendship. Since I'd like nothing more than to be your friend, Annie, I'd like you to wear it."

She gave her head a little shake. "Bartholomew, I barely know you. I'm not sure—"

"You've made me feel welcome here. That means a lot to an old man alone in a strange place."

"You're not an old man," she blurted.

He smiled. "I'm glad to hear you say that." And there was something in his eyes. Interest? In her?

"For now, Annie, let this gift be my way of saying thanks."

"There's no need to thank me."

"Let me put it on you," he urged. "Just to see how it looks."

Reluctantly she nodded. She sat up enough so Bartholomew could fasten the chain at her nape. The cool stone rested on her chest, just below the collarbone. It felt good there, and she couldn't help but smile.

"It looks lovely on you, Annie. Won't you keep it? Just to humor a lonely man? A man who . . ." He lowered his eyes. "A man who has grown quite fond of you in a remarkably short time."

She caught her breath, searched his face. He was an attractive man. Dignified and easy to talk to. So easy, in fact, that she suddenly felt she could tell him anything, trust him implicitly. But she wouldn't lead him on. "It's far too soon for me to think about—"

"I only want us to be friends, Annie," he said softly. "For now."

"Friends is all we can be," she told him. "I loved Richard more than . . ." Her voice trailed off.

"I know," he said. "But everyone needs a friend, don't they, Annie? Someone to talk to? To confide in?"

Sniffling, she nodded. "It would be nice," she said, "to have a friend." She fingered the tourmaline. "Thank you, Bartholomew."

"You're more than welcome, sweet Annie."

He rose to leave, pulling his coat more tightly around his shoulders. "Sleep well, Annie. And remember that if you need anything, I'm only a phone call away."

"That's kind of you."

"That's what friends are for."

She sat still for a long time after he'd left,

but sleep was not a possibility. She wasn't disturbed about Bartholomew's interest. She'd been honest with him from the start, and she thought he'd got the message. It was Richard who kept her awake. That face, so sad and confused, rainwater dripping from his brow as he stared at her.

She most certainly had *not* seen Richard on her porch. And she most certainly was *not* suffering from any kind of mental crisis. If losing him hadn't driven her to the loony bin, nothing could. So this hadn't been a delusion, but simply an *illusion*. A dream. She'd been through the loss of the only man she'd ever love. She'd dealt with it. And just because she was living under the constant, unending strain of pretending to be getting over it, when deep down inside the pain was just as fresh and raw as ever, was no reason she should start hallucinating. She *had to* pretend. Her concerned friends and neighbors, not to mention her parents, would have hounded her constantly if they knew the pain she still felt with every breath she drew, the gnawing ache inside her that never seemed to die.

God, it had been months before everyone in this little town had stopped staring at her with curious, concerned eyes. As if they'd all been expecting her to suddenly turn into a babbling lunatic before their eyes, without advance warning. She'd had to fight to get her job back. And she couldn't even blame the school board for their hesitance, since it was based largely on their fear. Who wanted a crazy woman teaching tenth-grade English? She'd seen a *therapist*, for heaven's sake.

No, all that had happened tonight had been a bit of overactive imagination. It wouldn't do to overreact to this. Not at all. Just looking around her, she knew that she was fine. She looked around her old house to find everything in it just the same. The water spot on the living-room ceiling was still there. Richard had repaired the roof, so it no longer leaked, but he'd never got around to painting the ceiling. She'd have to do that. And the curving mahogany banister still gleamed. She and Richard had sanded off the old varnish and replaced it with several fresh coats. They'd done most of the woodwork in the house together. Except for that upstairs bathroom. She'd have to do that alone. Yes, everything seemed solid and real and just as it had been before. Nothing was distorted or hazy. None of the furniture was talking to her. She didn't see eyes peering at her from the light fixtures.

She was fine.

The telephone shrilled, and she jumped to her feet so suddenly, she thought she'd pulled an abdominal muscle. Grating her teeth against a stream of cuss words, she frowned. Who'd be calling her at four in the morning?

Richard?

"Oh, for God's sake, stop it!" She yelled at herself, but instead of her words sounding like a reprimand, she felt more like she was whistling past a graveyard. She snatched up the phone.

"Annie-girl?"

Annie-girl. It was María, Richard's beautiful, blind mother, who'd given her that nickname when she'd been little more than a baby. No one else had ever called her Annie-girl . . . except Richard. Annie had always loved the way it sounded, flowing from María's lips with a slight Spanish accent. Almost as much as she'd loved hearing Richard say it. Now, though, it sent a shiver up her spine.

"María, what in the world are you doing up so late? Are you sick? Is everything all right?"

"It's Richard," the soft, melodic voice told her. "He's near, Annie. I feel him. He's . . . he's coming back. He's coming back to us!"

Chapter Two

∽ "Heard you had a spell last night."

Annie frowned hard at Harry Hayes, Otselic Valley High's principal, and blinked away her surprise. He stood in the doorway of her classroom, leaning against the jamb, arms crossed over his barrel chest, trying for all the world to look as if it were a casual question. But she saw the real concern in his eyes. It was enough to make her forget to smile at the way the tilt of his head was just enough to make his bald spot reflect the gleam of the overhead lights.

She closed her textbook without slamming it and managed to keep her voice level. "Where on earth did you hear that?"

"The new guy—what's-his-name—in Octagon House."

"Bartholomew Cassius," she filled in, banking the anger trying to surge through her. Bartholomew had likely meant well. He'd never deliberately do anything to hurt her.

Now, why in the world am I so sure of that?

67

"He was worried," Harry went on. "Said I ought to keep an eye on you."

Eyes were already on her. Annie felt them as strongly as a physical touch, and when she turned, it was to see Sara Dawson sitting alone in the back row, staring at her. She hadn't noticed her there before. Sara must have stayed behind when the others left at the sound of the bell. And now that Annie saw her, she was eager to get rid of Harry so she could talk to her. Something about the girl touched her, but Annie couldn't put her finger on just what it was. For a second she stopped listening to Harry and just looked at Sara.

Her beautiful pale skin was in stark contrast with the dark birthmark on her neck, and even with her solemn dark eyes that met Annie's and seemed to say that they knew.

Knew what, Annie wondered, frowning.

"So, are you okay?"

She snapped her attention back to Harry, feeling a little guilty for ignoring him. Since Richard had died, he'd been sweet to the point of being sickening. It wasn't his fault she didn't appreciate so much concern for her well-being. That she sensed hidden motives behind every seemingly kind gesture. To someone as sensitive as she'd become this past year, his concern felt more like an invasion of privacy.

"Fine," she told him. "I'm fine."

With a look that said he doubted it, one that had her wondering just what else Bartholomew had told him, Harry shrugged. "You're sure? Dr. Cassius seemed to think—"

"Look, it was a dizzy spell. I blacked out for a few minutes. That's all. Probably low blood sugar or something." She bit her lip and told herself not to sound so defensive. It wouldn't do to give Harry cause to start worrying about her ability to handle her job.

"So it was purely physical?" he asked, confirming her worst fears.

"Of course it was, Harry. Look, my obstetrician and I have everything under control." She forced a smile. "You worry too much," she told him, trying for a lighter tone.

"Only because I care." He returned her smile. "You know we're all like family here, Annie. So if you need anything . . ."

"I know," she said.

He nodded, still looking doubtful, then turned and left the classroom. Annie watched him go, wondering how she was going to manage to reassure Harry and restore her own job security.

Sara rose and came to the desk, drawing Annie's gaze and her thoughts away from the retreating school principal. She didn't have any books with her. Had she left them behind, then? In the desk?

Annie marveled at the grace of her approach. Her long, slender limbs ought to be awkward, but instead she moved like a dancer. There wasn't another girl like her, Annie thought vaguely. Not one with such ethereal beauty or such grace. She'd only been coming to class for a few days, and she always sat alone, in the back.

She stopped in front of the desk and looked at Annie with those big dark eyes. They reminded Annie of María's eyes. So huge and so black. But María's saw nothing and Sara's seemed to see everything. Even invisible things.

What an odd thought.

Her voice as soft as a breeze, Sara said, "You have dark circles under your eyes."

"Do I?" Annie reached up as if to wipe them away.

Sara nodded, searching Annie's face. "When Lyle Stromwell dropped his book a few minutes ago, you jumped out of your skin."

"It startled me." Annie drew a breath and tried to see this girl as what she was, a child, not an all-knowing oracle. "Is there something I can do for you, Sara?"

She nodded precisely twice and held Annie's eyes with her own. "Trust yourself. It's important, Annie."

That was it. Then she just turned and left. Annie rubbed her temples with her forefingers and told herself she really ought to start her maternity leave soon. This was getting to be too much. Nothing she couldn't handle, though, she reminded herself. She was tough. She'd survived hell, she could certainly survive one bad night and a strange young girl who spoke cryptic words that suggested she might just know Annie's deepest secrets.

Funny about Sara Dawson. The way she never said a word or raised her hand in class. The way the other students ignored her as if she wasn't even there. Annie had given her a couple of days to get settled in, but soon she'd have to call on her to answer questions or contribute to classroom discussions, try to get her to open up a little. The girl had never spoken a word aloud, except when she and Annie were alone together.

That's good. Think about Sara instead of your own problems. Distract yourself.

She shoveled a stack of papers into her soft-sided briefcase, locked the desk drawer, flicked off the lights, and headed out of the building.

Sunshine greeted her, and the warm wind carried the scent of dying autumn leaves. She schooled her facial expression to reflect that of a young mother-to-be, out for a walk on a beautiful afternoon, and headed down the street, waving at the students she met along the way. Smiling her false little smile until her face felt frozen.

Bartholomew had been talking to people about what had happened last night. Even if he meant well, he ought to know better. A retired psychiatrist ought to understand a little bit about confidentiality and discretion. Thank God she hadn't told him more.

At any rate, no one who glanced her way today would see a sign of trouble in her face. Even if it killed her, she would keep smiling.

She turned left onto Mariposa Road and sashayed over the Otselic River's minuscule bridge as if she hadn't a care in the world. She had to wait for a tractor to pass before she crossed the road by the little two-pump gas station and headed into the South Otselic Store. She had no doubt she could sustain the mask a bit longer. She'd had lots of practice.

She'd been too sick to eat that morning. Not morning sickness. That had passed by the fourth month. This was something else. Something deeper and, she suspected, more emotional than physical. Seeing Richard last night . . . or rather, imagining she'd seen him, had brought her pain back to its screaming, burning pinnacle.

But she had to eat, for the baby's sake. And school lunch had been meatloaf, a nightmare in itself. So she'd skipped it, and now she was queasy and dizzy, and it was probably as much from going hungry all day as from the recurring memory of her husband standing in the rain.

Leslie grinned at her from the other side of the counter. "How's that little one doing today, Annie?"

"Sleeping," she replied. "This kid never starts kicking like a mule until around midnight. Then, look out."

Leslie laughed at that. "What can I get for you?"

"I'm starved." Good touch, she thought. Everyone always thinks a good appetite equals good health. No one worries about you when you're hungry. "Could you make me a turkey sub with the works?"

"Glad to. Just be a minute."

Leslie went to work. When her back was turned, Annie let her aching facial muscles relax and wondered what she looked like. Empty? Heartbroken?

She gave herself a mental shake and wandered to the back to examine the videos. It might be a good idea to keep herself distracted tonight. She was already dreading the thought of another night alone, missing Richard. Maybe dreaming up his image again.

She'd already seen most of the movies on the rack, but there were one or two new ones. While she was examining them, the bell over the door jangled. Annie glanced up and saw the back of a tall, broad-shouldered man. He was facing the counter, but she would have known him anywhere, and her entire body went stiff. She couldn't move, couldn't speak. She couldn't even breathe.

His golden hair was longer than before. Wilder looking. His arms were bulging with more muscle, and his shoulders seemed broader beneath the long black coat he wore. But there was no doubt in her mind that she was looking at her husband.

Impossible! He's dead!

But he wasn't dead. He was right there. And Leslie was looking right at him and showing no signs of distress. She'd known Richard! Why didn't she recognize him?

Or maybe the better question was, was she even seeing what Annie was seeing? Or was this some kind of illusion?

She edged toward the far wall, ducking into an aisle and along it to the door. He couldn't see her from beyond the shelves. She kept low and hurried. She had to get a better look at him. But for some reason she couldn't explain, she was almost afraid of having him look back. Of meeting his eyes. Of feeling that old connection . . .

The aisle ended, leaving a brief open area between her and the counter and the exit. She'd step out there for a closer look. Only for a moment. His back would still be to her, but maybe she'd see enough to convince her this was just a man who resembled Richard. Drawing a breath, she stepped forward—and came up short against a chest that was harder, broader than she remembered. And yet the same. So incredibly the same.

His hands clasped her shoulders to steady her, and she looked up, blinked her eyes, and looked again. Her world was spinning away. She was staring into her husband's eyes.

"Excuse me," he said. "Are you all right?"

She opened her mouth, but no words came out. She could only gape and blink again. God, he was looking at her as if he didn't know her! But his hands were so warm and so familiar. And they squeezed her shoulders, exerting gentle pressure.

She started to shake. She wanted to run away. She wanted him to bend closer and kiss her mouth the way he used to. She wanted Leslie to shout his name and ask where the hell he'd been. She wanted to die. She wanted to live.

His eyes widened then, and he sucked in a sharp breath, his gaze falling briefly to her lips. And then his hands fell away, and he turned and walked out the door abruptly, as if something had frightened him as much as the sight of him had frightened her.

And why the hell did Leslie calmly watch him walk out of here with a diet cola in his hand? Why wasn't she screaming her head off? Did she sell Coke to dead men every day? Good God!

As he walked out the door, he turned and glanced over his shoulder. Right at Annie. His eyes met hers for only an instant. He frowned, maybe at whatever he saw on her face, and he was gone.

Annie's legs finally came back under her control. She forced herself to the counter and braced both hands on it to keep from falling flat on the floor. The shaking intensified until it encompassed her entire body. The world was spinning away into madness, and no one seemed to notice. No one but her.

"Here's your sub—Annie? God, you're white as a sheet? Are you okay?"

Annie blinked at her friend, wondering what on earth was wrong with the woman. Leslie had known Richard.

"That man . . ." It was all she could get out before her teeth started chattering. She clamped them together and envisioned herself clamping down on her self-control as well. She was not going to lose it like this. Not here. Not now. Leslie would be dialing nine-one-one if she kept it up. And there was no reason for it. There was a perfectly logical explanation for all of this. More calmly, she said, "That man. Do you know him?"

"The one who was just here, you mean? The ebony-haired, black-eyed pagan god you tried to mow down? Gee, Annie, is he what's got you looking so queasy?" She seemed relieved. "Can't say I blame you. He's something, isn't he?"

"His hair was . . . it was blond."

Leslie frowned, worry creeping back into her eyes and her voice. "No, Annie, it was dark. *Really* dark. He's new in town, I guess. I've only seen him a couple of times."

Annie shook her head. "Leslie, his eyes are blue." Then she cleared her throat. "I mean, they looked blue to me."

"Jet-black, hon. Must'a been a trick of the light or something." She tilted her head. "Are you *sure* you're okay?"

"Yeah." Annie was barely aware of muttering the word.

Leslie held up the wrapped sub, and Annie stared at it for a long moment before she remembered that she'd ordered it. She met her friend's eyes again and saw the speculation taking solid form there. The worry. The pity. The oh-my-God-I-think-she's-losing-it look.

Annie got control. Tenuous, at best, but control all the same. She forced her face to obey her commands. Forced a normal look to replace the stunned expression she had to have been wearing. Finally the worry in Leslie's eyes eased.

"Trick of the light," she said quickly, and even managed a self-deprecating shake of the head for good measure. "Right, that must've been it. Thanks for the sub." Too many words would not be a good idea. Too many words and she'd be blurting something stupid. She took the sub, paid for it, and wandered out the door. And for the first time since Richard's death, Annie wondered if maybe she was losing her mind.

She was disturbed when she got home. Her hands shook uncontrollably, and she tossed the sandwich into the garbage without a second's regret. She was sick. Her head throbbed, her stomach clenched and unclenched as if a fist were brutally massaging it. God, what was happening to her?

She paced, wondering what to do. Should she call a psychiatrist?

No, because she'd have to make an appointment, and who knew how far away it would be? Besides, she was not delusional. She was the sanest person she knew.

So maybe this was physical. Maybe something was going on with her body that was making her see things. Distorting her vision or her perceptions or something. She went to the telephone stand to look up the number for her obstetrician, but the telephone book wasn't where she'd left it.

He'd looked so real! So real and alive and wonderful that for the briefest instant she'd been tempted to fling herself into his arms and sob her heart out.

It would feel so good to have Richard's arms around her again. Just once more, to have him hold her and . . .

And she *had* seen him—*clearly*. There'd been no trick of the sun, nothing distorting her vision. How could she plainly see Richard's golden blond waves on a dark-haired man? How?

Oh, God, she was frightened.

No phone book in sight. She turned in a slow circle, scanning the room, and the shaking that emanated from her core intensified.

Forget the damn book. She'd just call Information and get the number.

She pressed a hand to her chest as if that would calm her racing heart, and she felt the pendant lying against her skin.

Bartholomew! Yes, she should call Bartholomew. He could help her. He was close by, and she could trust him.

Trust him, when he blabs your business all over town?

But he meant well, she told herself. And she ignored her better judgment, deciding to call him. But in her state, she couldn't remember his number either. She could get *that* from Information, though. She reached into her pocket for a pen and instead found a folded slip of paper she didn't remember putting there.

And suddenly she went very still. As her hand closed around it, a soft, soothing warmth spread into her palm, up her arm, all through her body. She withdrew the paper, staring at it. It was almost pulsing with an unseen energy. She unfolded it, but her hands shook so badly, she couldn't read it even when she held it in front of her nose.

Annie licked her parched lips and smoothed the paper onto the gleaming hardwood telephone stand with sweat-slick hands. Why was she feeling this sense of importance about the note? Why was she bothering to read it at a moment of such intense crisis? She was supposed to be calling Information, getting a number, asking for help. . . .

"It's all right," the note said in an spiky scrawl. And it was as if someone were holding her hand, squeezing it, whispering the reassuring words right into her ear. *It's all right. Everything's going to be all right. Really, it is. I promise.* And for some reason, Annie believed the voice.

She opened her eyes and read the rest of the note. "It's all right, Annie. *You're* all right. Believe that, with everything in you. Soon you'll understand." It was signed S.D.

Sara Dawson?

Annie shook her head. Sara hadn't given her any note. How . . . ?

The trembling was beginning to ease. She had no idea why, or how, but it did. She forced her breathing to slow and regulate, and her stomach stopped churning.

A blanket of warmth and comfort settled around her shoulders. What had happened? What had changed?

Annie blinked rapidly and looked from the paper to her hands holding it. Steady now. Her pounding heart had gentled. Her pulse no longer throbbed in her temples. The dizziness, probably brought on by spiraling blood pressure, was easing.

What the hell?

The words of a child—words that had nothing to do with what was going on in Annie's mind—had calmed her as surely as a shot of Valium. Why, for God's sake? And what did the note mean? Sara couldn't have known of Annie's troubles. So why say "It's all right," as if offering comfort? And what did she mean by "Soon you'll understand"? Understand what? Not these hallucinations she seemed to be having. Sara had no way of knowing about them.

Did she?

Annie couldn't help picturing the quiet girl with her strange, soulful eyes. No. No, of course she couldn't know. She was a young girl, not a psychic.

Still, for some unidentifiable reason, a frantic call to her doctor or to her retired psychiatrist neighbor regarding strange and troubling symptoms no longer seemed nearly as important as having a serious discussion with young Sara Dawson.

Chapter Three

∾ Annie couldn't explain the sense of calm and well-being that descended over her. She was curious, of course, about Sara. Disturbed that the girl seemed to know so much about Annie's personal life. But not upset for some reason—as she probably should be.

Later. She'd be upset later. First . . . she'd just talk to the girl. Find out who'd been telling tales. It was obvious Sara meant well, even if she had been listening to gossip a bit more than she should.

Annie picked up the phone, and the number she dialed was one she knew too well to have to look up. She only prayed Mrs. Watkins would still be in the office at this hour. Chances of it were pretty good. The woman spent more time at the school than at home. Nothing went on there that she didn't know about. Hell, they barely needed a computer system with her around.

When her crisp-apple tone came through the

line, Annie almost breathed a sigh of relief. "I'm so glad you're still there. This is Annie Nelson, Mrs. Watkins. Could you do me a favor and pull the file on one of my students? I need her home address and phone number."

Mrs. Watkins, as usual, was only too happy to be of help. "Which student, dear?"

"The new girl in English Ten. Sara Dawson. That's D-A-W—"

"Ms. Nelson . . . Annie . . . there's no new girl in that class."

Annie bit back her impatience and tried again. "Of course there is. She just started a couple of days ago. I don't know, maybe she's not on the computer yet, but her name is—"

"There is no Sara Dawson registered in this school, Annie. And there hasn't been a transfer since Bobby McArthur last May." Her voice softened to the tone of a worried mother. "Now, honey, you know me. I'd know if there was."

She *would* know if there was. So why *didn't* she? There was a long pause as Annie blinked at the receiver.

"Dear, are you all right? You want me to send someone over there? What's—"

Annie glanced up, her eyes drawn by some force beyond her control. And she saw him. Richard, lumbering down the road in that old familiar gait, making a beeline for her front door.

He looked so good.

She wanted to run to him . . . and she wanted to run away. She longed for him. She was terrified of him. Was he her husband or a stranger? A lover or a ghost? Reality or madness? She didn't scream. She held the phone in an iron grip. "I'm fine, Mrs. Watkins. Thank you." And she replaced the receiver.

She got to her feet, turned the lock on the front door, and watched as he came closer. He looked toward her, but she didn't think he could see her through the sheer curtain. It was dim inside, but still bright out there.

"I love you, Richard," she whispered. "But please go away. Go away and leave me alone."

Then she turned and walked through the dining room and the kitchen to the back door. And as soon as she was outside, she ran.

She couldn't look out again and see him standing on the porch, staring back at her. Not now, not after all this. She needed help, someone she could talk to about this, so she could figure out what was going on, why she kept seeing Richard's face on some other man. Some stranger. And there was only one place she could go to get it.

Octagon House. Bartholomew Cassius. He

could help her. And he would; she knew he would. She cut through the backyard and around behind the house next door. Then she raced to the road and crossed it, heading onto Mariposa. She glanced over her shoulder and saw Richard, his back to her, mounting her front steps now, ringing her doorbell. If he turned around . . .

She ran faster, not even slowing her pace when she'd passed the gas station and was beyond his range of vision. She pressed on, and her legs cramped, and her lungs burned. Hot tears squeezed out of her eyes from the exertion as well as the trauma. She was pushing herself too hard, but she couldn't stop. With every stride she felt sure the devil himself was on her heels, chasing her, gaining on her.

She turned the corner onto Gladding Street and picked up the pace again, jogging past the school. Her lungs were screaming now. Fire burned up the backs of her calves, and her heart thundered. She stopped at the foot of the steep incline and stared up the road just ahead of her.

Octagon House was up there. It sat like a squat emperor on a hillside throne, its dark window-eyes gazing haughtily down at her, reminding her for just a second of Bartholomew's eyes. Just as glassy and emotionless. A ripple went up her spine, momentarily chasing her panic into a quiet corner. Something cold touched her nape, and a warning prickle crept along her arms.

Don't go up there.

She shook herself free of the ominous feelings. It wasn't difficult. She only had to picture the man she'd seen standing, dripping wet, on her porch, staring in the window at her. She only had to picture herself screaming as she looked out at the face of her dead husband.

Desperation tugged her onward. Of their own volition, her fingers found and caressed the pink tourmaline suspended around her neck. It warmed at her touch. And as she drew closer, she knew she was doing the right thing. Something in the house seemed to draw her, call to her, and the unreasonable fears faded as this new sense of purpose took over. A sense that not only did she want to go there, she *must* go. It was too potent to resist.

"Ms. Nelson," someone called. "You all right? You look a little . . ."

She shook her head, waving a hand to silence the encroacher. Her eyes never wavered from their focus on the house. The feelings of confusion lost ground with every step she took. The sounds of her own inner fears seemed to come from a distance as the lure of Octagon House grew stronger. Once or twice she tried to shake the eerie sensation like a dog shaking water from its fur, but it clung.

Her pace slowed. One step at a time, she moved up the hill. And the farther she went, the more trancelike her state became. She could barely feel the pavement beneath her feet now. And her eyes picked out the flat, tar-coated octagonal roof in the distance and fixed themselves on it, on the way the blackness shimmered in the early autumn heat.

She barely registered the cries at first. Terrified screams gradually penetrated, and then the rumble of tires on rough pavement, moving at high speed, and the blast of a horn.

The screaming had form. Words. And it took a second for their meaning and the urgency in their tone to penetrate her fogged mind.

"Look out! I can't stop! Get out of the way!"

She was jolted out of her spell. And as if released, her gaze sprang away from the heat shimmers emanating from the black roof and widened at the danger right in front of her. The car swerved crazily, barreling down the steep incline, its nose seemingly aimed right at her midsection.

She made a move as if to lunge out of the way, knowing already that it was too late. There wasn't even time to scream.

And then something hit her, but it wasn't the car. Just as big from the feel of it, though.

Like a torpedo launched from the opposite side of the road, a body flew into her, taking her with it into the ditch at her left. Somehow the projectile she'd boarded turned as it flew, landing hard on the ground beneath her, cushioning her fall. She felt the heat of the car as it careened past, heard the impact of it hitting something farther along the road, then the long, lonely sound of the horn.

There were voices, shouts. Feet pounding over pavement. Annie shook herself, automatically encircling her belly with both arms, her first thought for the baby. But there were arms already there. Big, strong arms, that held her gently from behind and beneath her. And there was a hard body stretching the length of her back, and a breathless whisper, close to her ear.

"Are you hurt?"

She didn't turn. She couldn't, the way he held her. "I . . . no."

"And the baby? It's all right, you're sure?" As he spoke, one of his palms flattened against her abdomen. Right on cue, the baby kicked, hard and furiously. And there was soft laughter in her ears, bathing her neck.

Laughter so familiar she choked on a sudden rush of tears. Oh, God, it still hurt so much to hear that laugh. It would be so good, so damned good if he really were Richard.

This delusion—or whatever it was—was looking better all the time. Maybe she ought to stop fighting it. God, if these arms around her could only be his. That breath in her ear . . .

A sob broke from her chest. She couldn't stop it. Another followed, and then another. Tears flash-flooded her face. She cried so hard, she shook with it. Because it seemed very much as if her husband were holding her to him right now.

Gently, still protecting her bulging middle, he moved her off him. Annie covered her face with her hands, embarrassed and shaken. Terrified to look up and see Richard's face on a stranger. Terrified that she wouldn't.

She sat on the ground, legs folded to one side, face hidden, and fought to control her tears.

Strong hands grasped her shoulders, kneaded them. "What is it? You're hurt after all, aren't you?"

"No," she managed between sobs. She knuckled the tears from her eyes and drew a shaky breath, head bowed.

He eased her to her feet, still holding her, treating her as gently as if she were made of porcelain.

"I'm all right now," she assured him. "Really." She told herself it was true. She was all right. She could get through this just fine.

There was no more running away. It was time to face this thing. Time to see the truth. She blinked several times and tested her vision by counting her own fingers. Then, drawing a deep breath, she lifted her head and blinked the tear haze from her eyes. She would look at him. She would see that he wasn't Richard. She'd see the dark-haired stranger, maybe, or someone she knew, but not Richard. She turned her head and looked at him.

Her jaw fell, and she blinked faster.

"Oh my God." She didn't run from him this time. She couldn't. He was too real. And she had to be sure. . . .

With shaking hands, she touched his face. It didn't alter or vanish as she half expected it would. It was real. It *felt* real and familiar and wonderful. Her fingers dived into his golden hair, felt its texture. And the tears flooded her eyes, blurring her vision, and she pressed her lips to that beloved face again and again, muttering his name and a hundred other things, until the words and the kisses tangled in one another and tripped in their haste to reach him. She felt his body tremble, felt his arms close gently around her, saw his eyes flash as they met hers. And then she just nestled herself against him, let him hold her, buried her face in the fabric of his shirt. He even *smelled* like Richard. She'd be content to stay wrapped in these strong arms forever.

The way he felt when she pressed those tear-soaked, salty kisses to his face was beyond his understanding. Something rushed through him. Something more than the adrenaline surge he felt in the heat of disputes or battles, or the satisfaction he felt when a mission was complete. It was like . . . joy. Only stronger. Wilder. More fierce and intense and urgent than that. And his arms went around her without his consent, though if he'd given the act any thought, he wouldn't have resisted. He *wanted* to hold the small, beautiful, tortured woman. He'd wanted to hold her for some time now. To take away her anguish. To absorb it into himself if necessary—anything to ease her pain.

As soon as he closed his arms around her, she relaxed against him and his heart leaped in reaction to the way she felt there. Boneless. Shivering. Clinging to him as if she'd sink to the ground without his support. And the thought came to him that perhaps she was hurt after all. Automatically he scooped her up, surprised again at how light she felt. And he carried her easily, even while battling the eerie sense that he'd done so before. And no, not on that rainy night when he'd first seen her, but even before then. There was something so very familiar about the way her head rested against his shoulder, the touch of her hair on his neck, and the scent of that hair. There was something familiar about wanting to protect her. To take away her pain. Her soft breaths on his skin tickled a memory to life, but it was buried too deeply to identify.

She didn't speak to him. Just pressed her face into the crook of his neck and dampened his skin with her tears. He made his way back down the narrow road, past the school building. That was where he'd imagined she was going when he'd realized that she had left the house. And when he'd caught up to her, seen her apparent rush, he'd thought something urgent there must need her attention.

But the urgency in her step had eased at the base of this hill, and she'd gone on slowly, almost mechanically. Why had she wandered farther? What had drawn her into a brush with death?

He glanced over his shoulder at the steeply rising road behind him, but saw no one. And he dismissed his curiosity in favor of more immediate matters as he approached the wrecked car, its nose embracing a telephone pole. A woman babbled all but incoherently to the emergency people on the scene. Luckily for everyone involved, the volunteer fire department was practically within shouting distance.

The woman driver looked unharmed.
Thankfully the paramedics could devote their
attention to the one in his arms. The delicate
beauty who called herself Annie, and who'd
somehow become precious to him. At the
touch of her hands, he'd been enchanted. It
was like magic. Protecting her, seeing her safe
at any cost, had suddenly taken as on as much
importance to him as protecting the child she
carried. But protecting the child was his mission. He wasn't supposed to care for the
mother.

She stirred in his arms, and as he lowered
his gaze to her face, he saw her wide emerald
eyes staring up at him as if she were seeing a
miracle. Tears filled those huge round gems to
brimming and spilled over. Slowly, like glyc-
erin, they slid down her cheeks.

He stopped walking, shocked into immobil-
ity by the sight of those tears and the look in
her eyes. They bathed him with emotions,
those green eyes. They caught him and held
him, and he couldn't move in the force of their
grasp. There was a power emanating from
those eyes. Something stronger than Sir
George's magic, more binding than his own
vows. It gripped him by the heart and held
tight, shaking him right to the core.

A young woman ran toward him. Even as

she barked questions, though, he couldn't free his gaze from Annie's. She seemed to be searching him, inside as well as out, and her face registered nothing less than sheer adoration. Her lips kept parting as if she wanted to speak, then closing again, her words aborted. She shook her head several times as if to clear it. Blinked, rubbed her eyes, and stared some more.

"Annie! Annie, listen to me," the other woman snapped, her voice loud and firm but calm as she vied for Annie's attention. "Are you in any pain? Were you hit? Annie?"

The woman with the short blond hair kept after her until Annie broke eye contact with him and turned her head. Her voice a harsh whisper, she rasped, "Rebecca, *look*. Look at him."

"Rebecca" frowned, shot him a cursory glance, and focused on Annie once more.

"Yeah, I see him. So what?" She inclined her head toward a gurney, and Ren bent to lower Annie onto it.

"It's Richard," Annie croaked, her gaze darting back and forth between him and Rebecca. "Don't you recognize him? It's *him*."

The woman gave her head a shake, glanced at him once more, and then, slowly, her entire countenance altered. She looked frightened as her sharp eyes met Annie's. And her voice changed. Became softer, as if she were speaking to a child.

"Take it easy, Annie. Come on, look again. This guy doesn't look anything like Richard." She knelt beside the gurney, as if to see better, moving Annie's hair out of the way, probing her scalp. "Did you hit your head? Is that it?"

"The car didn't hit her," Ren explained, hoping to help in some way. "And when I knocked her out of the way, she landed on top of me. I don't think she hit her head."

"It *is* him!" Annie sat up on the gurney while Rebecca tried to urge her to lie back down. "Tell her, Richard. Tell her it's you!" Her eyes were wild, and he worried that maybe she was suffering some kind emotional trauma—perhaps from the shock of this near miss. The other rescue workers had stopped what they were doing now, and turned to stare at her, pity and a sad sort of unsurprised concern etched on their faces. And when Ren looked beyond them, he saw others. A crowd of them, adults and teenagers alike, gathering on the school's front lawn. Craning their necks. Whispering. Several were shaking their heads sadly. "Poor Annie," someone whispered.

"She's only confused," Ren attempted. "My name is—"

"Nelson," Annie said, her voice louder now,

more insistent. "Richard Nelson. And I'm *not* confused." With a strength that surprised him, she shoved off the restraining hands and got to her feet. "What's the matter with you people? Don't you think I know my own husband?"

"Husband?" he echoed, jolted.

But before he could say more, Annie was in his arms again. Clinging to his neck, shaking violently. Sobs racked her small frame, and tears dampened his shirt. She kept saying that name over and over again, and the sound of it brought a burning to his own eyes, a tightness to the center of his chest that couldn't be explained.

His arms went around her, and he wanted nothing more in the world than to protect her from any more pain. She stiffened when the one called Rebecca jabbed a needle into her arm. And then she slowly went limp.

"Don't leave me again," she whispered, just before her eyes closed. "God, Richard, I need you so much. . . ."

He held her tighter to keep her from falling. Richard, he thought. The name felt odd. Not new. Not unfamiliar or strange. More like an old favorite shoe that hadn't been worn in a long time—so long, it no longer fit. And he wondered if he'd ever been this man she called Richard. Maybe a lifetime ago. A lifetime he'd since forgotten. And if that were the case, then Sir George had lied to him.

He'd never have believed that possible.

"It's a very mild sedative," Rebecca explained when he searched her face. "She needs to calm down or she'll send herself into an early labor."

Ren nodded, easing Annie onto the gurney again. She seemed so tiny, so in need of protection. And he couldn't help but wonder how any of what he was beginning to suspect could be true. It seemed impossible to believe that he—or any man—could forget a woman like her.

As Rebecca hovered over Annie, Ren stepped aside. His gaze shot once more to the hill behind them and then slid to the smashed car. A man was wriggling out from beneath it.

"Brake fluid all leaked out, Mrs. Pike. There's a hole in the line. Lucky you didn't get yourself killed."

Ren frowned and his gaze was drawn up the hill once more. A man stood there, on the roadside in front of the odd-shaped house. Tall and slender, he stared down at them, and Ren could feel the touch of those black eyes even from here. Their gazes met, and the thin man smiled very slowly.

Chapter Four

෴ Warmth. Calm. Peace.

As Annie slowly came out of sedation, she felt as if she were enveloped in a huge, fluffy cloud of well-being. And as her mind cleared, she focused on that feeling, trying to seek out its source.

It radiated through her every cell, but as she concentrated, she realized where it began. A trail of comfort led down her arm to the warm pressure surrounding her hand. And another path to the source of this feeling of peace seemed anchored at her forehead, where a soft hand was stroking her hair in a gentle rhythm. And more of the serenity was found in the soft clarity of a strong young voice—a girl's voice—singing a lilting song that sounded like a lullaby.

Annie opened her eyes, then closed them and opened them again. Sara Dawson sat in a chair beside the bed. The girl held Annie's hand and stroked her face. She stopped sing-

ing, bent close, and pressed a soft kiss to Annie's cheek. Her smile was gentle; her eyes,
knowing and serene. Always so serene, those
beautiful eyes of hers.

"You're awake."

Annie nodded. "I guess so." She looked
past the girl, taking in the whitewashed walls,
smelling the sterile, all-too-familiar scent of
hospital antiseptic. For a second, panic seeped
into her veins like ice water, and her hands
pressed to her belly.

"It's Community Memorial," Sara said.
"And you're fine. The baby, too." She didn't
say those things the way most people would,
as if they were well wishes or positive
thoughts. She said them with authority. "I
thought you'd feel better knowing."

Annie narrowed her eyes, studying the
smooth young face, searching for answers.
More and more it seemed to her that this was
no ordinary girl. "Sara, what on earth are you
doing here?"

"I thought you might need me." She
squeezed Annie's hand before letting it go.
"You're upset. You read my note, didn't you?"

Annie nodded. "But I didn't understand
what it meant. Sara, you know nothing about
what I'm going through right now. You
couldn't."

"But I do."

Again Annie fell silent. She finally cleared her throat and forced herself to speak. "Tell me, then. What do you know about me or . . . or Richard?"

Sara tilted her head. "I know you're not insane. You're the sanest person you know. That's what you're always saying, isn't it?"

Annie gaped. The girl was so new in town. How could Sara know Annie had been driven very close to the point of questioning her own sanity?

But wait. Sara wasn't registered in school. And Annie had never seen her speak in front of anyone but her. She remembered how she'd thought the other day that her students ignored Sara, as if she wasn't there.

What if they weren't ignoring her? What if she really wasn't there? What if she's some kind of . . . of . . . what? Guardian angel?

Ridiculous!

"You have to trust yourself, Annie. Trust your mind, your senses. Believe what you see with your own eyes."

"If you knew what I'd been seeing lately, you wouldn't say that." Annie let her head sink deeper into the pillows. "Who are you, really, Sara?" And she eyed the girl's haunting eyes. "*What* are you?"

Sara only smiled. "What I'm not is more important," she said. "And I am not a figment of your imagination. Look at things, Annie. Analyze them, but don't doubt they exist. There are more things in the world than you know. More things than anyone knows."

Annie sat up a little, frowning. "What do you mean by that?"

"You must stop questioning yourself. That's the first thing. You can't win this battle unless you find the strength inside you, Annie. It's true, what Richard was always telling you. You *are* a strong woman. That's part of the reason you were chosen—"

"Chosen?" Annie shook her head rapidly, then paused, eyes widening. "How could you know Richard used to say that?"

"Find the strength inside you, Annie. Find the woman you were before Richard went away. She's still there. I know it. Your baby needs that old Annie, not this frightened, uncertain woman you're becoming. You—"

"Who are you?" Annie frowned at the lovely girl and shook her head in confusion. "God, Sara, who *are* you, *really*?"

Sara bit her lip, rising from the chair with a quick glance toward the door. "I need a glass of water."

And without another word, the girl walked into the small bathroom attached to the hospital room. She pushed the door a little but didn't close it all the way, and then Annie heard the water running.

God, what was this all about? Who was Sara? Annie knew, deep in her gut, that she wasn't just an ordinary girl playing head games with a teacher. Sara wasn't cruel. She was kind—good, through and through. Annie felt it in her touch, saw it in her eyes. The girl truly seemed to want to help.

And she *had* helped. Oddly enough, the only times Annie had felt relaxed and calm lately had been when Sara was nearby. She felt closer to the girl than she should, given their brief acquaintance.

The water was still running, the door still stood partly opened, yet Sara hadn't come out.

Annie slipped from the bed and got to her feet. She had to grip the back of a chair for support when a wave of dizziness washed over her, aftereffect of whatever drug they'd given her. She fought it and won. Then she started toward the bathroom.

Someone else was coming in. She heard the door from the hall open, heard two solid steps.

"Annie?"

She knew that voice. But she couldn't turn around and face him. Not yet. She stepped up to the bathroom door and pushed it open.

The faucet spewed clear frothy water into the basin. A mirror over the sink showed Annie the reflection of a small room. A small, *empty* room. Sara wasn't there.

Annie shook her head slowly, sinking to her knees, forgetting for a moment to hold on to the wall for support. "My God, it's true," she whispered. "She's not . . . not real. Or . . ."

Strong hands clasped her shoulders, drawing her backward until she leaned against jean-clad legs. "It's all right, Annie. I promise you, it's going to be all right."

His hands ran down her arms, then clasped her waist and lifted her gently, easily to her feet. "Come on, we can't have the doctors seeing you like this."

She bit her lip and turned slowly. The big hands on her waist loosened to let her turn, but never let go. They still rested there when she faced him.

"Who *are* you?" One trembling hand lifted to touch the face she still dreamed about every single night. "My God, are you real? Are you a ghost?"

"I'm real. I'm here to help you, Annie."

"Help me do what? Go completely insane?" Her words came out as whispers as her fingers touched a lock of his hair, rubbing its silken texture between them. "Is it you, Richard?"

The man closed his eyes as if her words caused him immeasurable pain. "I'm not your husband. My name is Ren."

"Ren," she repeated. "Richard Elliot Nelson. A man who could be my husband's twin, whose name is an acronym of his initials. Am I supposed to believe this?"

"You must believe it."

She had to force her hands to her sides, to stop from touching him, feeling his hair, as if to assure herself he was really here. "They never found the body," she muttered, almost to herself. "Were you hurt, Richard? Did you lose your memory and wander away? Is that it?"

With his two large hands he cupped her head, holding her gently but still making her look right into those eyes. "Listen to me. Your husband is dead. I'm not him. My name is Ren, and I'm here to help you."

She shook her head slowly, closed her eyes. "I didn't need any help. I was doing just fine on my own . . . until you showed up."

"You are perfectly sane," he told her. "Everything you're experiencing now has an explanation, Annie. That's the first thing you have to accept."

Annie tried to swallow the lump in her throat and, failing, went ahead and spoke around it. The result was a voice that sounded as if it were being filtered through gravel. "Of course I'm sane," she whispered. "I'm . . . the sanest person I know." He nodded, apparently approving of the statement. Annie couldn't take her eyes off him. If she was sane, then he was a liar. He *was* Richard. She was standing here looking at him, and his denying it was so ridiculous, it was almost laughable. "I guess it's the rest of the town that's gone crazy," she went on. "When Leslie saw you, and Rebecca, they said your hair was dark. They said you—"

"I know. Annie, it's best not dwell on that right now. These doctors in this place, they need to see that you are fine. If you keep insisting I'm your dead husband, they'll have you committed to an institution. I won't be able to protect you there."

Her eyes flew wider. "Protect me?"

Voices came from just beyond the door. The handle turned. "I told them I'm your husband's cousin," he said quickly. "Annie, it's important you listen to me. You must tell them the same. For the sake of your baby."

"My baby?"

He smoothed one hand down over her hair. "Trust me, Annie."

The door opened and a doctor entered. She wore round bifocals with tortoiseshell frames, and her hair was carrot orange.

Annie looked at the woman, then at the man who claimed he wasn't her husband. Then she turned slowly, walked to the window, braced her hands on the ledge, and stared, unsee-ingly, outside.

"How are you feeling, Annie?"

"Fine." She wasn't, though. *Trust me*, he'd told her. How could she trust him?

How could she not?

"I'm Dr. Maxwell, staff psychiatrist."

Surprise, surprise. They sent me a shrink. Well, who'd have guessed?

"You're fine, physically, Annie," the woman went on. "I just have a few questions I'd like to ask you before we let you go home. It's rou-tine, you understand. You were a little diso-riented right after the accident. Which might be perfectly normal. But I have to be sure, given . . ."

"Given all the stress I've been under," An-nie filled in. "Fragile-looking females like me aren't supposed to be able to handle so much stress, after all. Especially pregnant ones."

She turned away from the window and looked at Ren standing there, still wearing his long coat. He smiled. It was a familiar smile, one that crushed her heart to dust. She didn't know what the hell was going on. She didn't know if he was her husband's twin, if he was lying, or if he simply didn't know who he was. She only knew she had to find out.

Dr. Maxwell nodded. "I'm afraid that's en-tirely true," she said. "Thank goodness we fragile females surprise them sometimes. We're tougher than we look, aren't we Annie?"

"Tougher than they can even imagine," Annie said.

The doctor nodded, seeming reassured. "You certainly look better than when they brought you in."

Annie shrugged.

Dr. Maxwell pulled off her glasses, using them to point at Ren . . . or Richard, or whoever he was. "Annie, do you know this man?"

He met Annie's gaze, giving her an almost imperceptible nod.

"Yes," she said. She concealed her turmoil beneath a cloak of calm. It wasn't as hard as she'd thought. After all, she'd been doing it for quite some time, now, hadn't she? Hiding her grief. Pretending she was getting over losing him just the way people said she should. She cleared her throat. "This is my husband's cousin, Ren. I . . . I didn't recognize him at first. It's been a long time."

Dr. Maxwell nodded, sliding the glasses onto her nose, lifting the top sheet from the clipboard she carried. "Would you describe him to me?"

Annie blinked. Great, a trick question. She looked at him again, stared right at his long, golden blond hair, and took a shot in the dark, based on Leslie's words at the store. "He's been called an ebony-haired, black-eyed pagan god."

Dr. Maxwell lifted her head and her eyebrows at the same time. She smiled when her gaze met Annie's, and she looked a whole lot less serious than before. "Colorful, but accurate. So do you still think he looks like your late husband?"

Annie closed her eyes. *Lie. Lie through your teeth if that's what it takes to get out of here.* She cleared her throat. "It's more in the bone structure than the coloring."

"Annie always was the only one who could see the resemblance between us," the ghost, or whatever he was, added. And he sent Annie a warm, approving look.

"Well, I'm glad to see you're all right, Annie. You can go home just as soon as we get your release forms together." Dr. Maxwell tucked her clipboard to her side and slipped her glasses into her pocket as she strolled out of the room.

Annie stared at the man, fighting with everything in her to trust what she was seeing, not to begin questioning herself, her judgment, her own senses. It was difficult when everyone else seemed to be seeing some totally different person. "Your hair is not black," she whispered.

"No. No, it's not."

She nearly sighed in relief that he had confirmed it. "Then how . . . why . . . ?"

"It's better not to ask."

"I'm asking anyway."

"There are things I can't tell you." He closed his eyes, lifting a hand to touch her shoulder. "Let me take you home, Annie. And I'll explain as much as I can."

He wouldn't, though. She knew he wouldn't. He couldn't explain what was inexplicable.

Ren couldn't explain it to her because he didn't understand it himself. He took her home. She said she was tired and didn't want to talk to him anymore tonight, and he could see she was on the brink of exhaustion.

He walked her through the big house, and a flash of familiarity rushed through him in nearly every room. As he ran his hands along the hardwood banister, he saw, for just an instant, an image of his hands rubbing it with rough-textured sandpaper. His own hands applying new varnish to restore the gleam to the smooth wood. And beside them, a smaller pair of hands. Hands that looked like Annie's. He held her arm as he took her up the stairs, and unerringly he found her bedroom.

She was exhausted. Too exhausted to protest his presence with any vigor. "You shouldn't be here" was about the extent of it.

"I'll go. As soon as you fall asleep."

They'd given him a small paper packet of pills for her, and they'd seen to it she'd taken one before leaving the hospital. Sedatives, they'd told him. Mild but effective. They must be effective, or she'd be arguing about his presence more than she was, he decided. Or maybe she wouldn't. Maybe she was as glad to have him here as she'd seemed at first. She slid into the bed, burrowed under the covers he tugged up over her, and looked him in the eye. "I want you to leave."

"I will," he lied.

From the bed she stared at him through sleepy eyes. "No, I don't," she whispered. "Not if you're my Richard. I don't ever want you to leave again."

And that was all. She fell into an unnatural sleep. Emotional exhaustion, Ren guessed, was even more to blame than those small white pills. He'd given her a terrible shock and a lot to deal with tonight.

Ren took off his sword and laid it in a corner, then covered it with his coat. He sat down on the small stool that rested near the dressing table. And he stared into the oval mirror, seeing his true self. How could she see him? Why wasn't she fooled by his disguise the way everyone else was?

He looked again at his reflection, only not the one in the mirror this time. This one smiled back at him from a photograph framed in pewter. His hair was shorter, and he wore a tux. In his arms he held the most beautiful creature ever to draw breath. Annie, glowing with happiness, her eyes shining with unshed tears. Her small body swathed in white satin, pearls, and lace.

The dress she wore in the photo was a bridal gown, and the groom holding her close was . . . Ren.

Good God, it was true, then. He *had* been her Richard.

He turned slowly to gaze at the heartbroken woman who lay in the bed, crying softly now and then, even in her sleep. Annie . . . she'd been his wife. Was it possible? Could any man have loved a woman like this one and then forgotten her?

But it had to be true. And she must know him well—as well as he knew himself. *Too* well to be fooled by the Cloak of Disguise.

And he couldn't tell her. Because if she knew the truth, it would only be harder in the end, when he had to leave her again. As he must, according to his vows.

But would she see through his lies as easily as she saw through the disguise?

And why, as he heard her soft sobs, saw the tears glittering on her cheeks, did he feel his own eyes begin to burn?

He was still there.

Annie blinked him into focus. He'd drawn the padded stool from the vanity up beside the bed and fallen asleep there, his head pillowed near her feet. Sun streamed through the window, its amber rays igniting his golden hair. He'd removed the long, dark-colored coat he wore, and it hung in a corner, and she briefly wondered what he'd hung it on. But what mattered was him, not his coat. Why was he still here?

She'd told him to go. He had said he would leave as soon as she fell asleep. She had wanted him to go . . . hadn't she? God, if she had, then why was she feeling such overwhelming joy to see him here now? No, she knew damned well she hadn't wanted to wake up and find him gone again.

I'm not your husband, Annie.

His words floated back to her, bringing a pang of sadness so intense, her eyes welled with tears. He said he wasn't Richard. But how could he not be?

He lay there, looking in sleep so much like

her husband that it was impossible to believe he could be anyone else. So much so that any second now, she fully expected him to open his eyes—Richard always woke within a few minutes after she did—and send her that lazy, sleepy smile she'd missed for all these long months.

But he wouldn't, would he? Because he wasn't Richard. Why was that so clear to everyone who saw him—everyone but her?

He stirred and his eyes opened, focused unerringly on hers. And then he smiled, and her heart melted into a trembling puddle in her chest.

She hurt. Looking at him brought all the pain she'd been fighting right back to the surface. How dare he do this to her? How dare he walk into her life and plunge a hot blade into her heart by telling her he wasn't Richard?

She sat up in bed. He lifted himself away from her mattress, his smile dying at the look on her face.

"What are you doing here? You told me you would go."

"I'm sorry. I was only trying to ease your mind so you could rest. I lied to you, Annie. I can't go."

"You can't stay."

He rose, pushed a hand through his hair in

frustration, but still kept those familiar blue eyes pinned to hers. "Annie, I know this is painful for you. If there were any other way—"

"If you can't be him," she whispered, "then please, for the love of God, get out of my house. Get out of my life. Can't you see what you're doing to me?"

She'd meant to shout at him, but the words sounded more like a desperate plea.

"I was sent here to protect you, Annie. I can't leave. Not yet. I have to stay right here, in this house."

She was stunned. She stared, just shaking her head.

"It's important, Annie."

"No. Nothing is this important. I can't have you here; I can't look at you, see you standing there claiming you aren't Richard and looking too much like him to be anyone else. Nothing is important enough to go through this."

"Not even your child?"

Annie lunged out of the bed and stood facing him. "What *about* my child?"

He lowered his gaze, regret for what he'd said written all over his face. "I can't—"

She gripped the front of his shirt in fists that shook almost violently. "Damn you, Ren, or whoever the hell you are, if there's something going on that involves my baby, you'd better tell me and tell me now, or I'll make you wish you'd stayed wherever you came from."

He stood still, utterly still, just staring down at her. Then his hand rose, and slowly stroked her hair. "There it is," he said softly. "You've found it at last, haven't you, Annie? You've got so much strength inside you, you know that? I can see it in your eyes."

She bit her lip. Richard had said something so similar to her, how many times?

"Hold on to that strength, that anger," he said. "You're going to need all of it for the battles we'll soon have to face."

Annie closed her eyes. God, it felt good when he touched her. She wanted so much to believe this was Richard, here, speaking to her so gently. And with every word he said, every expression that crossed his face, she was more convinced.

She grated her teeth and faced him again. "What are you saying? Is my baby in some kind of danger?"

He nodded grimly. He clasped her hands in his, removing them from his shirt, lowering them, flattening her palms to her swollen belly, covering them with his own.

"Who are you?" She lifted her gaze to his, staring deeply into his eyes. "Tell me the truth."

His sigh was deep and coarse. "I come from

another realm, Annie. One most people don't even know exists." He was quiet, pensive for a very long moment. Then he drew a deep breath, seeming to choose his words carefully. "I've broken rules already by telling you as much as I have. Suffice it to say, Annie, that there are forces out there, good and evil so powerful, you couldn't begin to imagine them. There are those who wish to keep this child from being born. And there are those like me, who'd die to protect it."

"Why?"

"I can't say any more. I'm sorry."

It was madness, what he was telling her. Utter madness. But his words, his voice, rang so true.

"I'm not asking you to believe me. I'm not asking you to do anything at all, except let me stay. Let me protect you until your child is born."

Let him stay? She'd cut off a limb to keep him with her now. He had to be Richard. And she'd find a way to prove it, make him admit it, or make him remember if he'd somehow forgotten all they'd been to each other. She frowned, lifting her gaze to his and replaying his words in her mind. *Until your child is born.* A lump came into her throat as she whispered, "And what then?"

Ren cleared his throat. "Then . . . I go back."

Annie closed her eyes and silently vowed that he wouldn't. She wasn't going to lose him. Not again.

Chapter Five

∾ He'd done it. He'd convinced Annie of the lie he'd told her. That he wasn't her husband, had never been her husband. Maybe. She seemed to have accepted it, for now. Or perhaps she made herself accept it only because it was less painful that way. Or perhaps she was lying, pretending to believe him when in truth she knew better.

For some reason that latter theory seemed the most valid. And it disturbed him. He couldn't be what he'd been to her. Not now. Not emotionally, not physically. Desire was a thing that didn't exist for him. And his love belonged to the cause of good. Not to another living soul.

For whatever reason, Annie appeared to believe him. She called him Ren. Still looked at him with wonder in her eyes, but addressed him as a stranger. And she accepted his staying with her . . . for now, she'd said.

He'd never felt so awkward before. So

119

clumsy and large and likely to say or do the wrong thing and put the pain back in her eyes. He was a Hero, for God's sake! Why *would* he feel this way?

But as he walked her to school that morning, the sense of déjà vu was so strong, it dizzied him. The urge to hold her small hand tightly in his large one, or worse yet, to cradle her in the crook of his arm, was all but overwhelming.

He couldn't stop himself from watching her as she walked along beside him. The way the wind caressed her fiery hair amazed him. And the sun glinting from her jeweled eyes. And the silken texture of her skin.

He couldn't remember ever being this entranced by the way a woman looked. He tore his gaze away, tried to watch where he was going instead. She seemed stiff, tense as she walked with him, but the second his head was turned, he felt her looking at him. Her gaze roamed over his face like a living thing. And it was warm, enticing.

He turned toward her. She looked away.

She was still hurting; Ren couldn't deny that. Still trying to reconcile the man who'd forced his way into her life with the man she'd loved and lost. He hoped she could go on believing what he'd told her, that they were two separate men. But he was afraid she wouldn't.

She'd seen through his disguise so easily, it stood to reason she'd see through his lies as well. But her face, her eyes, revealed nothing. Except an excrutiating blend of pain and pleasure.

The scent of autumn hung heavy in the chilled air and made the day seem so crisp, one could take a bite of it. But above that scent, he was all too aware of hers. The soap she used, the shampoo, the skin lotions, and her own womanly musk combined to intrigue him and made it impossible not to lean slightly closer just to inhale the fragrance again. How could such a subtle scent play such havoc with his mind? It seemed so enticingly familiar. It tickled at the back of his awareness, nudging some hidden memory and drawing away before he could place it. Over and over again, like the ocean's waves teasing the sandy shore. Retreating. Teasing again.

He looked down at her, and she promptly shifted her gaze elsewhere. He noticed for the first time that she had a tiny parade of pale freckles marching across the bridge of her nose.

Seventeen of them. Don't you remember, you counted them once?

Ren frowned at the voice within but stared harder at the freckles—until she turned and scowled at him.

"What are you looking at? Do I have food smudged on my face or something?"

"No. And how could you? You didn't eat this morning."

"I did so."

"One slice of unbuttered toast and a minuscule glass of milk are not a meal."

"Yeah, well, I'm sure you'll understand if I say my stomach isn't quite calm this morning."

He blinked and lowered his eyes, ashamed to be the reason for her lack of appetite. "I'm sorry for that."

"Don't worry about it. I took my vitamins."

That eased his mind a little.

"Do you walk to school every day?" he asked her. "Even in the winter?"

"It's good exercise." She looked at him a little oddly, as if awaiting his reply.

"In snowstorms?" he asked her. "In below-zero weather?"

As her lips curved upward at the corners, she averted her face. "Gets the blood circulating."

"You're crazy," he told her.

"That's what Richard always said. Every time we had this discussion. Must have been a dozen times or more." And she looked at him, and there was a sparkle in her eyes that hadn't been there before.

He said no more, since they were arriving at the school building. He cupped her elbow in his hand as they started up the steps. At the contact, she stopped walking, closed her eyes, and drew a shaky breath. But she didn't take her arm away. She seemed to gather strength from his touch as she stiffened her spine. She drew a deep breath, opened her eyes, and began moving again.

As they entered the building, she spoke in a low voice. "I've told you how odd this is going to look, you coming to school with me this way."

"And I've told you that I'm not letting you out of my sight."

"Mrs. Nelson?"

They both stopped walking when the dark-haired woman approached. Annie frowned at her. "Yes?"

"Mrs. Wright. Tammy's mother," the woman explained. And Annie nodded as if she'd finally placed her. The woman reached her hand out to clasp Annie's shoulder, and her face seemed perfect for someone attending a funeral. "How are you?" she asked, and the words were laden with meaning.

"I'm . . . I'm fine." If Annie seemed confused, Ren was right with her.

"That's good," Mrs. Wright said, offering a weak smile. "That's very good. You just remember, when the burdens get to be too much for you, let the Lord carry part of the load. I know He's always been there for me."

"Thanks. I'll . . . uh . . . I'll remember that."

"We weren't meant to bear our grief alone, Annie. That's what He's there for." She patted Annie's shoulder once more, gave her a brighter smile, and moved away.

Annie stared after her for a second, the skin between her brows forming an accordion. Then she gave her head a shake and turned toward a classroom. But she stopped in the doorway. Her pretty mouth fell open, and her eyes widened in surprise, only to narrow, seconds later, in what looked like fury. And it was aimed at the little round fellow sitting behind the desk.

"Excuse me." She seemed to grow a few inches taller as she strode into the classroom and addressed the man who was arranging photographs in a horseshoe pattern. "Is there something I can do for you?" she asked him.

He glanced up, brows raised. "I don't think so. But I'll let you know if I need anything. New schools are always an adjustment." He gave her a smile, then glanced past her to meet Ren's gaze, and his smile died.

"Then maybe you can do something for me," Annie went on.

"Sure, just ask."

"Well, for starters you can tell me who you are, and why you're sitting at my desk." She had not returned his smile, Ren guessed.

"I . . . that is, I'm . . . Oh, my. This is embarrassing. I'm—"

"He's Marvin Kestler, Annie."

Annie whirled, and Ren turned to see the man who'd spoken, standing in the doorway.

"Harry, what the hell is going on here?"

Harry came the rest of the way inside, passing Ren as if he wasn't even there, and approaching Annie. He put a hand on her outer arm, giving her a sappy smile that was obviously forced. Ren stiffened, sensing the man was about to insert a blade between Annie's ribs.

"Annie . . ." Harry sighed deeply, and his hand on Annie's shoulder stroked a small circle. "Are you all right?"

"Why the hell does everyone keep asking me that?"

He let his hand fall to his side at the anger in her voice. "Because we care. Look, I heard about what happened yesterday. And—"

"*How*, exactly, did you hear about it?"

"Come on, Annie, it happened a few yards from the school. Half the town witnessed it. Did you really think I *wouldn't* hear about it?"

She set her jaw and crossed her arms over her chest, just above her swollen belly. "It was an accident, Harry. A near miss. I wasn't hurt. You can see by looking at me that I'm fine now."

"Physically," he blurted, then bit his lip and averted his eyes. "Look, you've been under an incredible strain. Everyone knows it, and believe me, we've been in awe of the way you've carried on in spite of it all. But Annie, you could only take so much. And we understand. We do. We just want you well again. That's all."

"We?"

"We've discussed this and we agree it's time you started your maternity leave."

"Who do you mean when you say 'we'?"

He shifted his weight from one foot to another. "Dr. Cassius and me, mostly." He lifted his gaze to hers. "And the Board of Education, of course."

Ren saw the way Annie flinched in surprise. "Bartholomew?" Her voice held a hint of hurt, maybe a touch of betrayal. Ren felt a stab of something very similar to jealousy then, but of course, it couldn't have been that. Knights didn't feel such things.

"He's terribly worried about you, Annie. And so am I. In fact, he wants to help you. Look, we know how hard this past year has been on you. And now with the baby so close, and—"

She jerked her arm away from his touch. "There is *nothing* wrong with me, dammit. I can still do my job."

"Maybe I ought to leave," Kestler stammered. He elbowed past them and hurried out the door, but Annie didn't seem to notice.

Harry sent Ren a meaningful glance, as if suggesting he ought to leave as well. Ren gave his head a slight shake.

Annie didn't see or else just didn't acknowledge the exchange. Ren saw how much color her cheeks had. He saw the gleam of unshed tears in her eyes. He stood closer to her side, then stiffened in shock when he felt her small hand slip inside his. Her fingers twined and squeezed, and he returned the pressure so automatically that his own action startled him nearly as much as hers had. She'd taken his hand when she'd needed his strength. And she'd done it before, hadn't she? He knew it. Something about the anger, the flash of life in her eyes right now triggered the knowledge in his mind. How he'd love to see it again.

"Harry, you could have spoken to me about this. This is one hell of a way to let me find out I've been replaced."

"Not replaced, Annie. This is only temporary. And I tried to call you about it last night but the phones—"

"My fault," Ren interrupted. They both

glanced at him as if they'd forgotten his presence. Annie seemed to suddenly realize that she clutched his hand, and she made a move as if to remove hers from his clasp, so he held it tighter. "I'm sorry, Annie. I took the phones off the hook last night. I wanted you to rest."

This drew a deep frown from Harry. "This guy is *staying* with you?"

Annie closed her eyes. "Is the board going to dictate my personal life now, as well as my career?"

"Annie's husband was my cousin," Ren cut in, not wanting her to let her anger destroy her position at the school. "Naturally, I want to be with her now, since he can't be here himself." He felt her hand tremble a bit when he said it. God, could the loss of one man still hurt her that much?

Her eyes opened and she faced Harry. "You don't have to explain anything to him, Ren. It's not his business. What *is* his business is running this school, and so I guess I have no choice but to honor his decision." She licked her lips. "But I don't have to like it.

"Annie—"

"Too late to apologize, Harry. I'll just go now. I hope I'm right in assuming my job will still be here after my maternity leave is over and I'm ready to come back to work."

He licked his lips. Ren felt a warning prickle

dance up his nape, and he saw Annie's anger surging to the surface again.

"Say it," she told him. "Will my job be here, or won't it? You said this leave was temporary. Was that the truth or a bald-faced lie?"

"The truth." He shook his head. "But this . . . isn't about the pregnancy, and we both know it. Look, take all the time you need. Have the baby, get your strength back. But most importantly, Annie, *get well*."

"Too vague, Harry. I want specifics."

He shook his head. "All right. Fine, you want specifics, here they are. You need to get some therapy. See someone. The school board isn't going to risk you having some sort of breakdown in the middle of a class, so unless you get help, you're unemployed. Now, Dr. Cassius has said he'd be more than willing to—"

Annie swore, using a phrase Ren wouldn't have believed was in her vocabulary.

"I'm sorry, Annie. But you're slipping. We've all seen the signs. Passing out during that storm the other night and saying you'd seen someone outside your house. And then your behavior in the store the other day. And what happened yesterday, the way you ran through town and right into the path of Hetty Pike's car. The way you freaked out afterward. Not recognizing your husband's cousin. Thinking he was Richard..." Harry blinked, and Ren thought for a second he detected a hint of moisture in the man's eyes. "Dammit, Annie, I know how much you loved him. Hell, the whole town knew. You two were joined at the hip for as long as anyone can remember, even when you were just kids. Honey, I know how hard it's been, but it's over now. He's gone. You have to get yourself together and move on. You need some help, Annie. It's understandable—"

"My job hinges on it. That's it, basically?"

With a heavy sigh, he nodded. "The board held an emergency meeting last night, Annie. We all care about you, but the welfare of the students has to come first. We want you to get help."

"And I shouldn't bother showing up here again without a note from a shrink saying I won't go berserk and start offing my students, right Harry? God, I don't believe this."

Releasing Ren's hand she turned and stormed out of the room, out of the building, right into the rush of bodies coming in. Ren was after her instantly, but he could barely keep her in his sight with all the students surrounding her. He dived into the crowd of them, shouldering his way through, battling visions of her swollen, delicate body being trampled beneath all those Reebok-clad feet.

When he finally found her, she stood frozen near a huge yellow bus. She was staring off into the distance, across the newly mown grass that surrounded the brick building. Just staring. And he wondered about Harry Hayes. He wondered if the man truly cared about Annie, as he seemed to. Or if he was, perhaps, working for the side of evil. Using her own feelings against her, working to systematically destroy her and thereby gain access to her child.

He knew there was a dark knight stalking her—Blackheart, if this mission was as important to humanity as Sir George had claimed. The dark side would send their fiercest warrior. But Ren had no way of knowing who the man might be or what form he might have taken to accomplish his evil mission. Like Ren, he'd likely come into this realm in disguise. So could he be posing as Annie's Harry Hayes?

"Annie?"

She blinked and brushed the tears away from her eyes. "I shouldn't be mad enough to strangle Harry," she said softly.

"Probably not."

"He really does care about me. He just doesn't understand."

"How could he?"

"And he has to look out for the kids. I mean, I wouldn't respect him if he didn't."

"Of course," Ren said.

She knuckled her cheeks dry, shook her head. "But it still infuriates me." She took a deep breath, held it a few seconds, let it out slowly. When she lifted her head and looked off in the distance, her face cleared a little.

"Feel better?"

She nodded but didn't look at him. Instead she lifted a tentative hand and waved. And in a second, she smiled very slightly.

"She's an unusual girl. So beautiful and . . . and odd."

"Who is?" Ren asked.

Annie pointed. "Sara. Right there, by the maple tree." She looked at Ren as he sought, and didn't find the girl she was pointing out. There was no one by the maple tree. "I've been trying to figure out why she's here, where she came from. But I suppose I should just accept her presence and quit questioning it. She's so supportive and kind of soothing to me. I like her."

Ren squinted, shaded his eyes, stared into the distance. But there was no one in sight. He looked down at Annie and frowned in confusion. A cold chill slid up his spine, and he slipped his arm around her shoulders before he thought better of it. "Come on, Annie. Let's go."

She nodded, waved once more toward the

girl only she could see, and leaned into his embrace as they walked.

And Ren felt a blade slowly slicing off a paper-thin portion of his heart.

She stopped walking, stepped away from him, and looked up into his face. "You didn't see her, did you?"

Ren set his jaw, met her crystalline green eyes, and knew he couldn't lie to her. He shook his head.

She bit her lower lip. "And now you're wondering if maybe Harry's right. If I'm slipping just a little bit."

"Annie, I never said that."

"You know me better than to think that way," she told him. "I didn't lose it when you died; I'm certainly not going to crack up now that you've come back."

He studied her face. Calm, rational. Loving. "I'm not Richard," he said.

"Right. I keep forgetting." She reached down, plucked a bright yellow buttercup from the ground, and held it under his nose.

Ren frowned down at her, completely at a loss. And then he sneezed.

"Richard was allergic to buttercups," Annie said, tossing the little blossom to the ground. "Quite a coincidence, isn't it, Ren?"

"Don't, Annie. Stop trying to see him in me. It will only cause you more pain."

She shook her head, held up a hand to cut him off when he would have said more, and started walking again. She walked briskly. He wanted to tell her to slow down, to take it easy, but he was afraid to say anything just now. Afraid of making her more suspicious, more unhappy, than she was already.

She left the road, crossed through a grassy lot that served as a town park, and only stopped when she reached the edge of the river that bubbled and tumbled along. Sitting down in the grass, she stretched her legs out in front of her.

The place was familiar to Ren. For some reason he knew that the blackberry patch was off to the right on the far bank even before he looked up and saw it there. And the way the willow tree seemed to bend over the water, like an old man trying to get a sip—he'd seen it before.

Annie leaned back on her hands. "Sit beside me, Ren."

He did, very close beside her. And he tried not to look at her. He told himself to study the water instead. But it didn't stop the rush he felt coming in his mind. Something had happened here. He saw, in blindingly rapid flashes, a checkered tablecloth spread on the grass, a bottle of wine, Annie's bare feet dangling in the water. . . .

She sighed. "You have no idea what he meant to me," she told him. "If you did, you wouldn't keep telling me to stop trying to convince myself you are my Richard, come back to me. Because you'd know how impossible it is for me to give up."

Ren closed his eyes, but still the flashes came. He saw the two of them, him and Annie, splashing each other with the river water, laughing out loud. But they were younger. Teenagers, perhaps.

"The closest thing I can liken it to is losing a limb," she went on. "Only it's worse. Almost as if I were sawed in half. He was part of me, you know. And when he left it was as if that part of me, the very best part of me, left with him."

He saw them fall to the ground together and saw himself catching her in his arms, kissing her until their laughter died and an innocent, timid passion replaced it. He saw his own hands, trembling as they fumbled with her clothes, removing them piece by piece. . . .

"I forget when I sleep, you know," she said. Her voice was softer now than before. "I forget he's gone, sometimes, in my dreams. So that every morning when I wake it's like losing him all over again. The experts told me it would get easier with time, but it only got worse. Hell, how could it not?

"Annie, you have to get past this."

"Don't." She shook her head at him, blinking the tears from her eyes. "Don't tell me to get over it. We didn't love like other people love. What we had ... it was bigger. It was deeper. It was like a living thing, the love we had." She closed her eyes. "How could you forget that?"

He wanted to take her pain away. He wanted it more than he wanted to draw another breath. But he couldn't tell her that memories were assaulting him even now. That maybe he hadn't forgotten. That perhaps she was right, and their love had been as powerful as she claimed—more powerful than Sir George's magic. So powerful, he'd been mourning its loss as much as she had, though he'd never known what exactly he'd been longing for.

This was the first place he'd made love to her. Ren knew it as surely as he knew that the man she was crying for was sitting beside her now. It was killing him not to tell her. But if she was in this much pain now, what would she feel when the time came for him to leave her again? God, it might destroy her utterly.

He lifted a hand to brush the tears from her eyes. "You can't surrender to your grief, Annie. And you know the reason as well as I do." He glanced down at her swollen belly, and she lowered her chin. "Your baby needs you." *Our baby needs you.*

"Our baby," she told him. And those two words were like blades sinking into his heart. She squeezed her eyes tight and nodded. "You're right. I know that. My grief, my need to get to the truth, can wait. Our baby's safety comes first. But I'm not going to give up, Ren." Her eyes opened, meeting his. "I can't."

"And you can't afford to be distracted by your wishful thinking either. This battle is going to take all your concentration, Annie. All your will."

She nodded, seemingly accepting that, and Ren felt he'd been given a reprieve. He had to convince her he wasn't her husband. But it looked as if it would be difficult. Perhaps impossible.

"Tell me this," she asked him. "Why do these . . . dark forces . . . want to hurt my baby?"

He wasn't supposed to tell. It would be breaking one more of Sir George's rules. Well, he'd already bent them. And he continued to bend them because he cared more about this fragile, strong, stubborn woman with every breath he drew. That was certainly a breach. A serious one. But dammit, he couldn't lie to her more than he already had.

He took her hand in both of his. "Annie,

your child is going to become a great leader. One who will bring about sweeping changes, good changes. Ends to war and disease and famine. Annie, this baby is special. Vital."

She blinked and ran her hands over her belly. "*My* baby?"

"Yes."

She shook her head slowly in wonder. Then she smiled. "Naturally. How could Richard's child be any less?" She picked up a rock, tossed it, and watched it plop into the water. "Trust the universe to pick the perfect father for such an important little one."

"But do you trust *me*?" Like her, he picked up a rock and flung it with a twist of his wrist. It skimmed the water's surface, hopping four, five, six times before sinking out of sight. He hadn't realized he could do that.

She hadn't answered him. He turned to see her staring, wide-eyed, at the ripples his stone had left in the water.

"Annie?"

She blinked, shook herself, and finally looked at him. That wonder was in her eyes again. "Yes," she whispered. "Yes, I trust you."

He became lost in those jewel-green eyes of hers for long moments. And then he blinked because he saw the way they softened, the yielding, the longing that blossomed in their glittering depths. And he knew what she wanted.

Her body seemed to sway toward him just a little, but he caught her shoulders and held her steady, keeping a bit of space between them. As his fingertips sank into the flesh of her shoulders, an urge to pull her closer rose up inside him. Inexplicable, but nearly irresistible. And he felt, like a shadow from the past, a distant memory. One so sensory and so vivid, it was as if it were happening again at this very moment. He felt the touch of her skin against his. The gentle friction, the heat. The taste of her came to life on his tongue, the feel of her mouth opening to his, the sensation of invading that damp satin paradise, of possessing it.

The sensations made him dizzy. His heart hammered against his chest, and he fought to keep his breathing regular. Trying to act perfectly normal was a difficult thing when he could almost feel his mind absorbing the memory and trying to reproduce it. How could he hope to hide his memories from her, to disguise the growing feelings in him? Especially when he couldn't for the life of him look away from the plea in her crystalline eyes. Especially when he was suddenly yearning to taste her lips. To feel, for the first time in what seemed like centuries, the stirrings of physical desire.

Dammit, he wanted to feel again!

It was Annie who looked away.

And Ren was left feeling as if he'd been on the verge of something wonderful, only to have it pulled just beyond his reach. And that gnawing emptiness, that ache that had haunted him for as long as he could remember, came back to him full force. And for the first time, Ren thought he knew what it was he'd been longing for so much. What it was he'd been missing.

It was Annie.

Annie, the woman who had been his wife. The love they must have shared. God, he'd been grieving for her as much as she still was for him. Only he'd been unable to identify the source of his intense sorrow.

But he'd felt it all the same. Even with his memory of her erased, his feelings for her— perhaps his love for her—had remained locked in his heart. And now that he understood that, he wanted more.

She got to her feet, and when she struggled, he was quick to grab her shoulders again, to help her. But she pulled away from his grasp, cleared her throat, straightened her hair, though there was no need. And then she averted her face, and he wondered if there were tears burning in her eyes, ones she didn't want him to see. He kept his gaze averted, too, as they walked together back to the house she'd once shared with the man she'd loved. And he felt once again like an invader in a sacred place. Even though he knew, more than he'd known before, that he wasn't.

Chapter Six

∾ "Mother, no. No, I'm fine," Annie said into the telephone receiver, hoping to ease the worry in her mother's tone. "I promise, you'd know if I wasn't."

"How can you say that?" Georgette asked. "Darling, you've been in the hospital, and you never even called us! You were nearly run down by a car, and now I learn you've got some stranger living with you! What on earth is going on?"

"It's reassuring to know the town rumor mill is still in working order," she muttered.

"Don't take that tone with me, Annie. I'm concerned. Now, about this stranger—"

"He's *not* a stranger." *Far from it*, Annie thought. *I'm pretty sure he's my dead husband.* She could just imagine her mother's reaction if she blurted *that* tidbit out.

"Well, he's not Richard's cousin, as you and he are claiming, that's for sure! María says—"

"You told *María* about this? Mom, how could you?"

"She's your mother-in-law. She has a right to know. And she says there is no such person as this Ren fellow you claim is Richard's long-lost cousin. So if he's told you he is, he's a con man. And if you aren't being misled, then you're deliberately lying."

"Oh, for heaven's—"

"We're coming over there. And we want some answers, young lady. I'm not going to have my grandchild raised in such an . . . an *unstable* environment. Some drifter under the roof! It's . . ."

She went on, but Annie rolled her eyes, shook her head, and tuned her mother out. She marveled that the small-town grapevine had reached her mother's neck of the woods so fast. Georgette and Ira lived three hours north, at the base of the forest-coated hillside that was Mystic Lake's home. Her horses usually kept her busy enough to leave Annie alone, but not this time.

Annie closed her eyes as her mother's voice rang on and on. Then she felt a warm, big hand close over hers, and the receiver was gently taken away. She glanced up when Ren spoke.

"Georgette? Hello, this is Ren, the man who's staying with your daughter."

Annie groaned inwardly.

"Of course. I'm looking forward to it. But I'm not sure it's such a good time for Annie. She's exhausted, and the whole idea of my staying with her was to ease the burden. She needs her rest."

She groaned out loud this time. Ren only smiled at her.

"Yes, I know Aunt María gets confused that way. She doesn't remember me, I'm afraid. I haven't seen her since I was a little boy. But it's probably for the best. When we were small, she used to get Richard and me confused. It was right after she'd lost her eyesight, you see. And our voices were similar, so . . ."

Annie blinked in surprise. There were few people on the planet for whom her mother cared more deeply than María Nelson. She'd taken to Richard's mother like a sister, and she'd do anything to keep from hurting her.

"Exactly, Georgette. That's a good idea. I'm sure that would be the best way to handle it. Questioning her about me will only dredge up painful memories. She's suffered so much already." He paused. "You're a kind woman. Okay, then. Good-bye for now."

He hung up and turned to look at Annie. And his smug expression was so familiar, it hurt. "She's reassured. She's not coming over . . . yet. And you're off the hook."

At that moment there was little doubt in Annie's mind that he was Richard. Richard, who'd always been able to sweet-talk his meddlesome, well-intentioned mother-in-law no matter what the circumstances. Exactly the way Ren had done, just now.

Dammit, she had to be nuts! But she also had to know more about him. He'd claimed he was not her husband, he'd told her he didn't know her, but she found herself wanting to prove him a liar. She wanted to be right about this. Wanted it so badly that maybe she was imagining the signs she kept seeing. Like the way he skipped the stone on the water that morning. Just as Richard used to do. He'd tried teaching her the trick of it when they were kids, one summer day on Mystic Lake. And even then, there'd been ... something special between them. Something neither of them recognized or understood, but both of them felt. Some tie that bound their souls together even before physical attraction had entered into their thought processes.

It was the same something she felt stirring between her and Ren right now. She'd realized it when he'd looked into her eyes, when he'd almost kissed her.

It was too much to believe in, too much to hope for. But all day it had been niggling at her brain. And as she pondered the idea, the pain that had been with her for so very long seemed to ease a little bit. The depression that had made her feel her legs were made of lead and her mind was stuffed with wet cotton balls began to dissipate. And instead, her brain filled with ideas and plots and plans of how she could test him to prove or disprove her theory.

How the hell had he known María was blind?

The rest of the day passed quickly. The first one she remembered spending without battling constant depression and pain. She smiled more often than she had in eight long months, and she cooked a real dinner instead of grabbing a sandwich.

She found him in the nursery. He'd taken all the various crib parts up there and was sitting on the floor with them spread around him. It brought a lump to her throat to see him working so calmly in the very place where she would have expected to see her husband. And she hesitated in the doorway.

He looked up, met her gaze, and glanced down at the partially assembled mess in front of him. "I should have asked first. Do you mind?"

Her knees trembled. She wanted to cry, but

she didn't. "No. No, I don't mind at all."

He smiled, and as his eyes traveled over her face his smile became a grin that took her breath away. "You have sauce on your chin."

Her stomach clenched into a knot. She ran the pad of her thumb over her chin, remembering the way Richard would kiss such spatters off her face and claim he was only tasting dinner.

"I made lasagna," she managed. It had always been Richard's favorite. "Do you like it?"

It seemed he had to think about his answer. He tilted his head to one side, frowning. "I think so. It's . . . it's hard to remember."

"Why?" She watched him carefully as she awaited his reply. "Has it been such a long time?"

He nodded, that sad, haunted expression darkening his eyes. "Longer than you know. But it's more than that." His eyes narrowed as he searched for words. "I'm not like other men, Annie."

"You never were," she said softly.

He frowned at her, but apparently decided to let it slide. "White Knights don't . . . feel things the way mortal men do."

And it was Annie's turn to frown. "Don't they?"

"Carnal urges aren't a part of our makeup. Hungers and cravings—"

"And desire?"

His eyes met hers, darkened slightly just before he averted them. "We eat because it keeps us strong. But I can't remember the last time I actually took pleasure in a meal."

There was more he wanted to say. Maybe that he couldn't remember the last time he'd taken pleasure with a woman either. But he clamped his jaw and erased the look in his eyes. An act of will, a deliberate covering up of his feelings. She'd done it herself often enough to recognize it when she saw it. What was he trying to hide? Ren rose and brushed his hands together. "It certainly smells wonderful," he said.

She stepped closer to him. "You used to say my lasagna was the next best thing to sex."

His face reddened a bit. "Not me. Your husband. I keep telling you—"

"Right." She smiled a little. "You're not him. Funny how I can't seem to get that through my head." She shrugged as if it didn't matter. "Richard was in ecstasy when he ate my lasagna. It's just dripping with peppers and onions, imported cheeses, fresh spinach." She sniffed the air. Saw him pretending not to do the same. "I make this garlic bread with it and serve it hot, so the butter just melts into

it. Richard always loved to mop up the extra
sauce with a slice of hot garlic bread."

"It sounds . . . very nice."

"It's ready and waiting." She stepped aside
to let him pass. He searched her face, wary of
her, suspecting a trick, no doubt. But then he
gave his head a shake and left the room.

Annie followed him down the stairs. He
paused only long enough to wash his hands,
and when he came to the dining room, he sat
at Richard's usual spot at the table. She didn't
have to tell him, hadn't given him a clue to go
by, hadn't so much as set a place for him yet.
Just motioned for him to sit, and waited while
he did.

She tried not to take that as yet another sign
that he was lying when he said he wasn't Richard. She had to be objective. She had to be *sure.*

She put the food on and watched him again.
Left-handed, just like her Richard. Everything
. . . *everything* . . .

The way he chewed, the amount of salt he
sprinkled on his food, the frequent, overlong
chugs of the milk they had with dinner. And
he could deny it until hell froze over, but she
knew damned well he was enjoying every
bite.

He broke off a piece of garlic bread and
swiped it through the sauce on his plate. Then
he froze, blinking down at the bread in his

hand as if surprised to see it there. He lifted his gaze, met her eyes.

She tried not to look smug. "Care for some more?" she asked.

He shook his head no, and dropped the bread on his plate. He looked confused. Maybe even a little bit scared.

Annie tried to tell herself not to get her hopes up too high, but her mind wasn't listening. With every breath he drew, she was more convinced this man was her husband. And that might be dangerous. The practical part of her—the tiny part that clung stubbornly to the idea that believing that would be surrendering to an impossible fantasy—insisted that it was dangerous. Very dangerous. But the rest of her was relishing this time with him. Needing it, thriving on it, drawing strength and warmth and even life from it. She hadn't felt this alive in a very long time.

"I'll get the dishes," he told her, rising from his chair and reaching for her empty plate.

"No, that's—"

"Rest," he said softly. "You look exhausted, Annie."

It was more emotional exhaustion than physical. Annie knew that, but she nodded anyway. She stretched out on the sofa with her feet up, rubbed the small of her aching back, closed her eyes, and listened to the comforting clink of dishes and the gentle splashing of water coming from the kitchen.

Sometime during the night, she thought she heard footsteps. Her first thought was of Ren ... Richard—the two blurred together in her mind. But then she stiffened a little. The steps were slow, calculated, creeping. As if the walker didn't want to be heard.

Sit up. Open your eyes. Call Ren.

The tourmaline pendant that rested on her chest seemed to vibrate and grow warm. It was nothing. It was only Ren, and if he was being quiet, it was simply because he didn't want to wake her. Absently she lifted a hand to stroke the pulsing stone at her throat. Soft sleep spread its velvet cloak over her and she embraced it, burrowing deeper into its arms. She dreamed Ren *was* Richard. She dreamed he came to her and took her in his arms and swore never to leave her again. Never. No matter what. She was so happy, so very happy.

She didn't *want* to wake because there was a part of her that knew this heaven was only a dream. To wake meant to lose him again. So she hugged sleep tighter and held her husband in her dreams.

*   *   *

She needed the rest. He couldn't bring himself to disturb her. Besides, if he woke her, he'd have to face the growing knowledge in her eyes yet again.

He'd relished the meal she'd prepared. The flavors had come alive on his tongue as none ever had before—or none that he could remember. The spices. The gooey cheeses. The sauce. It had been so good, he'd nearly wept.

God, what was happening to him? Something inside him, some dormant part of him, seemed to be reawakening. Sensory memories were returning and becoming more than just memories. They were coming alive. In him. A White Knight! It was unheard of. And unacceptable.

And looking at Annie only made the sensations he had no business feeling all the stronger. So he wouldn't move her to her own bed or wake her. He'd let her rest on the sofa where she'd fallen fast asleep.

He checked the locks and turned off the lights, and then he went to her, to tuck a blanket around her. As his hands smoothed the cover over her shoulders, she stirred, smiled a little in her sleep. Ren went still. Her dark lashes rested on her satin cheeks. Her hair spread out over the small throw pillows like a cloud. He battled an urge to bury his face in that fragrant mass of silk. Curiosity assailed him. Could he take as much pleasure in the scent of her hair as he had in the meal? Would it really damn him beyond redemption to find out? He bent closer, nuzzling locks of her hair with his face, inhaling that succulent fragrance that was hers alone. And a pleasure that was almost painful swirled in his mind. He didn't know why this was happening, but it was.

His chest brushed hers as he leaned over her, and a jolt of liquid heat shot through him, so potent and shocking, it nearly knocked him to his knees.

This was unwise, what he was doing. He could lose his very life for it. He straightened away from the sleeping angel, forced his gaze away from her, and went upstairs to finish assembling the crib. Anything to distract him from the thoughts plaguing his mind.

But as it turned out, it took a good deal more to make him stop thinking about her, stop *feeling* for her.

He'd never intended to fall asleep in the nursery, on the undersize crib mattress he'd been using for a seat. He couldn't believe he'd managed to doze at all, when he shook himself awake later. It was totally unlike him to doze unintentionally.

But when the sharp and acrid scent reached him, he knew with a surge of alarm exactly what had lulled him into unconsciousness.

There was an odor in the house. The odor of natural gas.

"Annie!"

Ren leaped to his feet, snatching up his sword and belting it around him with his heart pounding. He raced into the hall, down the curving stairs. In complete darkness he made his way to the bottom, not daring to so much as touch a light switch. Gas filled the room, the air so dense with it that he nearly collapsed before he reached Annie. And Ren knew that a single spark could send the entire place up in flames. So no lights. No telephone. No time to do anything other than scoop her into his arms and get out.

Air. God, he was dizzy! Disoriented! Weak.

He stumbled to the sofa where she lay, and gathered her into his arms. Pulling her close, he hugged her to his chest and spoke to her, but she didn't respond. As he turned toward the door, his knees gave out. He fell to the floor, still holding Annie, and knelt there clinging to her, blinking in the darkness, searching for the door. His eyes burned. He couldn't breathe. He finally got to his feet, only to fall again.

Damn. He'd drop her, hurt her or the baby if he kept this up. To hell with standing. He remained on his knees and made his way to the door. By the grace of God, he found it, but his fingers fumbled awkwardly with the lock. Finally it sprang free, and he got the door open. It was all he could do to throw himself, still clinging to Annie, through the opening.

They spilled together onto the porch, and he cushioned her with his own body. Ren gasped, inhaling great gulps of fresh night air. His head cleared slightly, slowly, and he breathed deeper, fighting for strength. He had to help her, had to see to it that she and the baby were all right. He got to his feet and scooped her up again, staggering down the steps and away from the house and its noxious gas, not to mention the looming danger of an explosion. And when he'd gone what his fogged mind judged was a safe distance, he gently laid her down in the dewy grass and knelt beside her, bending over her, feeling his heart shatter in fear for her.

She was pale, her face standing out against the night's darkness like the face of a ghost. He caught her fragile shoulders, shook her gently, then harder. No response. "Dammit, Annie, be all right!" He wasn't supposed to feel this way. But knowing it did nothing to quell it. He cared for this woman in a way he was only beginning to understand.

There was nothing. She wasn't breathing. The child's life hung in the balance. Ren bent closer, covering Annie's mouth with his own and forcing precious oxygen into her lungs to feed her—and her child. *His child.* Over and over he blew life into her body. And he heard his own heart pounding in fear all the while.

She coughed, pushing him away to gasp on her own. She choked and drew deep, shaky, noisy breaths that had an edge of desperation to them.

"Annie," he whispered, stroking her hair away from her face, holding her as she dragged in gulps of air. "Sweet Annie, are you all right?" He rubbed her hands and her arms vigorously, as if he could rub the life back into her. God, she was cold. He stroked her face and her eyes opened. She met his gaze, blinking, and then lifted her arms weakly to encircle his neck. Ren gathered her to him, held her hard, and rocked her slowly.

"What . . . ?" She drew another ragged breath, her body all but limp against his as she struggled to speak.

"Gas," he told her. "The house was filled with it." He held her away from him just a little, enough so he could search her face. The way her head wobbled made it obvious she could barely hold it up.

"Listen to me," he said as her eyes fell closed again. He shook her gently until they opened once more, unfocused and dazed.

"Did you hear anyone in the house, Annie? Did you see anything?"

She blinked vaguely.

"I have to know." Ren shook her a little more.

She smiled a little crookedly at him. "Don't leave me, Richard. Not ever again, okay?"

"Annie, come on. Sit up. Breathe. Deeper, come on."

She inhaled as he instructed. Exhaled. Dropped her head down upon his shoulder. "I love you so much, Richard," she whispered.

He closed his eyes as the pain took a large hunk of his heart this time. Soon there would be nothing left of it. "I know," he told her, his voice coarse and barely audible. "I know. Come on, breathe some more. Rest here. I have to go to one of the neighbors. I have to call an ambulance. . . ."

"No. Don't leave me." She clung to his neck with renewed strength.

Ren sighed and stroked her hair. "I'm not leaving you. I promise, I'm just going to get help. You need help, Annie."

She shook her head, lifted it. "Tell me you love me."

"Annie—"

"You still do, don't you?" Tears threatened, filling her green eyes to brimming. *"Don't you?"*

Ren swallowed hard. It was the gas. She was muddled, disoriented, only semiconscious, he told himself. She'd pass out again within a minute or two and probably remember none of this when she awoke. "Of course I do," he said to comfort her. He'd have said anything then if it would help her.

"Then say it," she demanded. No. Not demanded. It was more like a plea. "Say you love me."

He shook his head slowly, not knowing what to do. "I . . . I love you, Annie." And as he spoke the words, he knew he'd said them a thousand times before. It was as if one of the countless veils between Ren and his past had been removed. The words were warm and real and familiar. And . . . they even felt . . . *true.*

"Again," she whispered.

"I love you." He ached inside. For her. For himself. For what they must have had, what they'd lost.

Annie leaned up and pressed her lips to his.

God! It was heaven and hell all at once. To know what kissing her must have been like for him once. To know it could never be that way again because he was incapable of experiencing passion. He kissed her. Because he wanted to kiss her. He wanted to know just a hint of what he'd left behind.

Dammit, it was unfair and cruel and probably the most unknightly thing he'd ever done, kissing her when she was in this condition. But he did it anyway. And he wasn't supposed to feel anything. He wasn't *prepared* to feel anything.

But he did.

A shivering heat uncoiled in his belly as his lips moved over hers. Her tender mouth parted, and instinctively he took it, gently but greedily, because her taste made him hunger in a way he'd never hungered before. In a way he was supposed to be incapable of. So he gave in to it, telling himself it would just be this once. He fed from her sweetness, and she seemed to offer more. And Ren was flooded with sensations as his mouth mated with hers.

It was only when her lips slackened and her body went rag-doll limp against his that he stopped. Her arms around his neck loosened, and she dropped her head to his shoulder once more.

Desire pooled in his groin like lava, and his body responded in a purely mortal way. God, he wanted her. He wanted her more than he'd wanted anything in his life, that he could recall. Swollen middle and all.

He eased her to the ground, untwisted her arms from around his neck, and got to his feet.

"Don't call an ambulance. She's fine."

Ren nearly jumped a foot in the air as the

soft, gentle voice addressed him. The girl sat on the ground beside Annie, holding her hand. But she hadn't been there a second ago. . . .

"The baby, too," she went on. "She didn't inhale enough gas to do any real damage. You don't have to leave her. You don't have to make that call."

Ren shook himself. "Of course I have to. I can't be sure—"

"I can."

He narrowed his eyes on the girl. Lovely, to say the least. The most stunning young woman he could remember having met. So much wisdom in those eyes of hers, and a strange crescent-shaped birthmark on her neck. There was love shining from her eyes. For Annie?

"I'm sorry, Sara," he said, watching for her reaction. "It is Sara, isn't it?"

She nodded.

"I thought so. But I can't take your word for it. For all I know you might be the one . . ." He bit his lip, realizing he'd been about to say too much.

"The one who's out to keep the baby from being born?" The girl grinned at him. "If you only knew how funny that is. But look at me, Ren. Do I look like a Dark Knight to you?"

She didn't, but that was beside the point.

They were tricksters, the dark ones. And he'd already known the enemy would likely be in disguise.

"Touch me, then." She offered her hand. "Go on. You know what happens when a White Knight holds the hand of a dark one. Do it."

"It's forbidden for a White Knight to take the hand of a dark one," he told her. But something in her eyes made him lift his hand all the same. Ren closed his hand around her much smaller one, half expecting a lightning bolt to knock him to his knees. But it didn't. Instead he felt a comforting warmth moving from her palm to his and back again. Something softer and sweeter than anything he'd ever felt before.

She squeezed his hand before taking hers away, and then averted her eyes, blinking rapidly, almost as if tears were threatening.

"Who are you?" he asked her.

She shook her head. "I can't tell you that. Rules. You understand."

"Rules," he repeated. But he was puzzled. If she wasn't a Dark Knight, then who was she? And what did she know about the other realm? How could she know about White Knights and dark—or about him?

"I know what I have to know for now, Ren. Soon I won't know any of it. I won't remember

ever having known. And I know you understand *that* as well. But for now I just do. Accept it. And accept that just as I know these
other things, I know that Annie and the baby
are fine and healthy. Out of danger for the moment, thanks to you." She took Ren's hand in
her own, placed both on Annie's abdomen,
and closed her eyes.

Ren felt the child Annie carried twist and
perhaps stretch, as if waking from a deep nap.
The image of that made him smile, and he
glanced up at the young girl. But she was
gone. Odd, that he still felt her holding his
hand as if she remained. Very odd.

"Wake up, now, Annie-girl. Come on. Open
your eyes."

She heard his voice as if from a great distance, deep but quiet. Strong, but barely an
echo. As if he were far away. And that thought
sent a chill through her body. She didn't want
him to be far away. Not ever again.

"Richard," she whispered. "Don't go. Don't
go, Richard . . ."

"Ren," he said softly, and his voice was
closer now, clearer, but for some reason it had
gone hoarse. "It's Ren. Remember?"

She blinked until she was able to focus. Not
an easy task, with the way everything seemed
to be weaving in and out of its natural shape.

Her head pounded like a heavy-metal drummer, and she seemed to be lying in a pile of fragrant hay with her head and shoulders cushioned by Ren's lap. When she stared straight up, it was to see his worried face looking down at her. He smiled a little and picked a bit of hay from her hair.

She didn't sit up. Sitting up, she sensed, would make her head hurt more. And she was tired, so incredibly tired. "What's going on?" she asked him.

His smile faded. "You don't remember?"

The intensity in his eyes burned through her, and she knew then that something was terribly wrong. Closing her eyes, searching for the memory of what had happened last night, how they'd ended up sleeping on a haystack, only resulted in making her head ache more.

"Something happened last night, obviously," she told him. "Something that must have driven us from the house, into this—" She looked around. "Barn?" Frowning, she met his eyes again, her head still cradled in his lap. "Why did we sleep in someone's barn?" Then, slowly, a memory did come. But not of last night. It was from a long time ago, and it made Annie smile despite the throbbing in her head.

Ren's face turned curious. "What?"

"I was just remembering . . . the last time we fell asleep in a pile of hay."

He looked away. "Annie, don't—"

"My parents were away. We had the whole place to ourselves, but we couldn't even wait long enough to get to the house that night. We'd barely finished tending the horses when you scooped me up and carried me off to the hayloft."

He shook his head in denial.

"That hay was so scratchy," she said. "And I thought we'd never get the hayseed out of our hair. Of course, we didn't notice any of that until morning." She reached up to touch his face, drawing his gaze back to hers with the action. "You made love to me all night long in the hay, Richard. Don't you remember?"

"It wasn't me."

She sighed in disappointment. But at the same time, she felt a slight tensing of his body, and the place where her head rested on his lap seemed to be coming to life.

"I thought you time-traveling-hero types couldn't feel desire," she teased.

His face reddened a little, and he eased her out of his lap and got to his feet. "We don't."

"But you do."

"Annie," he said slowly, firmly. "You fell

asleep on the sofa last night. Do you remember that?"

She sat up, massaged her forehead, and thought back. And then she nodded. She did remember. It was right after dinner, right after she'd watched this man who claimed to be a stranger sit in Richard's chair and wolf down a plateful of Richard's favorite food in exactly the way Richard would have.

"Yes, I remember. I must have been more tired than I thought." Again she shook her head in bewilderment, gazing at the rough wooden beams and hay and rusting stanchions in disbelief. "I don't even remember leaving the house. What did you do, scoop me up and carry me off to the nearest haystack for old times' sake?"

His dark blue eyes narrowed as he faced her again. "This is important, Annie."

Sighing, she finally shrugged. "So tell me what happened after I fell asleep."

"I didn't want to wake you," he said. "So I left you where you were. Try to remember, Annie. It's important. Did you wake up at all after I went upstairs?"

She frowned even harder at the seriousness of his tone. "No. I don't think so." He watched her so intently, as if willing her to remember something. "Richard—"

"It's Ren, dammit." He bit his lip, lowering

his head. "Sorry. Annie, my job here is to protect you and the baby. You're not making it easy."

"If you think I'm going to make lying to me easy for you, Ren, you're sadly mistaken. I want the truth." She searched his face and saw his frustration. "But for now I'll settle for knowing what happened last night, and why my head feels as if it's going to explode."

A frown of concern appeared on his brow, and he moved closer, kneeling in front of her, his big hands framing her face while his fingers gently massaged her temples. "I didn't realize you were in pain," he said. "Are you all right?"

She closed her eyes and let herself relish his touch. She'd be all right if he'd just keep touching her forever; she knew she would. Richard used to massage away her headaches, just like this. Why wouldn't he admit who he was? Could it be that he truly didn't remember?

"The forces I'm here to protect you against made a move against you last night," he said, and his hands fell to his sides.

Her eyes flew open. "How?"

His face was grim. "The pilot lights on the range in your kitchen were blown out, and the gas turned on. By the time I realized what was happening, you were unconscious." He lowered his head. "I never should have left you alone."

"But you were only upstairs, and . . ." Annie sucked in a sharp breath, looking down at her belly. "The baby?"

"The baby is all right."

He said it as if he had no doubt, and for some reason Annie believed him. But she was stunned by what he'd just told her. Stunned and terrified. "I can't believe someone . . . someone tried to kill me last night. In my own home. I just—"

"Not kill you," he told her. "It isn't allowed."

Her mounting panic skidded to a stop, and she tilted her head to one side. "Come again?"

Ren paced away from her. "They can't deliberately murder a mortal being," he said as matter-of-factly as a driving instructor explaining the rules of the road. "They're trying to make you miscarry with this gas ploy, same as they were with that car racing down the hill toward you. The impact probaby wouldn't have killed you, but—"

She shook her head. "If they can't kill a mortal, then how can they try to kill my child? I don't understand."

He nodded patiently. "Birth is the crossing over, Annie. From the unseen, magical realm to this one. Until he or she is born, the child is fair game."

She lowered herself to the hay-strewn floor, stunned. "So last night was an attempt to murder my baby?"

Ren sighed hard and came to her side. He bent over her and cupped her face in his big hands. "I'm not going to let that happen, Annie. I swear it to you."

She couldn't get over the impact of it. Someone had come to her home last night, while she slept, and made an attempt on the life of her unborn child. Good God! The very thought of it . . .

"Annie, try not to dwell on this. I'm here to protect you and I will; I promise you that. I told you you'd need all your strength for this battle. It's time to call on that strength now."

"I can't." She blinked away the nightmarish thoughts and fears racing through her mind and stared up at him. "How can I?"

He stroked her face, her hair. "I do have some good news for you, believe it or not. I saw the girl last night. The one you call Sara."

She gave her head a shake. "You saw Sara?" Why did she feel such a twist in her heart at the mention of the girl's name? Why was she suddenly longing to see Sara again?

"Yes. She spoke to me. She's not of this world, Annie."

Annie blinked up at him. "You mean she's like you? Part of this realm you come from?"

"No. I'm not sure where she comes from. But I sense she's here to help you, just as I am. I think she can be trusted."

"I've always trusted her. From the first time I saw her," Annie whispered.

Ren nodded and looked away. "Maybe if I'd come disguised as a young girl, you'd have more trust in me," he said.

"I'd have more trust in you, Ren, if you'd stop lying to me."

"I haven't lied," he told her. "Not the way you think."

She stared into his eyes for a long moment, the headache slowly easing now, the fog in her mind lessening a bit. And she said, "You kissed me last night." Then she frowned. "Or did I dream it, the way I've dreamed it so many times?"

He seemed startled, even pained. "You'd stopped breathing. I resuscitated you."

Her smile felt bitter. "Oh." She lowered her head. "That's all it was, then?"

"All it can be," he said softly.

She got to her feet, turning her back to him so she faced the open barn door and the pink predawn sky.

"I almost wish I were the man you knew," Ren whispered from behind her, and he came closer. "I wonder if he knew how lucky he was to inspire this kind of fervent devotion in a woman like you."

Tears burning her eyes, Annie turned to face him. He was very close. And she was afraid. Sorely afraid that all the clues, all her instincts were wrong, and that he really wasn't Richard after all.

"I miss him so much," she said, but her throat had tightened up, so the words were hoarse.

"I know."

"Would you hold me, Ren? If you'd hold me . . ." A sob tore at her breast, breaking her voice. "I could pretend."

His arms closed tight around her, drawing her against him. Annie pressed her face to his shirt, and she held him hard and thought of Richard's arms. The way they'd always felt around her. Just like these felt now. Strong and safe, and so familiar. Ren's shape, the feel of his skin, his scent. Every breath he expelled whispered Richard's name to her. Every facial expression, every word he spoke. Every time he touched her. Maybe . . . maybe she wanted it to be real so desperately that she was imagining the myriad similarities. But there was so much.

He spread his palms over the small of her

back and rubbed small circles there, where she caught herself rubbing so often.

She tilted her head up and looked into his liquid blue eyes, eyes she'd looked into so many times in her dreams. It was killing her, not knowing for sure . . . wishing . . . wanting . . .

Wake up, now, Annie-girl.

Annie's thoughts ground to a sudden halt as his words to her earlier came rushing back. Annie-girl. He'd called her Annie-girl. Besides María, no one in her entire life had ever called her that, no one but Richard.

She bit her lip, tried to rationalize. She'd been asleep. She might have dreamed the words. She might have subconsciously twisted something else into the endearment she hadn't heard in so long.

But, God in heaven, she didn't think so. She'd heard it. And all the other rationalizations she'd been making fled into the darkest corners of her mind. He might skip stones like Richard, and share a fondness for oversalted lasagna, and he might have the same smile, the same voice, use the same figures of speech. But no one else would call her Annie-girl. No one but Richard. Not in a million years.

She swallowed the lump in her throat and tried to think straight. *I don't know how any of this can be. I just have to accept that it is, and go*

*from there. Like Sara said. Trust myself. Believe
what my instincts are telling me and go with it.*

"Annie? Are you all right?"

She couldn't stop staring at him. That face.
Those eyes. She knew her Richard better than
anyone ever had or ever would. And she
knew. She *knew*. How could she ever have
doubted?

What should she do now?

She didn't know. Only one thing was for
certain. Whatever she did, she would not risk
losing him again. She'd battle an army with
nothing but a squirt gun before she'd let him
go. Fate had torn her husband away from her
once, but some quirk of that lady had somehow sent him back. This time she'd have a hell
of a fight on her hands.

As Ren searched her face, Annie felt something cracking and peeling away inside her—
the shell she'd grown around the woman
she'd been. And she felt just a little bit of the
old Annie's strength and stubborness leaking
out through those cracks and seeping into her.
It was like breathing for the first time in eight
months. Like a sliver of light after endless time
enveloped in darkness. And she embraced it,
clung to it, and prayed she'd never lose it
again.

She had to confront Ren . . . Richard . . . and
force him to tell the truth—if he even knew

what the truth was. She had to have proof he couldn't deny.

The solution came to her like a whisper of a song dancing on the dawn's breeze and tickling its way across her ears to make itself heard.

The birthmark. Richard's birthmark, right between his shoulder blades. If it's there, then that's all the proof I need.

Annie swallowed hard, nodded once, and felt better than she had in eight long months. "Ren, do you think the house is safe by now? I really want to go home."

Chapter Seven

∽ Ren—Richard—had opened every window and door in every room, shut off the gas, and set up fans to clear the air in the house. He'd done all of it while Annie had gone upstairs to wash the hayseed from her hair and put on clean clothes. There was still a slight odor stinging her nostrils, but she was confident the danger had passed. He never would have let her come inside if it hadn't.

Now he was upstairs, taking his turn in the shower. And she was alone, with the opportunity she'd been waiting for all morning. Bolstered by the firm belief that she had every right to know the truth—more right than he had to keep it from her—Annie slipped up the stairs, quiet as a mouse. Her hands trembled a little. She supposed there was still a kernel of doubt in her mind. A tiny question. She might be wrong. He might truly be the stranger he claimed to be. But it was only nerves making her doubt what she knew in her heart to be true. It was her husband she was about to spy on. And she'd seen Richard's beautiful body too many times to let herself be embarassed by it now. No matter what he claimed.

She moved slowly down the hall and paused outside the bathroom door. She could hear the water running from within, could envision him standing beneath the spray. She touched the doorknob, turned it. Not locked. Why would he lock it? It wasn't as if he expected her to do . . . what she was about to do.

Slowly she pushed the door open, holding her breath, half expecting the hinges to creak and announce her presence. They didn't.

Inside, she could see him beyond the frosted glass of the shower doors, the hazy silhouette of his body. Her throat went dry and she swallowed hard, waiting until he turned his face to the spray, leaving his back to her.

She wouldn't get another opportunity like this one. Bracing herself, she moved forward and tugged the sliding door open. And just before he whirled on her, she saw it. The small brown mark right between his shoulder blades hadn't changed in the least.

"My God," she muttered. "I knew . . . I thought I knew, but now . . ."

"What are you doing here, Annie?"

She met his eyes, wide and alarmed. But she

could only stare up at him, shaking her head, working her jaw. It was true. There was no longer any doubt.

Sighing heavily, he cranked off the faucets and reached for a towel. Knotting it around his hips, he stepped out of the shower, gripped her shoulders, and searched her face. "Annie, what is this about?"

She looked over his shoulder, toward the mirror just behind him, saw the birthmark as clearly as she could see her husband standing in front of her, and said, "I used to tease you about your birthmark, Richard. I used to tell you it looked like a doughnut with a bite taken out of it, and say you must have been a cop in a previous life."

Frowning, he glanced behind him, following the cue of her eyes, and he could see his back in the mirror.

"Are you forgetting your lines, Ren? Should I help? You're going to tell me it's a coincidence. That it doesn't prove anything."

He faced her slowly. And he wasn't looking as if it were a coincidence. He was looking as if his deepest secret had just been broadcast on network television. His blue eyes were darker than she'd ever seen them. He shook his head, blowing air through clenched teeth.

"It's true, isn't it, Richard? It's really you." So much hope—more than hope, *certainty*—

surged in her heart that the organ strained to contain it all.

He looked at her for a long moment and finally looked away.

"For the love of God, Richard, don't lie to me again. Not now."

He closed his eyes slowly, expelling a deep sigh. "Yes. It's true. I was your husband."

She blinked in shock. Tough to believe she'd heard him right. She'd been fully expecting him to shoot down every bit of evidence she'd found. He'd been denying it for so long. She should be angry—but she couldn't. It made no difference to her now.

She moved toward him, not feeling her feet touch the floor. Her hands rose as if on their own, and she touched his face, pressed her palms to his cheeks, and cupped his chin. She felt a tear roll down her cheek as she searched his eyes, and she knew the desperation she felt must show clearly in them.

"Richard . . ."

"No." He caught her hands in his own, stopping them. "I said I *was* him. But I'm not the same man now, Annie. I don't . . . I don't remember."

"I don't care." The words came out as a whisper. And she knew it was crazy. She had him back, memory or not. She had him back! Her fingers inched upward, threaded into his hair. She clutched his head and drew it downward until his mouth pressed to hers. And she knew he wanted to resist her, to pull away, but he didn't.

"Annie," he muttered against her lips. And then he kissed her, his stiff back and shoulders bowing over her, his hard arms gathering her to him as his lips nuzzled hers. His eyes fell closed just before Annie's did, and she heard his coarse sigh of surrender. His mouth covered hers, captured it, drew on her lips as if in search of some forbidden nectar. His tongue slid inside to stroke the fires until they burned through her every cell. He tasted so good. So wonderfully familiar. And she knew it was all true. Because he'd confirmed it. He was Richard. He was her husband, and he was back in her arms where he belonged. No power on heaven or earth would take him from her again. She felt fierce and strong, determined and equal to any challenge. She wouldn't let him go. No matter what. Not ever again.

And then he straightened, and she saw both blazing desire and unbearable pain in his blue eyes. And he spoke the words she'd refused even to consider.

"I'm not the man you knew," he told her gently. "Not anymore. I can never be him again."

"You're already becoming him again," she whispered.

"Even if that were true, it wouldn't matter. I can't stay."

She shook her head in denial, but even as she did, she knew he fully believed what he was saying to her. It was in his eyes, in his voice—deep, trembling, and so, so sad. It couldn't be true. She refused to accept it. It would kill her this time. It would. There was no way she could survive losing him again.

"No," she whispered. "I won't let it happen."

"There's nothing you can do to prevent it, Annie. Nothing I can do either. It's the way this works." His voice was so sure.

She'd find a way. She would. She just wasn't certain how . . . yet.

"How long?" she whispered, not ready to argue over it. Not yet. Not while the chances were so good that it was an argument she'd lose. She couldn't bear to have him prove her wrong.

He closed his eyes and turned away from her. "I don't know. Until the child is born, I imagine."

She choked back a sob. "I won't pretend to understand any of this. I couldn't possibly. But I . . ." She what? She didn't know. She couldn't tell him she loved him because she didn't really know him. Not anymore. But, God, it felt as if she did.

"Richard—"

"Please, Annie."

She sighed but nodded. "Ren, explain this to me. What happened to you? How did all of this . . . ? I want to understand."

"I'm not supposed to tell."

"You owe me this." She touched his face with trembling fingertips. "If you can't be my Richard, at least tell me why."

Sighing heavily, he nodded. "You're right. I've put you through hell. I owe you an explanation."

"Thank you."

He met her eyes and swallowed hard. She saw the swell of his Adam's apple. "Can I get dressed first?"

She looked up quickly and saw a hint of humor in his eyes. It was Richard's. He was Richard, deep down. But she supposed she'd have to prove that to him before he'd believe it, or admit it. "If you have to." But she let her hand linger on the broad expanse of his chest for just a moment. "I'll make some coffee."

He nodded but said nothing as she turned and left the room.

An hour later she sat in the living room, across from him, trying to digest all the things he'd told her. He'd told the truth when he said his memory of his mortal life had been erased, along with visceral feelings and desires. She sensed his honesty. She'd always been able to tell when Richard was fibbing. So she knew he was being open with her, finally.

But she thought perhaps he wasn't fully aware of the other things she could sense. That his memory, and his feelings, hadn't been destroyed but buried. And that she could find them and bring them back to the surface again. She knew she could.

And she would.

"I came here believing this to be just another mission. My job was to protect an unborn child. I didn't . . . I didn't know who I'd been . . ."

He stopped and she got the feeling he couldn't go on.

"But why did this . . . this Sir George, whoever he is, send you? He must have known."

He shook his head, but Annie thought about what she knew of her husband, and she knew the answer. "It's because you're the best, isn't it? My baby is so important that he'd send you, in spite of all the complications, simply because you're the best."

Ren shrugged. "Maybe. I don't know. You weren't supposed to be able to recognize me. Sir George's magic was supposed to conceal my identity from everyone but myself."

"And that's why no one else recognizes you," she said, nodding. Finally understanding. "But nothing could fool me. You could have come to me with a bag over your head, and I'd still have known you."

"I'm just beginning to realize that."

"You haven't changed as much as you think you have, you know." She thought she detected moisture in his eyes. Maybe she'd given him enough to think about—for now. And maybe she'd know how to make him remember, make him love her again, after she'd taken some time to digest all of this.

She sipped the coffee. And for Ren's sake, changed the subject. "Will this Dark Knight try again tonight, do you think?"

Ren tilted his head, studied her face. "He might. I won't lie to you, Annie. But I'm not going to let anything happen to your baby. I swear it."

"Don't call it that." She said abruptly, a knee-jerk reaction to his words.

He frowned and leaned forward in his chair. Annie sat in a rocker across from him and saw his confusion. "What?"

"My baby. Don't call it my baby, Richard. It's your baby, too."

He paused, blinking. Then he looked away. "You have to stop thinking of that, Annie. I'm not Richard. Richard wouldn't have known how to protect you in these circumstances. I do."

Very calmly, she spoke her heart. "If you're not Richard, then who are you? How can you be my husband and not be? How can you be the man I lost and this ... this being you've become? It doesn't make sense to me."

She wasn't crying, hadn't raised her voice. She just sat there, questioning him in a voice gone soft and steady.

"I'm Ren, a White Knight. A Hero. Nothing about me is the same as it was in my mortal lifetime. I couldn't drive a truck now if you put me in one. But I know how to fight. I know the ways of magic, and the secrets that lie beyond this realm. I've seen the forgotten past as well as the distant future. Wonders you'd never dream of. Things Richard would never have believed in."

"You've only been away from me for eight months. Eight months." A little breath escaped in a rush as she shook her head. "How could you forget what we had in eight—"

"Time moves differently on the other side. And I'm constantly moving through it. For me, Annie, it's been years. Centuries."

Her gaze didn't waver. She shook her head, unsatisfied with his answer.

"Annie, when I . . . when I crossed over, the man I was before vanished."

"No." She rose from the rocker and moved toward him. She couldn't keep her feelings to herself. Somehow she had to make him know what she knew. "Your memory of him might have vanished, Richard, but the man is still there. I've seen him." She dropped to her knees in front of him, took his hands in hers. "They could take away your memories, Richard, but not your soul. Not your heart." She lifted her eyes to his, and she could see the old Richard there, so clearly, longing to get out. To take over. To come back to her. "And not what we had together. No force in the universe could take that away. It's still there. Sometimes I see just a flicker of it shining in your eyes."

He lowered his head, perhaps unable to face her just then. "No."

"You're lying. To me and to yourself. Or maybe you just don't realize it yet, darling. But I'm here." She laid a palm over the pounding in his chest. "Right here, in your heart. I am there always. I carved a place for myself inside you when we were only children, and you did the same to me. And there's nothing in the world that could take you out of my heart, and nothing you or anyone else can do to get me out of yours."

Ren closed his eyes. She was quiet, studying his face. "If you let yourself believe what you're saying, Annie, you'll only be more hurt in the end. When I leave."

"Is that why you won't admit that it's true? To spare me the hurt of losing you again?"

"I won't admit it because it's not true. I'm not Richard. I don't even remember having been him. I can't be what you want me to be, Annie."

"And you don't feel anything for me now," she whispered.

He lowered his head. "I'm sorry."

Annie sniffed, then ran one hand over his hair. "I always could tell when you were lying, darling."

He went stiff and lifted his chin. There were tears in his eyes. He *did* feel something for her. "I saw a damp spot in the nursery ceiling," he said, and she sensed he was grasping at straws. "I need to go up on the roof and take a look."

"You need to be alone, to figure things out. It's okay. I understand."

He shook his head and got to his feet. "Just yell if you need me."

"I need you, Richard. Don't doubt that for a minute."

Closing his eyes at her words, he finally turned and left her alone.

* * *

Fury! Damn undiluted fury was what Ren felt! The gods were having a hell of a laugh at his expense right now, weren't they? Sir George, out there somewhere watching him twist and writhe in agony! Was it so amusing? And what the hell had he done to earn this kind of torment?

He adored the woman! And it wasn't a new feeling, something that had developed since he'd returned. Although there was that as well. But what he felt—the emotion that choked him until he could barely speak—was old. And deep and real and raw. It was eternal. The fact that he couldn't remember it didn't stop him from feeling its resurgence. And the fact that the physical desire he must have once burned with for Annie was now little more than a dim echo did nothing to ease the longing for her in his heart. He wanted what they'd once had, craved the memories of their life together. He'd been robbed of all of that.

God, they must have been so happy. How could any man be less with a woman like her loving him as much as she obviously had? It wasn't fair, dammit! Why did he have to die young? Why the hell should she have to go through life alone, give birth alone, survive as a single mother to his child . . .

His child! And he wanted it. He wanted to be there for it and hold it and nurture it. He longed in his heart to be free of the vows he'd sworn. And he couldn't have fought the feeling, even if he'd wanted to.

He knew the rules. He was probably damned now. If he kept it up and he died this time around, even Sir George's magic wouldn't be able to bring him back. And he was beginning to wonder if that would be a bad thing. Because to go on living eternally, knowing he had a wife and a child out there struggling by on their own without him, would be pure hell. Damn fate and its tricks. Damn the world and everyone in it. Everyone but her. Everyone but his beautiful, sweet Annie. And their baby.

Ren sat on the roof pretending to inspect a nonexistent leak, and cursed the stars, the heavens, the gods. And still felt no relief.

"Bartholomew, it's good to see you." Annie stepped aside and let him enter. Bartholomew looked around, as if expecting someone else to appear, before taking a seat on the sofa.

"You don't look well, Annie. You're pale. What's wrong?"

Annie tried to smile, but the dim remainder of her headache made it difficult. The knowledge that she'd found Richard again, only to have to face the possibility of losing him once more, made it all but impossible. "Nothing. I'm fine, really."

He shook his head, his eyes inscrutable. It was the twist of one corner of his mouth that told her he knew she was lying.

"No, you're not. Darling, I know something happened here. I came by early this morning, just to check in, and found the doors and windows all open. Fans mounted in several of them, running full blast. And the entire place just reeked of natural gas. Now, Annie, if you're not going to tell me, then please, for God's sake, tell someone."

Her smile faltered. She blinked fast and remembered Ren's warning not to talk to anyone about him. He'd said the Dark Knight might be in disguise, that there was no way to know who could be trusted.

But this was Bartholomew! She knew Bartholomew would never betray her. Still, she had promised.

"It was nothing. Just a gas leak. I had to leave the house until it aired out."

"A gas leak?" Bartholomew looked skeptical.

"Yes." She shifted in her seat and avoided his eyes. "Can I get you some coffee, or—"

"So it's been fixed, then?"

"Well, of course, or we wouldn't be sitting here."

"Funny. I didn't see any repair trucks. No one from the gas company. How did it get fixed, Annie?"

She jerked in surprise. "Well, I . . . that is . . ."

"Annie." He shook his head, leaned close to her, touched her arm. She felt the warmth of the pendant he'd given her, and felt guilty for lying to him. "Tell the truth. You turned on the gas yourself, didn't you?"

"*What?*" She gaped at him for a moment. "No, of course not!"

He shook his head, bending closer to clasp her shoulders, his black, lifeless eyes nearly blazing. "I thought we were *friends*, Annie. I thought you *trusted* me."

"I do. But honestly, Bartholomew, that's such a ridiculous idea. I'd never—"

"Annie, you're not well. I'm an expert; I know the signs. And if you tell me you haven't been questioning your own sanity lately, then you're lying. I know. Don't you see that?" She lowered her head, but he caught her chin in one hand and forced her to meet his gaze. "You have, haven't you? Or perhaps you haven't, but you know deep down that perhaps you should be."

She fought the irrational and unexpected

surge of doubt that swept into her mind out of the blue. And there was a sense, a sense that the doubts weren't coming from inside her but from . . . outside. From somewhere else.

The pendant throbbed on her skin. Absently she stroked it and battled her own uncertainty. "Actually, Bartholomew, I probably did question myself once or twice, but now—"

"But now you're convinced there's nothing wrong. Is that right?"

She felt her brows draw together. "How did you—"

"It's typical, Annie. Darling Annie, I only want to help you; don't you know that? When you convince yourself that the delusions are real, that you were perfectly sane all the time, then the illness is winning. It's one of the worst possible symptoms. Don't give in to it! For God's sake, Annie, you have a baby to think about!"

"But I . . ." She shook her head, looking at the room around her for support. She closed her eyes then and heard Sara's voice telling her to trust herself, believe what she knew to be true. Ren was real! She knew he was, and he was Richard, and . . .

The necklace heated, burning her fingertips, making her realize somehow just how crazy all of this would sound if she should try to tell someone about it. *You see, I wasn't crazy. My husband just came back from the dead, is all. He needed to protect our child from unseen demons out to destroy it, and when it's all over, he'll go back to some other realm, and I'll be alone again.*

Bartholomew's arms slid around her shoulders. He held her to his chest and patted her back as she tried to understand why she should suddenly doubt herself this way. "There, now. It's not too late, I promise you, Annie. We can still pull you back. You can still be well enough to be a mother to your child. That's what you want, isn't it?"

"Y-yes. But I—"

"Just come with me now. Come with me. We'll go to a hospital, and I promise I'll see to it that you get better. I'll take care of you, Annie." He was touching the necklace now, stroking it slowly as he spoke to her. "You can trust me. You know that, don't you, Annie?"

Go with him? But that would mean being away from Richard. . . .

"Come on, Annie. We'll go right now. We'll get you the help you—"

"No!" She jerked away from his embrace and stood bolt upright. The chain around her neck snapped, and the pink tourmaline clattered to the floor. Her self-doubt seemed to desert her along with the stone. She was herself again, and she was certain of her own mind. Bartholomew was wrong, and she refused to let him interfere in this. "No," she repeated more calmly. "Bartholomew, I do cherish your friendship, and I can think of few people I trust more than I do you, but I sorely resent your coming here and implying that I'm having some kind of breakdown. I'm fine. Perfect. Better than I've ever been, and you're overstepping the bounds of friendship as well as your profession by talking to me like this."

She felt better. And maybe Bartholomew would say that was another symptom, but she knew it was because there was nothing wrong with her.

Bartholomew practically sagged in disappointment. "Denial," he said sadly. "Well, all right, Annie. All right, it has to be your decision." He crouched down, picked up the stone, straightened. "But know that I'll be here for you. If you ever want to talk about this, tell me what's been going on with you. I'll be here. You call me, night or day, if you decide to accept the help you so obviously need. Understand?"

She nodded. "I'm sure you mean well, but I'm fine. Thank you for your concern, Bartholomew."

"Here." He held the stone out to her.

She lifted a hand to take it from him, but something stopped her. A voice flitting through her mind, one a lot like Sara's, telling her no, don't touch that stone. So she lowered her hand, frowning, not understanding. And she heard herself say, "I think you'd better keep it."

Ren watched Annie closely enough to know she was safe, but he avoided being too close to her. He couldn't listen to her telling him about what they'd had. Not now. It was tearing him up.

Always he'd felt this gnawing, aching emptiness inside him. But he'd never been able to understand what was supposed to live there.

That emptiness was gone now. She'd filled it in a way he'd never imagined possible. But along with her, there was pain. The pain of knowing what he felt for her now was only a shadow of what he must have had with her once. And the pain of knowing he had to leave her again. There was no way around it. Over and over he played the oath he'd sworn in his mind. And the final words rang in his ears. *Should I break my vow to you, should I fail to obey, my fate will be death—the second death, from which there is no resurrection.*

God, how could life be so cruel?

Through the night he tried to find a solution, a way to end his time with her without breaking her heart. But he saw none. And he knew he was allowing that matter to distract him from the more important issue: protecting her from the villain until the child was born.

Annie was asleep now in her bed, the bed they'd once shared. But Ren was uneasy. More and more he felt the presence. Dark, menacing. A mental surveillance, a spiritual spy. One he could neither see nor fight, at the moment, but there all the same. Watching, waiting for an opportunity.

Nervous, he went upstairs and slipped into Annie's bedroom, feeling instinctively he shouldn't be far from her side tonight. And the second his gaze fell on her, lying in the rumpled bed, her hair spread over the pillows, a sheet clutched in her hand, he felt the tug of a distant memory.

He'd entered this room on their wedding night, to find her waiting there. The white negligee she'd worn was like gossamer, and her cheeks were stained pink. Those huge green eyes stared into his, waiting. He'd taken her hand in his, drawn her to her feet, and the sight of her had taken his breath away. He remembered the way her hands had trembled as they'd gone to the straps of the gown, and the contrast of her shiny red nails with her peach-toned skin. He recalled the way she'd lowered her eyes as she pushed the straps down and let the satiny fabric fall into a pristine pool at her feet. It hadn't been their first time—but their first time as man and wife. And he'd found it endearing that she'd be nervous. And he remembered, very distinctly, that he'd battled tears at the time. Awed by the fact that this wonderful woman had chosen him. Determined to give her the love she deserved for the rest of her life.

He felt that emotion welling in his heart again, right now, as he looked down at her sleeping there. And it remained, even after the brief memory had faded away.

Then he tilted his head. Her belly had moved. There, it moved again! Poked from inside by a tiny fist or maybe a little foot.

His baby, she'd told him. His child. Ren's own flesh and blood, and hers, growing there inside her.

Quietly he moved forward and eased himself onto the edge of the bed. She didn't wake. He moved his palms over her taut, expanded middle, only stopping when he felt the baby move directly beneath them. A minuscule fist— he was certain that's what it was—seemed to reach toward him, stretching her skin oddly, pressing right against his hand. Ren felt a hot tear slide over his cheek, and he lowered his head, pressing his lips to that tiny, thrusting hand. "My baby," he whispered.

Would he ever know the child? Ever hold it in his arms? Or would he be summoned back to the other realm the instant it drew breath?

He turned his head and rested his cheek against her warm skin, only the thin night-gown and Annie's flesh separating him from his child. Knowing this might be as close as he'd ever get.

She waited until he fell asleep there. Then she stroked his hair and silently cried herself back to sleep.

Hours later, in the darkest time before dawn, she woke. Ren had retreated to his chair beside the bed, where he sat sleeping. But something was wrong. She felt it, right in the center of her being. There was no sound, nothing she could identify. Just a cold sensation. A chilling . . . presence?

She slipped out of bed, rubbing her arms, then froze where she stood. The curtains billowed before an open window. Goose bumps raced up her nape.

"Ren?"

He came awake at once and sat up straight. "Ren, did you open the window?"

She knew by his expression that he hadn't, even before he told her so. She moved toward the window, and in the pale moonlight, she saw him. A dark form standing on the lawn below. Unidentifiable but menacing. He stared up at her, his face swathed in shadow.

Annie screamed.

Ren had her in his arms before the sound died, cradling her to his chest, stroking her hair. He looked out the window, too. "Where, Annie? Where did you see him?"

She turned, shocked that the form no longer stood there. "Right below us." She pointed to the spot.

Ren urged her toward the bed. "Wait here."

"No! Don't leave me!"

"I have to get to him, Annie. It's the only way I can stop him. Wait here. Lock the door." He pressed her onto the bed, whirled to close and lock the window, then snatched a sword from where it was leaning against the wall, covered by that long coat he always wore.

A sword. Good God.

Annie choked back her sobs, but she managed to get to the bedroom door and lock it. Then she crawled onto the foot of the bed, scurried up to the head, and huddled there. She couldn't stop shaking, even when she tugged the blankets up and clasped them just beneath her chin. Minutes ticked by, like slow-moving clouds on a still day.

God, where was Ren? What was taking so long?

She stiffened at a sound, a slight rattle, that came from the bathroom. Her gaze flew to the closed door and riveted itself there. Part of her wanted to scream, to run out of the bedroom. Another part feared running right into the arms of some unspeakable evil. She was imagining things. She was . . .

Oh, God! The knob was turning. The bathroom door was opening.

Chapter Eight

➣ Ren was chasing shadows when he heard her scream. He'd sworn he'd seen something dark slipping around the garage. Then behind the house, then among some trees out back. If he'd been as alert as he should have been, he'd have realized that he was being led farther and farther away from her. But by the time he realized it, it was too late. And he knew, dammit, just by the cunning nature of the trick, that the enemy he'd face this night was none other than Blackheart, the dark knight he'd battled so often and defeated only part of the time.

He whirled at the heart-wrenching shrieks and realized that at least three hundred yards now stood between him and the house. From here he could see the bedroom window. He could see her silhouette beyond the curtain, hands crossed protectively over her protruding belly—the haven of his child—as she backed away from some unseen demon, screaming again, ripping the night as well as Ren's heart with her cries.

Damn! He sprinted, sword in hand, pouring every ounce of his strength into each stride—and slammed into an invisible blockade, one he knew was constructed of pure black evil.

It was like being hit by a truck. The impact sent him backward, and he hit the ground hard. He shook himself. The blow had been significant, but he forced himself to his feet, grinding his teeth against the pain, blinking to clear his vision.

He'd encountered Blackheart's invisible barriers before. And he knew he couldn't break through this unseen wall on his own. He needed magic. *If* Sir George would still grant it. That would be the major question, wouldn't it? Ren had been cursing his vows of service, cursing Sir George himself. Longing to leave his duties and remain here, hungering for Annie in his heart of hearts. Had he gone too far?

He had to try. He dropped to his knees, lowered his head, and began chanting the words, calling down the strength of the Light. The power didn't originate with Sir George. Ren knew that. It only came by way of him. Its source was Goodness itself. And Ren was relieved and more than a little bit surprised when he felt it reaching him. Filling him with the power he needed to break through. Trans-

forming him from the semblance of mortal
man and raining down on him a new countenance—that of the White Knight he had become.

And Annie screamed again.

He had no face! The figure wore a black
robe, and the oversize, monk-style hood covered a black void.

Annie scrambled from the bed when the
bathroom door was flung wide, and the creature stood there like the shadow of death. Her
spine went so stiff with fear, she thought it
would snap, and an uncontrollable shudder
racked her. Her heart thundered as the dark,
menacing thing moved toward her, and she
lunged for the door. But this creature moved
faster. It put itself into her path, and she nearly
collided with it. She saw its cloaked arms rising as if to enfold her, and heard the movements of the fabric. She jerked to a halt just in
time and backed away. Her breathing was ragged and harsh, her throat bone dry as she
looked for a way out, a means of escape. But
it advanced on her slowly, and there was nowhere to go. The backs of her legs bumped
into the bed behind her. The monster crowded
closer, and she felt an unnatural chill in the
air, smelled the stench of pure evil. And she
knew that was what this thing was made of.

Fear clenched her insides, and she felt sick with revulsion.

"Get away! God, who are you? *What* are you? Why can't you just leave me alone!"

She clambered backward over the bed. A cold, clammy hand grasped her wrist, powerful fingers digging deep into her flesh as he twisted her arm. She screamed again, in pain this time. And again when its other hand rose and she saw the hypodermic it clasped. The thing lowered the needle toward her arm.

The baby! This creature was trying to kill her baby!

She strained to pull free of his grip as she stared in sick horror at that needle's deadly tip hovering a hair's breadth from her arm. With her free hand, Annie groped blindly. She touched the lamp, clutched at it desperately, and brought it down on her dark attacker's faceless head. Its grip faltered and she scrambled off the far side of the bed, nearly falling, but caught herself, and just as it lunged for her again, she reached the bathroom. She slammed the door behind her, threw the lock, and prayed Ren would come in time. But what if he didn't?

She whirled, knowing she had to protect her child at any cost. The window! It stood open, and she realized that must be how the fiendish creature had gotten inside. But it was small. Maybe too small?

She clambered up onto the counter beside the sink, knocking everything that stood there to the floor in her haste. She knew it was coming after her. She had to hurry.

It was difficult to focus. The ritual required concentration, and it wasn't easy to block out her screams. But he did it. And as he was slowly filled with the Light that was the source of his strength, he felt the transformation take place.

It took seconds, precious seconds that seemed to Ren like hours, but he knew when it was complete. Rising to his feet, Ren lifted the gleaming white-gold broadsword, now pulsing with power in his hands, toward the force field, and with a single swipe, cut through it. And then he was racing toward the house.

Something powerful slammed into the bathroom door. Annie swung her legs over the edge of the window. It slammed again, and this time the door rattled in its hinges and then cracked down the center. Annie tried to work herself through the small opening. But her belly was too round to fit. There was no room! The monster outside hit the door again, and the noise was nerve shattering, deafening, terrifying. God, what could she do? How could she fight this thing? Not jammed halfway through a window. She'd face it. Dammit, this was her child she was fighting for.

She pulled herself back inside, got to her feet, and faced the door, pressing her back into the far corner. Whatever it was, it was strong. She cried Ren's name when the thing hit the door again. This time the door caved in, and the evil black being seemed to grin at her, though she had no idea how she knew that. Somehow it made its amusement known. It was deriving some perverse pleasure from her terror. It loved this, loved fear. It thrived on torturing the innocent. It was going to enjoy hurting her, taking her child from her, watching her grief destroy her. And it let her know all those things without uttering a single word.

She wrapped her arms around her belly. "Get away!"

"At last," it hissed.

She pressed her back tight to the wall, would have gone right through it if such a thing were possible.

"I win," it whispered.

"Not just yet, Blackheart."

She nearly sank to the floor in relief when she heard Ren's voice come from behind the dark-robed creature. But then her eyes widened once more when the monster turned away and stepped aside, giving her an unobstructed view of Ren standing in the bedroom.

He was nearly blinding in his brilliance. Golden clothing. Tight-fitting pants hugged his calves. It wasn't a natural color, that gold. It was the color of purity, of goodness. And it gleamed. A white-gold breastplate rested protectively over his chest. And the sword he brandished was of the same glimmering metal. His eyes shone in a way she'd never seen. Almost feverishly they glowed, and it seemed to Annie there was even a faint light emanating from them—illuminated sapphires sparkling with rage and smelling battle.

"So, we meet again," the evil thing rasped.

"So we do, Blackheart. But you have me at a disadvantage. You've seen my human form. I have yet to see yours."

"At a disadvantage is where I want you, White Knight."

Ren nodded. "So now I know why I was chosen for this mission. I'm the only one who's ever defeated you."

"Ah, but you forget. The honor is mutual, Ren. I, too, am the only one ever to defeat you. Quite soundly on occasion. But nothing like I'm going to do this time."

"No, not this time," Ren said softly. He looked past the thing, met Annie's eyes, and held them with his own. "This time it's my very heart you're after."

"And this time, I shall have it." The black thing lifted a hand, and the air around him shimmered the way heat waves sometimes do over pavement. The shimmers darkened, and the waves took form. A black sword solidified in his hand, and as the shimmery darkness moved down his body, his robe altered, morphing like something out of a science fiction movie, until it became black armor. His breastplate, his helmet, complete with visor, were all black. His face, as before, was invisible.

He sidestepped back into the bedroom, and as the two began to circle one another, Annie trembled in fear. They brandished those swords as if they meant to use them. And for the first time she noticed that Ren's weapon was honed to a razor's edge. As was his opponent's. What if Ren was hurt? Killed? The Richard she'd known and loved could no more hold his own in a sword fight than she could.

Oh, God. Frantically Annie searched for something she could use to help her husband. Where were the damned shears when she needed them?

She heard a crash, and her wide gaze found the two of them again just in time to see Ren's sword flash toward the black one, leaving a glittering comet's tail in its wake. Shimmering sparks showed the path that blade had just taken, like a child's sparkler on the Fourth of July. She blinked.

The dark one ducked and rolled, avoiding the blow but nearly mowing Annie down in the process. He came to a stop just before crashing into her feet, and she hopped backward into the bathroom to avoid him.

A powerful hand gripped her arm from behind and tugged her out of harm's way. Gnarled fingers, oversize knuckles were all she saw. "What in the name of Goodness are *you* doing here?"

The voice was old. Ancient. Pure and powerful. She lifted her head to see a man who matched it, with powder blue eyes and wild snowy hair. His neat beard ran along his jawline and covered his chin, coming to a sharp, white point. The whiskers on his upper lip curved downward, merging with the beard. When she could tear her eyes from this stunning ancient man, it was to examine the ordinary clothes he wore, so at odds with his appearance. A suit, with a dark coat much like the one Ren wore. No doubt it hid a sword belted at his hip.

"Well?" he demanded.

"I . . ." She shook her head, then whirled at

the sound of steel on steel. The blows they landed were enough to kill normal men. The swords flashed again and again, collided over and over, sending showers of fiery sparks into the air at each and every impact. The solid oak chair beside her bed took a mighty blow meant for Ren, and split in two. If that blade had hit Ren instead . . .

He'd have been killed! She lunged forward, but the old man clasped her shoulders. "Leave my knight to his own powers, woman!"

She turned her head and looked him right in the eyes. "He's *not* your knight. He's *my* husband!"

The old man's shock didn't faze her. She didn't care that he reacted as if she'd slapped him, catching his breath, eyes widening. She only turned to watch the battle again, waiting for a chance to help Ren.

The old man put an arm around her shoulders, but his cold touch chilled her to the bone.

"I am sorry for you," he said, and she thought he meant it. "But he *is* my knight, and so he must remain. He swore a vow."

"He swore a vow to me before he ever knew you." Still she kept her gaze glued to Ren. He dodged a blow that would have taken off his head, and countered with a swipe of the fiery golden sword that should have broken his opponent's shoulder. He wielded the sword with the skill of an expert. A warrior. It was almost beautiful, as if the entire battle had been choreographed. Every blow aimed at him was deflected or dodged with dancelike grace. And for the first time, Annie realized Ren truly was different from the man she remembered. He'd changed, more than she'd wanted to admit.

"That was in another lifetime," the old man said. "One that ended. You should not even be here, witnessing this battle. It simply isn't done." He sounded as if he expected her to see his logic, shrug her shoulders, and concede. She couldn't get past the combatants and out of this house even if she wanted to. Which was beside the point, because she didn't want to. Not if it meant leaving Ren behind.

Instead of wasting her breath explaining all of that, she glared at the strong elderly being. "I won't let you take him from me again," she told him, dropping each word with an icy strength she hadn't even known she'd possessed. "Don't you doubt that."

She'd already returned her attention to the battle when he gasped. "Do you *know* to whom you speak, lady?"

She sent him a brief glance. "I think I do. But it doesn't matter. You could be the devil himself, or almighty God, and it wouldn't make a bit of difference to me. I'd fight either of them to the death for him. I won't lose him again."

A clash, and then a louder one, sent a wave of fear over her, and her gaze flew back to the battle just as the Dark Knight's blade struck home. Its black tip sank behind Ren's breastplate, and he gasped.

The black knight drew the sword away with a vicious wrenching twist, and its tip was coated in blood. The moonlight streaming through the window made the scarlet liquid shine as Ren fell to his knees. Annie leaped forward, screaming his name.

She heard the most evil laughter she'd ever heard in her life, and a voice of pure blackness poured into her mind, hurting her head. Its volume was deafening and seemed to echo endlessly, to come from everywhere all at once, and from nowhere at all.

"Give the child to me, woman. And I'll return your man to you."

She felt the old man's hands close on her shoulders.

"Come with me now," the dark thing urged. He lifted a gauntlet-clad hand toward her. "Take my hand. Surrender to me and I'll let him live."

"Go to hell!" she screamed.

The laughter came again, so loud she pressed her hands to her ears and squeezed her eyes shut to block it out. On and on it rang until she fell to her knees.

"Leave her!" The old man's voice was stronger, and the laughter vanished.

She managed to open her eyes again and saw the concern in the white-haired man's granite face, but she cared only for Ren. Her husband. Her Richard. She scanned the floor where he'd fallen, but he was on his feet again, and lunging toward the demon with murder in his eyes.

The black one whirled before Ren could strike him down, and then the two battled on and on, the sounds of the battle deafening as the two fought so rapidly, it became difficult to watch them. A mirror shattered; the items on her dresser crashed to the floor.

Annie pressed closer, straining to hold back her horrified tears. Ren's blade trailed fire and struck the dark one's neck, just below the edge of the helmet. The Black Knight wailed, a roar that echoed endlessly, and fell to his knees.

But Ren dropped as well, lowering his sword and glancing up into her eyes. He pressed one hand to his side, and she saw the blood oozing from between his fingers. God!

Suddenly the dark one shimmered and vanished.

"Draw," the old man muttered. "They'll meet yet again." Then his aged hand closed on Annie's. "I cannot let him stay," he told her gently.

She met his pale eyes and whispered, "And I can't let him go."

Then the mysterious man dissolved into a multicolored mist that evaporated before her eyes. Annie blinked in confusion but quickly dismissed it and turned, terrified of what she would see.

Ren was lying in the center of the room, on the floor, in his jeans and T-shirt. And the side of the shirt was crimson. His bloodied sword lay at his side, staining the carpet.

Failure tasted like gall, and Ren's mouth filled with its bitter flavor even as conscious thought began to recede. Worse than the red-hot pain in his side, worse than the weakness flooding him. Failure. He hadn't defeated his enemy. He hadn't saved Annie. He'd failed her, and his child as well. He'd failed them both.

Annie's hands ran over him like silk, her palms tracing his face, sliding down his neck to his shoulders. Her very touch chased the pain into a corner. Down over his chest, lower to his abdomen, and he knew she'd touched him this way before. But her sighs then hadn't been the distressed ones she uttered now.

Yes, just like this, he thought, at her warm

touch on his belly as she pushed his shirt up and away. Then she gasped and drew those satin, healing hands away, and he missed their touch the instant it was gone.

Poor Annie. She was afraid for him. Afraid of losing him. But she would eventually. Either to Sir George or to death.

He forced his eyes open, searched for her, and found her, bending over him again. Her auburn brows bunched together over those sparkling, damp green eyes. There were crinkles of worry on the freckled bridge of her nose. She pressed a wad of fabric to his wounded side. He heard water trickle. Felt her breath on his skin as she bent close to him. And for a time he wasn't fully aware of what she was doing. Only of her touch, her closeness. She smelled good.

"There. That's the best I can do, for now." Again her palm skimmed his cheek. "Be okay, hon. You have to be okay. I can't lose you again."

He tried to summon the strength to speak, but already she backed away, slid her arms around him, and tried to tug him off the floor.

"No." He'd meant it to be a firm command, but it came out as a weak protest. He shook his head and managed to lift a hand to her belly. "The baby . . ."

She reached for him again, but he shook his

head, the look in his eyes, he hoped, more forceful than the tone of his voice. He reached upward for the bed's edge, gripped it, and mustering every ounce of strength in him, he pulled himself up. He'd be damned before he'd allow her to injure herself trying to help him.

Despite his orders, she did help him. And the instant he collapsed into the bed, she was beside him again, checking and rechecking the wounds in his side, where Blackheart's blade had slipped behind the front edge of his breastplate.

"You need a doctor," she told him.

He only shook his head and closed his eyes. "Rest . . ."

"Will you die, Ren? Is it possible?"

He barely heard her. He was slipping into slumber, but she gripped his shoulders and shook him awake.

"I have to know. I don't understand how any of this works. Tell me, Ren, please, or I'll drive myself nuts worrying."

Blinking sleepily, Ren nodded. "I can . . . die. But only if . . . I break my vows."

She stared at him, pain in her eyes, but nodded slowly. "I see." But she didn't really. He knew she didn't.

Then, to Ren's surprise, she lay down beside him. Snuggling close, her head pillowed by his shoulder, she tugged the covers over them both and wrapped her arms around him.

"Annie—"

"Don't you dare say this isn't a good idea." She threaded her fingers into his hair and stroked him slowly, hypnotically. "And even if you do, I'm not moving."

Her warm breath bathed his neck. Her cheek touched his chest. He lifted a hand to touch her hair, then lifted the other, wrapped his arms around her, and held her close to him. And it felt as if he'd found heaven, peace, life, joy. God, he didn't want to leave her. Not ever. And that very thought might condemn him to death. If this injury was mortal, Sir George might not pull him through it. Once the vows were broken, the immortality was lost.

She pressed her lips to his throat. And Ren's child kicked him in the ribs. He smiled as he fell asleep.

"Richard . . ."

She kissed his eyelids one at a time until he woke and rolled toward her with a playful growl. Then prying one eye open, he glanced at the clock on the nightstand.

"You're a brat, Annie-girl. It's only four-thirty. I don't have to get out of bed for an hour."

Her smile was slow and filled with meaning. Her green eyes sparkled with mischief. "I know."

And she traced a little pattern over his chest with her fingertips, then retraced it with her lips.

Ren's eyes opened wide, and the dream he'd been dreaming vanished. Only it didn't, really. Because in the dream he'd been lying in the same bed, beside his beautiful Annie. Even now she nestled closer, smiling in her sleep, her tousled hair hiding half her face. She spread her hands against his chest and kneaded his skin before settling down again. Ren groaned inwardly and closed his eyes.

God, he wanted her. He hadn't believed it was possible for him to ever feel desire for a woman again. But it must be, because it was what he felt.

And he couldn't let it happen. If he made love with her, it would be the final betrayal of his promise to Sir George. And it would only be harder on Annie in the end, because either way, he'd have to leave her. And if he revealed to her that he did remember, that bits and pieces of their past had been floating through his mind, it would only hurt her more to see him go. Better she believe he'd forgotten. Better he convince her that he was an entirely different man now. If only she could detest him. If only . . .

She opened her eyes and propped herself up on one elbow. "How are you feeling?"

Miserable, he thought. "Better. You have a healing touch, Annie."

Her eyes changed, grew smoky, sexy. She lifted a hand toward him. Touched his face. And her desire radiated from her skin and her eyes and bathed him in warmth. He had to close his eyes against it.

Ren rolled away from her and sat up, swinging his legs off the bed. He pretended he couldn't sense the wave of pain that surged through her. The sting of his rejection. But he did sense it. And he felt like a bullet in the gun of a paid assassin. Moreover, he felt like a liar. He hadn't wanted to turn away from that look in her eyes.

He cleared his throat. "We should get an early start, Annie."

"An early start at what?"

God, her voice was soft, injured. He didn't—couldn't—turn to face her. "I think it would be best for us to leave here for a while. It will slow him down, give us a bit of an edge, and we need every advantage right now."

"Leave the house?"

"The house, the town. We'll make it difficult for Blackheart to find us. He'll track us down eventually, but it will take time. And all we need is time, really. Just enough time for the baby to be born. Then you'll both be safe. How long now until you're due?"

He heard her sigh before she answered. "A month. Four weeks. To the day."

"I'm sorry, Annie. If I'd defeated him in battle last night, this would have ended. I let you down."

The mattress moved and she sat up. Her arms slipped around his chest from behind, and her face rested between his shoulder blades. "You didn't let me down! God, you were hurt! I'd rather fight the bastard myself than to have to see that happen again."

Ren stiffened at her gentle embrace. In truth, it hurt him more than the blade in his side had. But to move away from her was more than he could do. "You shouldn't have seen it this time." He shook his head and searched his mind. "I don't understand what's happening, Annie. When the time of confrontation comes, the Hero and his adversary are supposed to be cloaked, concealed from mortal eyes. No one from this side is supposed to witness it. As far as I know, no one ever has."

"Well, *I* have, Ren." She sat up straight again and let her arms fall away. He could feel her eyes on him, though. "Haven't you figured it out yet?"

He rose and forced a distant expression on his face, the expression of a cold stranger, before he turned toward her. "It was a fluke. That's all. Don't read more into it, Annie."

She flinched as if he'd struck her, but kept her chin high, her spine rigid. "A fluke? Come on, you don't believe that. It happened because I'm supposed to be with you and you're supposed to be with me. We're a part of each other, can't you see that? We're only whole together. They're not going to separate us again. I'm not going to let them."

Ren wished to God she wouldn't think that way. "Annie, you're fooling yourself. It isn't going to happen. It can't."

She was so quiet, so hurt. He knew it. Damn, why did she have to go through all of this?

"So explain it to me," she said at last. And he knew she was making an effort to sound normal. As if she weren't cut and bleeding right now. As if he hadn't hurt her again with his cruel words. True, but cruel. "This . . . this Blackheart. You know him."

He nodded. "He's the strongest knight in the Dark Army. We've battled before, but not often."

"And did you beat him then?"

"Not always." He saw the hint of fear that crept into her eyes. It wounded him. "That's why I want you in hiding," he explained. "I can't be sure of winning the final battle. And he's here, watching you." She frowned and tilted her head. "He could be anyone, Annie.

When knights come to this side they're cloaked. I have no way of knowing what form Blackheart has taken this time."

She shook her head slowly. "I still don't understand. How can you win the battle if neither of you can die?"

"A mortal wound. A temporary death. If I've been true to my vows, Sir George will bring me back. If I've broken them, he can't. It's said Blackheart's lord will do the same, though I wouldn't trust that one's word."

"My God."

He looked at her, smiled crookedly, saw the flare of recognition in her eyes, and quickly erased the grin from his lips. "It will be all right, Annie."

She nodded and got to her feet. "I'm not sure I'll ever be all right again," she said, and he sensed the words came from her heart as much as from her lips. "I'll take a shower, and then we can pack."

The bathroom showed the stress of having contained pure evil last night. Or perhaps just the stress of holding one panic-stricken mother-to-be. The shower curtain was torn. Had she done that? The medicine cabinet's door hung from one hinge, and the contents were scattered in the sink and on the floor. Razors, aspirin, her vitamins. Wonderful. Her prenatal vitamins lay on the back of the sink, the cover off, spilled everywhere. And she was sure she hadn't done that. She sighed and shook her head. Why did that seem like such a big deal? She scooped the little capsules back into their brown bottle, keeping one in the palm of her hand. She popped the vitamin into her mouth, turned on the cold water, and reached for the glass on the edge of the sink.

The glass slid sideways before she touched it. It did a little suicide leap to the floor and exploded into a zillion shards. Damn!

"Annie?" Ren popped his head through the door.

She spit the pill into her palm and dropped it in the wastebasket, grimacing at the bitter taste it left in her mouth. She didn't remember them tasting so awful. Then again, she didn't usually hold them in her mouth so long. "I'm okay. Just a little accident." She could not swallow a pill dry, not one that tasted like that. Instead she screwed the cap on the bottle and made a mental note to take her vitamin later.

Ren met her gaze, scanned her body, frowned at the broken glass on the floor, and nodded. "Be careful," he said. "Don't cut yourself." And he said it as if he really cared. Then he ducked back out.

Her life was turned upside down, she

thought. But then she realized that at least it wasn't depressing anymore. She turned to adjust the water temperature in the shower. Oh, she was scared to death of this threat that loomed in the shadows. And she was dreading the day when Richard ... Ren ... would try to leave her again. But she felt ... different. Alive again. He was here, with her. She'd stopped mourning his loss. She could reach out and touch him, and he'd be there, real and strong and warm. She could talk to him and he'd answer her. Not just in her dreams but in his own strong voice. They had a goal, and they were working together to reach it, working together to thwart this unseen enemy and protect their child, just the way they'd worked together to create it.

Annie couldn't believe that this all hadn't happened for some reason. Why had he been sent back here to her? She'd heard him talk about other knights. Why not one of them? Okay, he was the only one who'd ever defeated this Blackheart creep. But she had a feeling there was more to it than just that. Because why else would she have been able to see him as he truly was when everyone else saw only the mask? And why was she the only one to witness that frightening battle? God, couldn't Ren see that it meant something? It had to.

But what did it mean? Maybe Annie was translating it all wrong, putting only the significance she wanted in place. She wanted it to mean that they were destined to be together, that no force on heaven or earth could tear them apart, that he was fated to come back to her and to stay, to be a father to their baby and—

Maybe he didn't *want* to stay. Maybe that was it.

Annie blinked in shock at this new, frightening thought. It hadn't occurred to her before, but now that it did . . . He'd told her he was incapable of feeling things like desire. She looked down at her swollen, misshapen body and closed her eyes. God, had she really been about to offer herself to him in bed this morning? Had she really thought she could rekindle his passion for her like this? She groaned and closed her eyes. No wonder he'd turned away so quickly. He must have known what she'd been thinking . . . wanting.

As she shed her robe and stepped into the shower, Annie wondered if there was a man in the world who'd rather live a mundane life with a wife and child than to be some kind of superknight traveling the cosmos with his magic sword to fight evil forces for the cause of good.

She didn't know. But she did know that if

there was one man who would choose his wife
and child over unending adventure, it would
be Richard. And she could make him want her
again. She had to. Because if she lost him
again . . .

But he said there was no way around it.
That he had to go back. And the old man had
told her the same thing.

While she showered, she heard Ren come
into the bathroom and pick up the pieces of
the glass she'd broken. She wished the pieces
of her broken heart could be swept up so easily.

Chapter Nine

∽ Ren drove, and as he did, he remembered. Not everything. Not his entire life before or their entire life together. But certain feelings crept up on him. There was a feeling to belonging somewhere, belonging *with* someone. And he'd had that feeling once. He'd stopped being just Richard and had become Annie's partner. People, friends, the entire community had begun seeing them as a team, a pair, a couple. Even before he'd married her. Long before then. It must have begun when they'd been little more than children.

When one was hurting, the other hurt. When one was happy, the other was happy. When one was sad . . .

She was sad now. And he felt it. It had been so long since he'd experienced this sharing of emotions. So long since another person's feelings had mattered so much to him. But hers did.

"It's going to be all right, Annie." Stupid

thing to tell her. He had no idea if it would or not. He had no idea if she could handle his leaving when this was over. But he thought she could. She was strong. Annie had always been so incredibly strong. He wanted to pound his fist on the steering wheel in frustration, but he restrained himself. For her sake. And he knew, only too well, that there would be time enough for the rage later. Endless time, without her.

"It will," she told him. "I'll be fine. Don't worry about me."

Ren blinked and glanced sideways at her. There was something different in her voice, in her demeanor, as if she was hiding behind something false. What was the matter with her? Her voice wasn't her own. A new one that didn't belong to her rang out in its place, holding no emotion, no tenderness the way it usually did. He studied her for a moment and saw a porcelain mask on her face. Expressionless, she stared straight ahead as if she was very deep in thought and maybe not liking what she was thinking.

"Annie?"

She only shook her head in a way that told him more plainly than words not to pursue the question he'd been about to ask. He frowned and decided to ask it anyway. But she was faster.

"Where are we going?"

He sighed, frustrated that she'd changed the subject, and determined to bring it up again later. But he could see something had upset her, so much so that she was hiding it from him. So he decided it would be best to put it off—for now.

"I studied a map last night. There is a place a few hours north of here. Secluded and safe. A lake in a forest. We can rent a cabin there."

She blinked but didn't look at him. Before his eyes, the color slowly drained from her face. "Mystic Lake?"

Ren cocked his head to one side. "How did you know?"

"Hell, Ren, it's obvious you're here to torture me. No better place to do it, is there?"

"I don't under—"

"Damn you for this. And damn you more for not knowing what that place is, what it means. God, Ren, how can you possibly not know?"

He shook his head. Keeping up with her changing moods was like running an obstacle course. Now she was angry, her fury snapping like an electrified wire, threatening to burn him. He knew he was hurting her again, tearing her heart out, but for the life of him, he didn't know why.

"Ren, your mother and my parents are the

owners. They rent out the cabins on the lower side of the lake, the ones you can drive to. But the one on the north side is for family only. It's utterly secluded. Dammit, Ren, it's where we met when we were little kids. It's where we snuck off into the woods to neck when we were teenagers. It's where we spent our honeymoon. Two weeks of uninterrupted conjugal bliss in a rustic, enchanted cabin smack in the middle of a magical paradise."

He didn't speak. He couldn't for a while. At least the mask had faded. Her pain was clearly visible now. The way her lower lip quivered, the way she caught it between her teeth and bit down hard to stop it. The moisture in her eyes, shimmering deeper no matter how often those thick velvet lashes swept it away.

"It's the place where our baby was conceived," she said softly.

"Annie, I didn't know—"

"Of course not. It's just another coincidence, right, Ren?"

She didn't really believe that. Maybe the name had stirred some long-dead memory of their happiest times together. Maybe he'd chosen it because of some subconscious longing to go back. Maybe. But he couldn't tell her that, could he? If she knew he was remembering her—remembering the two of them, together—it would only be harder on her in the end.

"We'll go somewhere else instead. I'm sorry, Annie. I honestly didn't know. I never meant to hurt you."

"Then why did you leave me?" She clapped a hand to her mouth and squeezed her eyes tight as soon as she blurted out the question.

He couldn't do it. Ren simply couldn't bear to sit there beside her and see her in so much pain. He pulled the car to the roadside and faced her, clasping her shoulders when she would have turned away.

"Listen to me."

She shook her head, averting her face even as the tears flooded over it.

"Listen," he repeated, holding her there. Then, as a sob tore through her chest, he broke. His will, his strength, they dissolved at that heartbroken sound, and he put his arms around her and drew her to him. Her eyes fluttered open and met his. He saw the emeralds swimming beneath her tears, and wanted nothing more than to take her pain away.

Her eyes widened, her lips parted to question him. But before a word could escape, he covered them with his own. And the taste of her mouth was all he remembered and more. Sweetness and life-giving nectar. His anguish died as Ren sank into a well of feeling. He could drown in these sensations and not mind. His hands moved into her hair, fingers stroking and twining, holding her head captive for his seeking mouth. He tasted her, delved into her with a questing tongue to find even more drugged honey. His mind seemed to melt away, and passion took its place in his brain. He loved her. He wanted her. Annie. His woman. His wife.

She clung to him for all too brief a time, and then she stiffened and pulled away.

"I don't . . . understand," she whispered, and the confusion in her eyes matched what he was feeling.

He straightened, the taste of her still on his mouth, her scent, her touch. He was more than a bit dazed as he searched her beautiful face, her eyes, so tormented and confused . . . and maybe a little frightened. Of him?

Ren blinked away the ecstasy-induced haze and tried to understand what she must be feeling. "I don't either."

"If it's pity, if that's what this was, then—"

"I don't know what this was," he told her. "But I promise you, Annie, it wasn't that."

She drew her legs up underneath her and leaned back against the seat, still studying his face. He wished to God he knew what she was thinking.

"Maybe . . . maybe going to the cabin is a good idea after all," she said very softly. Then she nodded decisively. "Yes. I want to go there. My mother's been bugging me to go there ever since . . ." She didn't finish the sentence. She didn't need to. "It used to be my haven. Maybe it's time I went back. Maybe if I'm there, I'll be able to figure things out."

He looked at her there for a long moment, even lifted a hand to touch her. But he lowered it slowly. He didn't want to hurt her again. He never should have kissed her that way because he was sorely afraid he'd given her false hope. It wouldn't happen again. He wouldn't let it.

He pulled the car back onto the road and drove. But his mind was on anything but the task at hand. Instead it was busy searching, seeking, striving to find an answer to all of this, a way to avoid hurting her. He knew one thing, and one thing only. He didn't want to leave her again. And there went another one of his vows, blown to bits. He was losing ground fast with Sir George. If he wasn't careful, this mission could very well end up being his last.

María sat in the overstuffed chair on the glass-enclosed porch, basking in the sunlight. It made golden stripes on her bronzed, wrinkled skin and in her still-dark hair. If Annie had known María was visiting her parents that day, she'd never have stopped by. She'd have just hiked up to the cabin without even letting them know.

Too late now, though.

"Annie, honey, I know I've been after you to take a vacation at the cabin," Georgette continued, her wheedling already becoming tiresome. "But, baby, not now. Not so close to your time."

"My time is a month away. Mom, I need to do this. Please, stop nagging."

"Your mother is only concerned about you," Ira added, ever Georgette's staunch defender.

"I know that, Dad. Look, it's only for a little while."

"Well, it's simply out of the question. That's all there is to it. You know the only way up there is on foot or on horseback, and you *must* know that pregnant women can't do things like that!"

"Mom . . ."

"I think she ought to go." The voice was laced with a Spanish accent, and all eyes turned to María.

Ren hadn't taken his eyes off the older woman since they'd arrived, and Annie had been wondering if he remembered her, felt any recognition at all. He hadn't said a word, probably for fear she'd recognize his voice and go into shock. Now he tilted his golden blond head and studied her. Annie, in turn, studied them both. There was no obvious similarity between mother and son. Ren was the image of his blond, blue-eyed father, who'd died long ago. But if you looked closely, you could see the likeness. It was in the bone structure of the face. The proud shape of the chin. The exotic tilt of Ren's sapphire eyes was the same as that of María's sightless black ones. Their smiles were alike, too.

"Why on earth do you think that, María?" Georgette patted her hand as she asked the question.

"Richard wants her to." María closed her eyes and nodded her head in serene certainty. "He's coming back to us, you know. Of course you know. I already told you, didn't I?"

"Yes, María. You told us." Georgette blinked her eyes dry and bent to kiss the leathery cheek. "We love you, sweetie. We know how much you miss him."

"He's near," María said softly. "Very close to us, right now. I feel him." She smiled dreamily, tilting her face toward the sunlight. "Everything will be fine once Richard gets back. You go up there to the cabin, Annie. You wait for him there. He'll know where to find you. It was your special place."

The four others in the sun-drenched room

went silent, and worried searching looks passed from Annie's parents to her, and back again.

María rocked in her chair, her smile appearing, sad and wistful. "I remember how the two of you would scamper in the woods and play in the water when you were little babies," she said, her voice a lilting song. "Oh, I knew my Richard had met his match in you, Annie, even then."

Georgette smiled. "I knew it, too. Remember how you'd follow him everywhere he went, Annie? My goodness, I'd never have believed—" She bit her lip, meeting Annie's damp eyes. "I'm sorry, sweetheart."

"It's okay, Mom. I remember it, too."

Her mother sighed, nodding gently. "I still think you ought to at least check with your doctor first," Georgette said. "If he says it's safe, I'll stop arguing. Maybe some time on the lake is just what you need after all."

"Of course it's what she needs," María said. "He's near, I tell you."

Annie blinked away her shock at María's perceptions. If she became as close to her own child as María had been to her son, Annie thought she'd be eternally grateful. To be so connected that she could feel his presence . . . It was uncanny.

Silently she walked over to where María sat

in the chair. She knelt in front of her, wrapped
her arms around her mother-in-law's fragile
frame, and hugged her tight. She didn't say
anything. She didn't know what to say. If Ren
truly did have to go back when this was all
over, it might be better if María never knew
about any of it, although Annie had a feeling
the woman already knew. In fact, she'd known
all along. Ever since the accident, she'd insisted her son wasn't really dead.

Sweet María. Annie thought maybe María
would recognize Richard just as she had, if she
had her sight. It was almost a blessing she
couldn't see him there, only to have to lose
him all over again. She'd never survive that.

Annie wasn't sure she was going to survive
it herself.

Ren had almost gone to the old woman, too,
when he saw Annie hug her. He wanted to.
And it took every ounce of his will to resist.
He couldn't because he had a feeling she'd
know exactly who he was if he did. So he kept
his distance, just watching her from across the
room and wishing he could embrace her.
Wished he could say to her, "It's all right,
Mother. I'm right here. I'm here with you."

But he couldn't do that either. He wondered, and not for the first time, if he'd realized what an incredibly lucky man he'd been

in his mortal life. How many men were loved as deeply and thoroughly as Richard—as *he*—had been?

Annie went inside to make her phone call. He'd started to go with her, but she'd told him she wanted privacy for the conversation. He gave it to her, though he couldn't help but wonder why.

He'd damned near changed his mind about the entire notion when he'd realized they would have to reach the cabin by horseback. Though Annie had said she could walk it, Ren felt hiking was out of the question. Horseback riding didn't seem like a viable alternative. But when Annie came back outside she nodded.

"The doctor says it's okay, but not to go faster than a brisk walk."

He was still having second thoughts, though, even as he helped Annie's father transfer the meager things they'd packed into saddlebags.

The two men stood in front of a small stable, a pair of fine Appaloosas patiently grazing nearby.

"Georgette and I stocked the place last month," Ira told him. "We were hoping Annie would spend a weekend up there with the two of us before the baby came. Course, we knew we'd have a fight on our hands." He shrugged, and there was sadness in his eyes.

"She's refused to go up there since Richard died. Can't say as I blame her. He was a good man, Richard was."

Ren nodded and continued packing the saddlebags. He felt Ira studying him whenever he wasn't looking. Typical father, wondering what this stranger's intentions were toward his daughter. Ren wished he could reassure him. But he was helpless to do so.

"I realize you're concerned about her," he said, knowing full well it wasn't nearly enough. "I am, too. I only want her safe and happy."

"She hasn't been happy in a long time, young man. Sometimes . . ." Ira shook his head and looked away.

"Go on, please."

He sighed. "Sometimes I wonder if she'll ever be happy again."

Ren nodded. He would have liked to tell the man not to worry, that he'd see to Annie's happiness if it killed him. But it was a promise he'd never be able to keep. Hell, if anything, he was only going to make her more miserable than she'd already been.

Ira turned away and fastened the saddlebag on the back of the horse he'd chosen for Ren. Ren had taken it upon himself to prepare Annie's mount, a gentle dapple mare. He knew horses, and he was taking no chances on loose cinches or spirited mounts.

"All set?" Ira asked him.

Ren nodded. "Shall we go get Annie, then?"

Ira inclined his head, and the two men walked toward the house. Inside, on the window-lined porch, Ren waited while Ira went on into the house where Annie and her mother were chatting. He would have gone, too, but the sight of the frail woman, sleeping now, in the chair by the window struck him into silent, motionless wonder.

There was an odd lump in his throat when he looked at her. She was his mother. She'd given birth to him, raised him, loved him, and mourned him. And somehow she knew he was near.

Quietly he moved close to her, bent low, and pressed his lips to her cheek.

She patted his face with a wrinkled hand, and a soft smile touched her like a ray of sunlight before she settled into sleep once more.

"I hope your doctor was sure about this, Annie. We can still change our minds, go somewhere else. It's not too late."

Ren made the suggestion as they stood beside the horses, beneath the golden sun. But by then Annie had begun to look forward to the trip. She could use some time to regroup, and the rustic woodsy setting at Mystic Lake might help her get calm and centered. She wasn't changing her mind now, and she wondered for a moment why Ren was having second thoughts.

Probably he was just realizing he'd be all alone with her up there. Really isolated, and what if she told him she wanted him then? Was that what he was afraid of? As if he couldn't fight her off.

She sincerely hoped he wouldn't try. It was going to be tough to work up the nerve to seduce her husband, to make him want her again. Especially when he'd made it clear he couldn't work up enough interest to want her back. At least she'd thought so when he'd bounded out of bed in such a hurry this morning, injured side and all.

But then he'd kissed her in the car.

Oh, hell, the man was confusing. He hadn't said he *didn't* desire her. He'd said he *couldn't*. And she'd give an awful lot to know for sure whether that was something that could be overcome.

He was frowning, coming to stand nearer her, his palms sliding protectively over her belly. Damn him and his conflicting signals. He'd drive her nuts.

"Annie, I didn't realize we'd be so completely cut off. I wanted seclusion but not total isolation. What if something happens?"

"Ren, there's a CB radio at the cabin," Ira told him. He stroked the Appaloosa stallion's sleek neck. "You'll be able to contact us at any time. And don't you hesitate to do it if you have to. That's our little girl you're taking up there."

"We could have her in a hospital within thirty minutes of your call, Ren," Georgette informed him. "Guarantee it. By chopper if necessary. There's a clearing just big enough to land one."

"See?" Annie told him. "No problem."

Ren shook his head, jaw set. "The horses are still a problem. Your mother was probably right about that. I don't think you ought to be riding just now, Annie."

Annie gaped in amazement. She'd never heard him say her mother was right about anything in her life! She almost said so, but that would have seemed odd to her parents. As far as they were concerned, she hadn't known Ren all that long.

Only all our lives, she thought sadly.

"Well, you're wrong. I'm not going to gallop, and the doctor says I can do anything I would normally do, as long as I'm careful. Horses are fine, at a nice, gentle walk. And you don't have a medical degree, so stop arguing about it."

Ren frowned. "Doctors have been known to be wrong."

"So have you, a time or two." She bit her lip and looked away. She'd also asked the doctor about sex. She felt incredibly self-conscious about that now. Ridiculous of her to be thinking about sex in her condition, even if the doctor *had* assured her that it would be perfectly all right. Same terms as the horse. Slow and gentle.

"You didn't tell him where we were going, did you, Annie?"

She snapped herself alert and shook her head. "No, of course not. I'm not stupid. I just asked if it would hurt me to ride a horse for a short distance."

Ren nodded but still looked uncomfortable. "And you're sure he said it would be all right?"

"Yes, Ren." But he was still looking skeptical, and she read his thoughts as easily as if they were written in ink across his forehead. Suppose her doctor was this Blackheart character, and suppose he told her it was okay only because he knew it wasn't?

"I've known Dr. Finnes for years, Ren. And besides, all my prenatal care books say basically the same thing."

At last his furrowed brow cleared, and he nodded. No more excuses, Annie thought.

Soon he'd be stuck with her, alone in that cabin. Poor guy must be terrified of what would happen then. She almost smiled. Then she nearly laughed at the irony of it. Eight months pregnant and thinking like a seductress. It was almost absurd.

Ren took Annie in his arms and lifted her right off her feet. He gently planted her in the saddle, still looking worried, and bent to adjust the stirrups for her.

She wanted to protest, and realized she was a little bit angry with him for no reasonable cause. Except that he didn't want her anymore. Didn't love her anymore. Didn't even remember their lives together. But she shouldn't be angry. None of those things were his fault.

"I like the other horse," she said with a frown.

"This one is the gentler of the two."

"Oh, and how do you know that?" Since when was *he* an expert on horses, anyway?

"It's in the eyes," he told her. "And the other one's eyes are filled with mischief." He mounted his ghost-colored stallion, moved it up beside her mare, and took her reins in his hands. With a click of his tongue, they moved off onto the trail that twisted through the trees.

*   *   *

Ren held tightly to the reins of the horse beside his, largely ignoring his own. He guided his mount with a squeeze of his thighs and a nudge of one heel or the other, or of a knee. And the horse responded as if by instinct, slowly picking his way along the trail, taking his time.

Annie's mount, too, seemed to know what Ren wanted from her. The mare snorted her impatience but kept to the plodding pace Ren had set. Annie, on the other hand, was anything but calm. She seemed excited and eager to pick up the pace. Every time he quelled her mare's tendency to go faster, she shot him a playful glare.

"Watch yourself," he warned, pointing out a low-hanging pine bough on her side of the trail.

She didn't duck. Instead she shoved the needled bough aside impatiently. "Give me the reins, Ren. I have ridden before, you know."

"Not very . . ." He bit his lip before he could finish the thought. He'd been about to say "not very well." Because the sight of her sitting so rigidly on that mare had given him another flash of memory. Of her falling from a similar horse, landing irreverently on her backside, and being furious with him for laughing.

He hadn't laughed at first, he recalled. At

first his heart had tripped to a stop, and he'd raced toward her, terrified she might be hurt.

But she'd been fine. Just angry. And he'd laughed at her expression and made her angrier. It was all he could do not to laugh now at the memory.

"Not very what?" There was a speculative gleam in her eyes.

"Not very relevant," he told her quickly. Maybe too quickly, judging by her frown. "Whether you've ridden before or not, it's not the same as now. Your center of gravity is different, and you have to be a hundred times more careful. That's all."

Her green eyes narrowed. She studied him until he almost squirmed in the saddle, and when he dared return her gaze, she tossed her fiery hair in a way that sent heat sizzling right to his toes. What man had ever believed a pregnant woman was not sexy? Not him. Not looking at her. She was regal and beautiful and strong and fragile all at the same time. She was desirable enough to make even a White Knight hunger for her.

He smiled at her. It was good to see her this way, haughty and confident. Much more like the woman he'd known so long ago. Maybe it was this change in her that was urging more and more memories to the surface of his mind. She was more like the woman he'd dreamed about last night. The depressed, haunted, teary female he'd found on his return hadn't been Annie. Not really. She'd been just a shell of her. Hollowed out, empty inside. *This* was Annie, filled with righteous indignation over his coddling.

God, but it was good to see her coming back to life. But would that life leave her when he did? Would she sink again into depression and despair? It wounded him to think that might be possible, but he was too realistic to discount it. She'd have the child: someone to love, to share her life with. Maybe that would be enough. Maybe the baby would keep her alive.

"There's a fork in the trail up ahead, as I recall," she told him. "Go left. Last time, we took the wrong way, and ended up . . ."

Ren's head came up, but hers lowered. He saw the blush creeping into her cheeks, and the way she tried to hide it. He didn't need to ask her to finish the sentence. He could guess what they'd ended up doing, if not where. It amazed him how many of the random memories he'd been discovering were of her. Of touching her, kissing her. Seems he'd had an obsession with making love to his wife, once upon a time. Not that it surprised him. He was rapidly reacquainting himself with the feeling. Even more so now, watching her sitting atop that mare so proudly and confidently. Watching the play of the sunlight that filtered down through the branches as it splashed random patches of color on her hair, her face. Watching the way she turned her head slightly in the direction of every bird's lusty song and seemed to absorb the music.

He nudged the horse left and kept hold of Annie's reins despite her objections. They rode in silence, until they came to a deep gully, its steep sides raw, unstable dirt and stone, its bottom far below. Ren halted the horses at the bridge that spanned the gaping chasm. He questioned its safety with no more than a look, a raised eyebrow.

"It's safe," Annie told him. "My father wouldn't have let me come up here unless it was."

"Are you sure? Annie, that's quite a drop. If it should give—"

"It won't."

Ren frowned at her, then glanced at the bridge again. "Stay here. I'll go over first, just to be sure. If it holds the two of us"—he patted his mount's neck—"then it will certainly hold you and the mare."

"Will you quit playing knight to my damsel in distress? I'm tougher than I look, you know."

"Old habits," he said. "Hard to break, you know."

"I wish."

He frowned at her, half afraid he understood that remark. She continued to protest, but he went ahead anyway. He refused to take unnecessary chances with his wife and his child.

God, when had he begun thinking of them in those terms? Ren sighed as he crossed the bridge, wondering just how thoroughly his feelings had already damned him.

Chapter Ten

 The cabin was just the way she remembered it, the dark, ancient-looking logs standing solid and strong. It was like a symbol of continuity—one thing that would never change in an ever-changing world. The full front porch seemed to Annie like an open-armed welcome. She wanted to run to it. She wanted to fling her arms around the cabin, hold it like a lost friend, and cry with it because they couldn't go back to those good old times. But instead she just sat astride a dusty Appaloosa mare and stared at it and tried not to cry. She hadn't been back here since Richard had died. She hadn't been able to face their haven without him. She'd vowed long ago never to come back here again because she'd sensed the painful memories would be too much.

Maybe they would be.

The windows met her eyes, and they understood. The surrounding pines whispered their sympathies along with their welcome, and the breeze that was their voice caressed her face and carried their scent. They knew as well. Everything had changed all around them, but here, they seemed to tell her, here everything was the same. It would be all right ... here.

She smelled the water, heard it lapping at the dock. And she wanted to see it first, before anything else. She gripped the pommel, swung her leg up in front of her, and then slid down to the ground.

"Annie!"

"What?" She looked up fast at his exclamation.

Ren shook his head and sighed his frustration at her. "Be more careful, okay?"

He'd softened his tone. It was an effort, she could tell. Hell, did he think she was too helpless even to get down off the horse on her own? She ignored him and loosened her pack from the mare. As she did, Ren climbed down and did the same. She was only mildly irritated when he took both packs, his and hers, in one hand and led his horse up to the cabin with the other. She was left with little recourse but to follow.

Ren tossed the packs onto the porch and turned to look around. He spotted the fenced clearing and the small but sturdy shed at its center. Then he faced her again. "I'll take care of the horses. Why don't you go on inside and rest for a few minutes?"

She sighed through her teeth and snatched the mare's reins away from him. "For God's sake, Ren, I'm pregnant, not comatose. Gimme a break." Then she stomped off toward the corral, leading the mare at her side. She only glimpsed Ren's puzzled expression briefly before she put him firmly behind her. She led the mare through the open gate, loosened the cinch, and tugged off the saddle.

And he was right behind her, impatiently taking the saddle from her hands.

She sighed and looked up at him. "You haven't changed a bit, you know that?" Then she bit her lip and averted her eyes because he had seemed startled by her words. "I mean, I'm not an invalid. I wasn't before, and I'm not now. Pregnant or otherwise."

"Did I say you were?"

He was all wide-eyed innocence, and she felt a prick of conscience at being so impatient with him. He'd always tended to coddle her. It wasn't the patronizing attitude that was irritating her. Being treated as helpless drove her wild, and always had, but not when it had come from Richard. His tender care had always gone hand in hand with his incredible love for her, and she'd cherished it. So it wasn't the care that was bothering her. It was that the love no longer came with it. And that he kept doing tiny little things to make her want that love back so much, she ached with it. The way he looked at her. The way he touched her. The way his voice went soft when he spoke to her, so much like it had before.

She had to look at the ground because there was a bit of that sparkle in his eyes right now. The one he used to get just before he'd sweep her up into his arms and carry her off to bed—or to the nearest possible alternative. She relaxed her grip on the saddle and tried to still the flutter of awareness in her belly.

"There's a place for the saddles in the shed," she said, wondering if she sounded as nervous as she felt. "And some brushes to rub the horses down."

"I'll get them."

He walked away, a saddle over each shoulder. She checked to be sure he'd closed the gate. He had, of course. Then she took the bridles from the horses and gave the mare a pat on the nose. Ren returned and patiently began brushing the stallion. He hadn't bothered bringing a brush for her. So she stood there watching him.

"When did you learn so much about horses? You used to avoid them like the plague."

He glanced up at her, smiling. "Had to

learn," he said. "Sometimes I'm sent to eras where they're the only mode of transportation."

"That must be something." She shook her head and sighed. "Sounds like every man's fantasy."

"Not even close," he muttered. And the way he said it . . .

Annie licked her lips and her stomach flip-flopped.

"You groom like a pro."

He smiled, his hands running slowly over the animal's sweat-dampened coat. And in a few minutes she was mesmerized by watching them. "You always did have great hands," she muttered. And by then she was running hot and cold remembering the kind of magic they'd once worked on her.

As if aware of her every thought, he stopped rubbing, straightened, and turned toward her. His gaze met hers, and she felt a current run between them. For a second she felt stripped bare, as if he could see everything going on inside her mind, and her heart, and even into the depths of her soul.

The feeling shook her to the bone, and she tore her gaze free. Was she imagining the flare of desire in his eyes? Or could it be real?

Before she could decide, he banked it and turned back to the horse as if escaping. With a sigh of frustration, Annie snatched up the blankets and bridles, and took them into the shed.

It was cool in there. Cool and dim and smelling of the hay that was stored overhead. Annie hung the bridles up, leaned back against a rough wood wall, and closed her eyes. This wasn't good. Initially she'd felt only emotions. Pain when she'd first seen him and he'd claimed he wasn't Richard. Then joy at learning he really was, and more pain that she'd lose him again.

Now, though, something else was slowly overwhelming her. And she supposed it was only natural that it would. She really should have expected it. She and Richard had always had an explosive passion for one another. Why would she think it would be any different now? She'd never stopped wanting him, craving his touch in the night. That hadn't changed.

It should have, of course. It was entirely different now. She wanted him more every time she looked at him. Unfortunately he didn't feel the same way.

Or did he?

Annie cleared her throat and straightened away from the wall. She'd better get back out there or he'd be wondering if she'd tripped and fallen.

When she emerged into the sunlight again, he was already working on the mare. It seemed she wasn't needed, so she went right past him, out through the gate and toward the back of the cabin.

"Where are you going?" He released the mare, and she trotted a few steps before finding a succulent patch of clover on which to nibble.

Annie didn't alter her pace. "Just out back," she called over her shoulder. "I want to see the lake." And then she was out of his field of vision. Heading over the well-worn path that wound its way through thin, scraggly grass, down a wildflower-dotted slope. At the bottom the lake spread out, still and shimmery as fine blue crystal in the sunlight.

Annie stopped for a second on the shore and just looked at the water. Placid, calm, soothing. God, she'd needed this. She just wanted to absorb the feeling of peace into her troubled soul. The sun glinted off the water's surface, twinkling playfully on her face. She smiled at the light and hurried out onto the dock that reached into the water like a broad, curious finger. Still stained dark brown like the cabin. Still in good shape. Solid. Unchanging. She took off her shoes, rolled up the legs of her pants, and sat on the edge, dangling her feet in the water. Cool, wet, energizing.

Last time they'd been here, she'd put on a skimpy bikini and Richard hadn't been able to take his eyes off her. And then she'd taken it off, and he . . .

Annie sighed and frowned down at the stretchy material sewn into the front of the pants she wore. Nothing sexy about them. Nothing she could do about it. God, why couldn't he have come back when she was in her normal shape? She'd have made him remember then. She'd have made him realize that he didn't want to go chasing dragons with his armor and his magic sword. She'd have made him want her again.

Hell, she was going to make him want her again anyway. Because if she could restore those feelings in him, then maybe she could restore his memory, too. And if Richard remembered, he'd never want to leave her again. He'd fight with everything in him to stay. She knew he would.

He'd never seen anything more alluring in his life than Annie the way she was right at that moment. Sitting on the dock, leaning back on her hands, bare feet toying with the water. Her long auburn curls spilled crazily over her shoulders, halfway down her back. And when the slightest breeze stirred, her hair came alive, moving, dancing in the wind. Reveling in it the way Annie was reveling in the sunshine. And the sun seemed to be reveling in Annie, making her hair gleam, her eyes sparkle. Glittering on her skin, kissing it the way Ren wished he dared.

He stood there, undecided, halfway between the cabin and the lake. He'd been intending to go down there with her. He'd even started that way, wanting only to get closer to her. Maybe touch her.

But as he stood there watching her, he realized that wouldn't be such a good idea. Not just now. No, he was in no condition to be near her. He was feeling too much—more than he could hide, maybe. He watched her for a moment, longing for her with everything in him. It was probably the only vow he hadn't already broken, the one about not making love to a mortal woman. And he was getting perilously close to breaking even that one. Damning himself.

But God, if he had to leave her, he might as well be dead anyway. Maybe it would be worth the price. His life for a night in her arms. Yes. Yes, it would be worth the price he'd have to pay, he decided. And then he closed his eyes and sighed deeply.

Yes, it would be worth what it might cost him—but not worth what it would cost Annie. It would be a hundred times harder to watch him leave her again if she had a clue as to how he felt about her. It would have to be.

Grating his teeth against the regret that swamped him, Ren turned and walked to the cabin.

Maybe she just wanted to be alone. Maybe she needed some solitude to get her thoughts together. Maybe that was why she didn't come inside for so long.

Ren had entered the cabin alone, noting the layout with approval. The bedroom on the first floor was a blessing. He couldn't see Annie climbing the ladder to the one up in the loft. Too dangerous.

He set their bags down on the floor just inside the door, beneath the tent-shaped rain slicker that hung from a peg, and moved through to inspect the premises. The first-floor bedroom was through an open door to the left; the loft, right above it. The main room sported old, overstuffed, comfortable furniture and a huge fireplace on the facing wall. The kitchen was off to the left. Propane powered the range, he guessed, having spotted the tanks outside. But there was a refrigerator, and lights. He marveled at the effort and expense it must have taken to get power up here. And he admired Annie's parents, and his mother, for having the sensitivity to use buried cable instead of stringing wire on poles and ruining the natural beauty of this place.

There was magic here. Ren could feel it all around him.

He glanced out a window. She was still there, on the dock. Hadn't moved. God, she was beautiful.

Ren shook his head and made himself busy. There was plenty to do, and she'd be safe as long as he could see her. He'd distract himself. Figure out how to operate the CB radio on the little table. Unpack their belongings. Get their beds ready. Make sure there were locks on every door. Although mere locks, he thought with a shiver, would do little to keep Blackheart from getting inside.

He glanced out at Annie again. She was running both hands backward through that mass of auburn curls, lifting them from her shoulders, tilting her face up to the sun.

Yes, he'd get their beds ready. And his would be up in the loft. As far from hers as he could get. He'd sleep in the shed with the horses if not for the threat to Annie and the baby. But he had to remain close enough to protect her.

God help him have the strength to stay in the loft all night.

* * *

Hours later, he'd distracted himself all he was going to. And she still hadn't come inside. He would have given a limb to know what he'd done to make her this angry with him. If, indeed, it was anger that was keeping her out there. Maybe it was hurt or sadness or shyness or . . .

Whatever it was, it was time she come inside. And if he had his way, it was time she stop being so damned stubborn and tell him what he'd done.

Ren strode down the slope to the dock, ready to insist on a full disclosure. "You can't stay out here all night you know," he informed her as he approached. "Now, Annie, I know something's eating at you, so why don't you just . . ." He frowned when he reached her, then crouched down beside her. "Annie?"

Her still, relaxed face didn't flinch. Her eyes didn't open. Like a careless mermaid sunning herself, she'd fallen asleep on the dock. Ren smiled to himself and reached out to push a lock of silken hair from her cheek. He'd imagined her out here fuming over some imagined slight all evening. But he thought she'd taken it a bit too far when the full moon had risen over the glistening water, and she still hadn't returned. Instead, she'd simply gone to sleep.

She didn't stir, exhausted, no doubt, from the turmoil of the past few days, the episode last night, the trip up here. God, he was pretty worn out, and he was a trained warrior. Maybe bringing her here had been a good idea after all. If she felt relaxed enough to go to sleep here by the water, she must be drawing some comfort from the place.

Ren looked around at the wide star-dotted sky and the tranquil water. How could she not take comfort here, in a place like this? It was little wonder they'd fallen in love when they'd met here, so long ago. And it was no wonder that love was powerful enough to surive, even now.

He bent over her and scooped her into his arms, lifting her easily. She must weigh very little in her normal state, as light as she was now. He knew her body. He'd felt her, touched her intimately in his dreams and tangled memories. What a strain on her small frame it must be to carry the baby inside her. How tired she must be by now of bearing the extra load.

Her head lolled against his shoulder as he started back toward the house. She stirred a little, only enough to slip her arms around his neck, though, and then she was out again. Ren couldn't stop himself from bending down and rubbing his cheek over the top of her head. Her soft, fragrant hair on his skin made him suck air through his teeth. Bad idea, that impulse. But he did it again.

He opened the cabin door with his foot and took her inside. He carried her into the bedroom and lowered her very carefully to the bed. Then he stood there, staring at her, longing for her.

He ought to wake her up. She should eat something. But she seemed so tired, and she was sleeping so soundly, he couldn't bring himself to do it. Besides, if she got hungry, she'd wake on her own, wouldn't she? Right now she obviously needed the rest. He brought a towel out of the small bathroom and dried her wet feet. She'd fallen asleep with them still dangling in the water, and the bottoms of her toes had wrinkled like pink raisins.

He grinned at the image.

Then he sat on the bed's edge and began to unbutton the blouse she wore. But when it spilled open, his hands stilled and his smile slowly died. Her breasts swelled like luscious fruits, ripe to bursting. Her bra hooked in the front and barely contained her. She hadn't been like this before. His dim memories had painted a false picture. Or maybe she'd changed.

Of course she'd changed. She carried his child.

Hands trembling for no reason he cared to identify, Ren lifted them to the front of the bra and released its clasp. Then he pulled it open, freeing her, and feasting his hungry eyes on her.

He told himself he'd done it only because the thing had looked so uncomfortable. And that now he would pull the covers over her and let her rest.

But he didn't move. He only stared. If ever there was the perfect vision of woman in all her glory, he was seeing it now. He couldn't force his gaze away from her. He wanted to hold her swelling breasts in his hands, to feel the weight of them pressing into his palms. He wanted to stroke her dark nipples and see them stiffen in response. He ached to touch her, to kiss her.

Her gasp and sudden movement took him by surprise. She jerked the blankets to her chin and rolled away from him. "Ren, what are you doing!"

"I . . ." He blinked, searched for words. "I was just . . . making you comfortable. So you could sleep. I wasn't . . ."

She lifted the covers, peeked underneath, then lowered them and closed her eyes.

"Annie, it's all right. I . . . we were married once. Don't be embarrassed."

She shook her head, but her eyes didn't

open. "How did you get me up here from the lake, Ren? A wheelbarrow?"

His jaw dropped. He expected her to laugh and look at him with a twinkle in her eye, but she didn't. "I carried you."

"Did you check yourself for damage? Could be a hernia lurking—"

"Stop it, Annie," he said softly. "You're no burden, even now with the baby."

She turned her face into the pillows, a deep muffled groan escaping her. When she spoke, her words were not only garbled but muffled as well.

He touched her shoulder, then rubbed it, helpless to think of anything to ease her apparent embarrassment. He still wasn't sure exactly what was wrong.

"Annie, come on. Don't cry. I was only trying ... I mean, I didn't *mean* anything. I wasn't—"

"You think I don't *know* that?" She lifted her head to ask that question. Then she dropped back onto the pillows again. "Ugh."

Ren gave his head a shake. He'd thought himself equal to anything. A warrior, skilled in many forms of battle, including the kind where minds warred rather than bodies. He'd considered himself a champion at outwitting or outfighting any enemy, anywhere. But he was out of his league with her.

Aloud he searched for logic.

"It's a difficult time for you, Annie," he said softly. "Coming back here. The memories must be hard to deal with. Maybe it was a mistake. Maybe we ought to go back."

"I love it here, you big dummy." But there was a threat of tears in her voice.

Of course she loved it here, he thought. Wasn't it obvious the way she was getting ready to cry her heart out?

"The pregnancy is probably getting to you, then. Is that it, Annie?" Of course it was. Hadn't he just been thinking how tough this whole thing must be on her physically? Hell, the emotional strain must be just as bad. "I've heard that the final weeks are always the hardest on the mother. Is that it, Annie? Are you worn out and tired of carrying the burden?"

She rolled to her back again, sitting up and tugging her blouse together. "Our baby is no burden, Ren. *I'm* not the one having a problem with it. Gosh, *I* know what I look like without this baby stretching me all out of proportion."

He lifted his hands, feeling all but helpless. "Well, so do I. I don't understand what's—"

"You do?"

All of the sudden moisture evaporated from her eyes. She sat up straighter, brushing her damp cheeks dry, blinking her eyes clear, sweeping her hair away from her face, and staring at him as if she could see his very soul.

"How, Ren? If you don't remember anything about our past together, then how do you know?"

"I . . ." Oh, great. He'd just about blown it. Think fast, he told himself. "The pictures!" Oops, he shouldn't have yelled it out like that. Dead giveaway. "The pictures in your house, Annie, the ones of our . . . your wedding. I've seen them, and . . . and Annie, you're beautiful in them."

Her eyes narrowed, and he knew he'd dropped the ball.

"Not to say that you aren't beautiful now. You are. Even more so." He pushed a hand through his hair. "You know that, Annie. It's not the first time I've told you."

She grimaced at him as if he'd just told her she had a wart on the end of her nose. "You're not going to say I'm glowing, are you? I often think that's a polite mispronunciation of "growing.' "

He allowed himself a cautious, tentative smile. So the problem was simply that she didn't feel very attractive right now. Unless he'd guessed wrong yet again. And she didn't want him or anyone looking at her. Why? Because she was afraid they'd confirm her suspicions? God, how little she knew.

"No, Annie. I'm not going to say you're

glowing, but only because I'm afraid you'll hit me if I do."

"Hmm, maybe you remember more than you're admitting." And now she smiled back at him.

"I'll just say that you're the most beautiful woman I've ever set eyes on. I believe if da Vinci were here right now, he'd beg to paint your portrait. And it would outshine the Mona Lisa as his greatest masterpiece." He studied her reaction, seeing the skepticism in her eyes, then seeing it fade a little. Ren wondered then if there was anything in the world more beautiful to a man than a woman who carried his child. He doubted it. "You're beautiful," he said again to cement it in her mind. He didn't want her to doubt it.

She shifted her eyes a little. "Yeah, well, so are forest fires, but that doesn't make you want one."

He frowned, tilting his head to one side. *Want* one? Ren suddenly had the distinct sensation of a light being turned on in a dark room.

"Forget I said that," she rushed on. "Look, I'm sorry I fell apart on you. Let's chalk it up to out-of-whack hormones and forget about it, okay?" She slid out of the bed on the opposite side and rubbed the small of her back. "Where's our stuff?"

Ren shook himself, blinking away the flash of understanding that had nearly blinded him. "I unpacked for you. Everything's in the dresser."

She nodded, not looking him directly in the eye, and went to take a nightgown from the oak dresser beside the bed, still holding her blouse together with one hand. Then she frowned and sent him a glance. "This is the only dresser in the place, you know. You can put your stuff in here, too, if you want."

"I took mine up to the loft."

She actually winced, and he wanted to snatch his words back the second they were uttered. Idiot!

"Oh." She blinked against the pain that showed so clearly in her eyes, and finally turned away in her effort to hide it from him. "I . . . thought you'd be using the couch. You knew it was a hideaway bed, didn't you? Stupid question. Of course you knew. I told you on the way up. Well, take the loft, then." She spoke rapidly, too rapidly, as if blurting things as they popped into her mind just to fill the silence. "Hell, Ren, if you get to feeling too crowded, try the damned shed. I'm sure the horses would welcome the company."

"Annie—"

She slammed the bathroom door behind her, cutting off his explanation. And what the hell was he going to say, anyway? He'd actually thought about sleeping in the shed. But not for the reasons she apparently imagined.

When had this change in Annie's attitude toward him begun? This morning, he realized slowly. In bed this morning, when she'd turned to him with desire shining from her gemstone eyes, and he'd turned away. He'd known his rejection had stung her then. But he hadn't guessed at the interpretations she'd put on it.

He'd never known anyone as volatile. In deep mourning for her husband one day, furious with him the following dawn, feeling rejected and unattractive by nightfall. She was like the wind, unpredictable and impossible to hold. And God, how he wanted to hold her.

And what she was thinking right now was making her more tense and unsettled than ever. Because what she was thinking, Ren decided, was that he didn't want her. And it didn't matter that he'd explained that he couldn't feel desire. She thought she should be able to get past that, to *make* him feel again. And she had. But he'd denied it, and she believed it was because of the child she carried. His child. God, didn't she know that made him want her even more?

So he was left in a no-win situation. If he could show her how very wrong she was, it would ease her pain. He knew that. But if he let her go on thinking the way she was, it would be easier for her to let him go in the end. She was angry with him, likely thought him a shallow fool to reject her because of a belly swollen with his seed. His own flesh. His baby. If it were true, she'd be right. But it wasn't true, and she was more wrong than she could possibly realize.

So what was he going to do?

He heard the shower running as he turned to pace the room. She'd take her time in the shower. That was another thing he knew about her. And he wondered if he knew it because of his experiences with her the last few days or because of the past they shared.

And did it matter? Probably not.

He shook his head. Impossible situation. Impossible decision. Tell her he was half out of his mind with wanting her, overflowing with feelings for her, and break her heart to bits when he had to leave? Or let her go on thinking him a shallow, vain idiot? Let her go on hurting over his rejection now, just to ease her pain later?

Damn, he didn't know what the hell to do.

Instead he tried to focus on ways to make Annie feel better for the moment. Her back ached. That much was obvious. And she was tired of carrying the extra weight, whether she admitted to it or not. He could only imagine what other aches she might have. And she wasn't looking well. Dark circles under her eyes, paler-than-normal skin.

She'd be damp and cold when she came out of the shower. Autumn's chill was beginning to work its way into the cabin. Okay. He could see to her comfort, if nothing else.

He turned down the bed for her. Dug a fluffy comforter out of the cedar trunk at the bed's foot, and laid it atop the blankets that were already there. He plumped her pillows. Then he turned off the light and lit the kerosene lamp beside her bed. Softer, more calming. The bed looked inviting with that amber glow spilling onto the white sheets.

He sternly told himself it was supposed to look inviting to her, not him. Then he moved out of the bedroom because telling himself the facts didn't alter the way he felt when he pictured her lying there, her hair spread on the pillows, her skin painted by the lamplight.

Ren laid a fire in the fireplace, touched a match to the kindling, and watched the flames curl up to lick at the logs. Resin hissed and snapped. Warmth spread from the grate into the room, chasing the chill away, and the fragrance of burning wood tinged the air with something cozy and nostalgic.

Then, remembering she hadn't eaten, he

checked the cabin's stores. Ira had said he'd stocked the place with supplies. The man hadn't been lying. The refrigerator was barren, but myriad packages filled the small freezer, and still more were stacked in every cupboard. He settled on a can of "home-style" chicken vegetable soup with seasoned croutons, and a mason jar filled with peaches so bright yellow, they almost glowed. Mentally he ticked off food groups. Dairy. He was lacking dairy. Probably the most important thing for her right now.

He dived into the cupboards again and found some canned puddings—made with real milk, the label said—and he opened one for her, stuck a spoon in it, and felt a little better.

Then he stopped what he was doing and smiled to himself, and if he'd had a mirror handy, he figured he'd have seen a pretty goofy-looking grin. But it felt good taking care of her like this. She deserved it. He'd missed the chance to coddle her, treat her like the most delicate bit of china, the most precious diamond. This was a time when most men really began to appreciate what they had in their wives. Watching her blossom and expand as the child inside her did. Feeling an awed joy over the incredible gift she was about to give him. Wishing to take some of the stress and the discomfort onto himself.

He'd missed so much.

His smile only died when he thought about how much more he'd miss in the future. His baby's first words, first steps, first day of school. His wife's joy and wonder in every achievement. The warmth of a tiny hand, enfolded within his own.

A hot blade slid silently through his heart, and Ren's hands trembled a little as he stirred the soup. Not now, he ordered himself, and for once his mind obeyed. He wouldn't dwell on the future. Instead he'd attempt to make up for some of what he'd missed.

And later he'd worry about the pain that was in all likelihood going to be with him for as long as he lived. Later, in that vast, dark future that loomed ahead of him, when he'd have to live without her. A fiery hell would hold more appeal.

Chapter Eleven

∽ By the time she came out of the bathroom, dressed in a big dorm shirt, her damp hair trailing down over her shoulders and leaving wet spots in the general vicinity of her breasts—not a good area on which to focus, he decided—Ren had a place set for her in front of the fireplace. She started to head past him, straight for the little kitchen, but did a double take and came to a halt.

"What's all this?"

"I thought you might be hungry."

She blinked, and her eyes seemed wary, as if she was wondering what he could be up to. But she dismissed whatever she'd been thinking and took the seat he pointed out, a big, friendly rocker with plump, quilted cushions lining it. She eyed the soup, the glass of milk he'd created when he'd found a box of powdered mix in the cupboard, the chocolate pudding, the small bowl of peaches. "I don't think I can hold all that."

"Why not? You feeling queasy?"

"No, but—"

"Then eat. Come on, Annie; it's good for the baby. You know that."

"I know." She went for the pudding first, pulling the spoon out of the can to lick it clean, making Ren's stomach knot with intense longing as he watched her. "Not bad," she said.

"You shouldn't worry about your weight right now, Annie. You'll take it off again in no time, once the baby's born."

She washed the pudding down with a sip of the milk and grimaced, setting the glass aside. "Won't matter then, anyway. You'll be . . ." She met his eyes briefly and looked away.

Gone, he finished in his mind. He'd be gone, and she couldn't get that out of her thoughts. Maybe that was adding to her impatience with him.

"I'm not worrying about my weight," she put in, probably just to fill the awkward silence. "I eat plenty. I wouldn't let anything as petty as vanity interfere with the baby's health."

"I know that. And besides, you have your vitamins."

"Yeah."

Tension. That's what it was. Thick and electric, it seemed to hover like an invisible wall between them. He couldn't think of a single way to break through it.

She finished half the pudding, licked the chocolate from her lips, and reached for the soup. Ren reached for his own, having forgotten it was there. Watching her eat chocolate pudding could, he figured, make a man forget just about anything. And for a while they ate, but Ren sensed it was more for something to do than because either of them actually felt hungry.

"You're really uncomfortable here with me, aren't you, Ren?"

She'd finished the soup. The bowl of peaches went untouched. Ren wasn't certain how to answer her question.

"Why do you say that?"

She shrugged and shook her head. "Just a feeling I get."

"You and your feelings."

She glanced at him sharply. He realized he'd slipped. He wasn't supposed to know how often she relied on her gut feelings to guide her. He wasn't supposed to know a lot of things about her. But more and more was coming back to him now.

"I just meant you shouldn't jump to conclusions. I'm enjoying this time with you, Annie."

"Are you?"

Her eyes were searching, questioning. "I

am. My only regret is that it can't last longer."

She lowered her head, and he knew she still hadn't given up on her crazy notion that he could find a way to stay. It wouldn't help her at all to know he wanted that as badly as she did.

The fire snapped and hissed, and she focused on the dancing flames. "We should make the most of what little time we do have," she said, her voice very soft.

"I thought that's what we *were* doing."

Closing her eyes slowly, she released a long sigh. "Not even close."

"Annie . . ."

Shaking her head, she got out of her chair, belly first, hands braced on the arms for support. "I'm going to bed now. Thanks for the meal. I'll do breakfast, okay?"

"Sure."

Then she was gone, and Ren sat alone, the emptiness inside him gnawing right to the bone. He'd never in his life been as lonely as he was at that very moment.

And just how the hell was she supposed to sleep? Now he was saying she was beautiful, plying her with pudding by firelight, acting as if . . . as if he cared about her, and maybe a little more than that. She'd caught the man undressing her, staring at her body as if he liked what he saw, for crying out loud. And yet he ignored her blatant hints as if she were speaking a foreign language. What the hell was going on with him?

When she thought he might desire her in spite of his claim that he was unable to, he turned away. When she treated him like a casual stranger, he seemed hurt. She'd seen an undeniable flash of regret in his eyes when she'd left him alone in the living room. Had he wanted her to stay? To invite him to come with her? Or was she imagining the things she kept seeing in his eyes? What in God's name did the man want?

Annie tossed uncomfortably on the bed for hours and never came a bit closer to knowing the answer. She knew what she wanted. But that was little help. She wanted him. She wanted to make love to him. No, she wanted him to make love to her. The way he used to, so that it was more than just sex, more than passion. She wanted to feel his love surrounding her and cradling her and warming her the way she used to feel it.

God, she missed that. The sense his lovemaking had always conveyed—that there was no one in the world for him but her. That nothing could ever come between them. That she meant everything to him. The feeling of being cherished, treasured. The certainty that he loved her above everything else in the universe that used to envelope her entire being as she fell asleep in his arms.

She wanted him back: that's what she wanted. She wanted him to remember, to be her husband again, to be Richard.

Maybe it simply wasn't going to happen. And maybe, she decided after hours of hopeless analysis, she wasn't going to sleep. She flung the covers aside and tiptoed to the door, peering through it.

The fire's lonely glow spilled into the rustic room, painting the dark wood with an orange wash. Wasted with no one there to enjoy it. The dishes had been cleared away. Ren was nowhere in sight. Up in the loft, she imagined. Probably figured she was too round and awkward to manage the ladder. Probably figured he was safe from her up there. And he was probably sleeping quite soundly without her.

It wasn't fair, she thought. She hadn't slept soundly without him in eight long months. His memory kept her awake and haunted her dreams. And now he was here, in the flesh, and still managing to haunt her.

But not for long. He'd leave her alone again sometime soon. And she didn't think she could bear it.

She needed air, space. She had to think this through, find a way to come to grips with it.

God, she didn't want her baby raised by a woman in constant mourning. What kind of life would that be? How would her child manage to grow into this great world leader if all Annie ever showed it was grief and sorrow?

She padded barefoot through the living room and slipped out the front door. The night air sighed its fresh breath into her lungs. It tasted of earth and pure water and pine needles. It was good. Somewhere a night bird crooned a lullaby that went on and on, the same three notes over and over. Continuity. She clung to the bird's song, loving the predictable pattern of it, wishing she could find more predictable patterns in her life. She breathed deeply and stepped off the porch, slowly making her way around back, toward the water. Stars glittered like diamonds on the lake, and a streak of silvery moonlight magically bisected the calm surface.

Annie sat on the edge of the dock and let her bare feet dangle in the pure water. María used to tell stories about this lake. She used to claim it was somehow special. Pure, she called it. One of the few lakes left in the modern world that was still exactly as it had been on the day it was formed. Unsullied by man and his toxins.

Annie sighed. Ren would be gone soon, unless she found a way to make him stay. Of course, before that would work, she had to make him *want* to stay.

"I just don't know how to deal with him," she muttered to herself and to the lake. "I don't know how to . . . how to relate to him. As a friend or a stranger or a . . ." She broke off, but the words whispered through her mind anyway. *Or as a lover.*

She waved her feet back and forth, feeling the brisk, chilly water rushing over them, invigorating her. She'd never had trouble relating to Richard before. But now everything was so different.

Or was it? Maybe she'd been looking at this all wrong. Richard had been away. She'd missed him terribly, and now he was back. Why did that mean anything had to be different? Annie sighed. "Because he's changed, that's why."

Closing her eyes, Annie envisioned Ren . . . Richard in her mind. *But there's so much about him that's the same. Everything, really. His personality hasn't altered. He likes the same foods and uses the same expressions. He's just as kind, just as wonderful. He's the same.*

Except for the armor and the magic, and of course, his memory and the fact that he no longer wanted her. He was a warrior now . . . but maybe the same man inside.

And what about her? Had she changed as

well? Maybe she had. God knew she was no longer the carefree, happy woman she'd been before. Now she was wary, a little bit unsure of herself, and hurting. Always hurting.

She searched herself for the woman she used to be, the girl she'd been before that. When she looked around this place, her haven, she realized she'd still enjoy climbing the trees and exploring the forests and skinny-dipping in the chill water. That part of her, the happy part, was still there, inside her. It was only being stifled by the pain of losing him. Maybe she could find a way to bring it out again.

Most important of all, her heart hadn't changed. She still loved him as much as she ever had. Maybe even more, now that she'd seen how empty her life could be without him.

She tilted her head, considering this. If neither of them had truly changed inside, where it counted, why not treat him exactly the way she would if he'd never left?

The wind picked up. It hummed in harmony through the highest branches of the nearby trees, sighed down to the lower ones, and whispered in the needles. Annie looked up at the starry sky. She smelled the pine sap, pungent and good.

"This place," she whispered, "is magic. Anything is possible here."

Annie didn't look down. She kept her gaze

skyward, let the peaceful night filter into her, relaxing everything it touched. It reached deep, this place, and shook the woman she'd been before, rousing her from a long slumber. Annie felt her old self waking, a bit groggy and a little unsure, but awake, at long last. And as she woke, she wondered why she'd wasted so very much time grieving. The old Annie wouldn't have. She'd have been relishing every minute she had with the man she loved. So what if he rejected her? At least she had to try. God, if she could only show him a fraction of what they'd had together, he'd never want to leave her.

She got to her feet, turning toward the cabin, but hesitated, a bit of her newfound courage deserting her. What she needed was a plan. And to formulate a plan, she needed a clear, sharp mind and just a little bit more time. Her gaze was drawn to the lake again. It lay as still as a dark mirror, its serenity beckoning her. And the girl Annie had once been smiled.

"Annie . . ."

She wasn't there. Her bed lay empty, rumpled. Her shoes and her jacket were right where she'd left them. Where the hell was she?

Ren couldn't believe he'd fallen asleep! Not now, not when Blackheart stalked his wife and his child like a madman. Besides, Ren thought as he frantically searched the entire cabin, he'd been wide awake for hours, chasing sleep until he'd given up ever catching it. He'd been unable to close his eyes, knowing she was lying alone in a big bed just below him. Three times he'd got up and gone to the ladder with every intention of slipping into her room. He'd slide into her bed and pull her into his arms and hold her. Tell her how much he wanted her. Oh, he couldn't make love to her, not the way he'd like to. He had no idea whether intercourse would be safe at this late stage of pregnancy. But there was more than one way to make love to a woman, and Ren had all but writhed in his lonely bed as the alternatives had twisted through his mind. A mind that was supposed to be incapable of stirring up such fantasies.

But each time he'd started to go to her, he'd stopped himself. He no longer cared that he'd be sentencing himself to death for breaking his final vow to Sir George. He no longer cared that his existence as a White Knight would end with the completion of his current mission. He wanted her. And he cursed whatever powers had decided it could be wrong for a man to want his own wife.

What stopped him from going to her, though, wasn't the consequence he'd face. It was the one she'd face. She'd be devastated when he left her, even though he'd be truly dying this time instead of returning to his service as a White Knight. It would hurt her just the same, maybe more, this way. He couldn't do that to her.

Ren put those thoughts from his mind now as he failed to find Annie in the cabin. She'd gone outside. God, why? Didn't she know that Blackheart could be lurking there, waiting? Didn't she realize the danger?

Shoeless, wearing only his jeans, and those unfastened, Ren raced out onto the porch, around the cabin, and down the grassy incline to the lake.

And then he stopped and caught his breath.

She was in the water, the wedge-shaped portion that had been transformed into quicksilver by the moonlight. She swam, her slender arms beaded with droplets as they moved. Then she stopped and floated, and her hair spread into the illuminated water around her, and Ren thought of mermaids and sirens.

She saw him, but she didn't smile. She only held his gaze steadily and paddled toward the dock where he stood. At the end of it, she stopped. She clasped the dock to keep herself afloat, her chin just level with the wood. And he could see the slim column of her throat, and the water beading on her shoulders, and the mounds of her breasts just above the water line.

He lost the power of speech.

"I wanted to swim," she said softly, as if that explained everything.

Ren cleared his throat. "I . . . I was worried. You shouldn't go out alone, Annie. Blackheart could be—"

"I don't want to hear about Blackheart. I just want to swim."

There was something in her eyes, something potent and brazen and deliberate. He tried to ignore it but knew he was losing the battle.

"How do you know it's safe? For the baby, I mean?"

Her lips curved upward slightly at the corners. "I asked the doctor when I called him from my mother's. I asked the doctor about everything I could think of, Ren. Everything I thought I might even remotely consider doing up here."

He almost choked. He blinked, thinking the expression in her eyes might be a trick of the moonlight, but it remained the same. Seductive, inviting.

"I . . . I think you ought to come back to the house, Annie."

"Well, I think you ought to come swimming with me, Ren. The way we used to do." She released the dock, turned, and pushed off, paddling away. Ren glimpsed the perfect white curve of her buttocks as she did, just for an instant. When she surfaced again a few yards away, she slapped her hands against the water, sending a light shower onto his chest. "So, you coming in, or what?"

She was smiling, impish in her delight. He couldn't help but smile back. God, the many moods of Annie never ceased to amaze. But this was one he liked, one he'd longed to see. She was happy. And if it took swimming naked in the moonlight to see that she remained that way, then he'd spend the rest of his time right there in the water with her.

He was lost then, and he knew it. It was too late to think about the consequences. Ren watched her for another full minute before he reached for his jeans and began to lower the zipper. He took them off and Annie stopped her playing. She came into the shallow water, just up to her shoulders, and she stood very still, her gaze burning over him. He stood in the moonlight, feeling those eyes on him, wondering if she'd turn away. Wondering if he wanted her to.

She didn't. She feasted on him all the while he undressed, until he stood naked on the shore, and Annie stared, not saying a word.

And when he stepped into the water, even its sudden chill didn't diminish the effect that longing in her eyes had on his body. He swam out to her, emerging right in front of her. And still she stood in silence.

He ought not to do what he was about to do, but Ren knew painfully well that the time for changing his mind was long past. He drew her into his arms, letting his hands slip around her wet body, running his palms damply over her back. And he kissed her. He pressed her mouth open and took it the way he'd been wanting to for so long, and he tasted everything he remembered in its velvet depths.

Annie shuddered in his arms.

"Do you know how much I want you, Annie? How I've longed for this? My God, it's been killing me." His words came in deepening gasps against her mouth, her face, her throat.

"No," she whispered. "I didn't know. I thought you couldn't—"

"So did I," he told her. "You made me feel again."

"It took you long enough to tell me."

"Somehow I can't believe you ever doubted it."

"I doubted," she said. "But I hoped...."

He ran his hands down her back, over her perfect hips; he closed his fingers on her buttocks and kneaded her. Then he lifted her, his hands slipping through the water, down the backs of her thighs, spreading them until they wrapped around his waist, above his hips. She leaned back in the water, floating, clinging to his shoulders. Ren bent over her, capturing a full, ripe breast in his mouth, nuzzling it until its nipple stood erect and throbbing, and then licking it mercilessly. He braced one hand in the center of her back to hold her to his mouth. The other, he brought around, between them, and downward, his fingers dipping into the wetness between her legs.

God, though it would kill him to restrain himself, he would. But if it was the last thing he lived to do, he'd see her in ecstasy. He'd see the way her face twisted in sweet agony with the pleasures he'd bestow. She'd never forget him.

His fingers dipped lower, parted, touched. She gasped and her eyes flew wide open. And he watched her. Dipping his head to torture her breasts with his mouth, he kept glancing up to watch the expressions flit over her face. When his fingers probed inside her, her eyes closed and her lips parted. And when he withdrew them slowly only to insert them again, deeper, and pulled back and thrust again, faster, faster each time, she set her jaw, clenched her teeth. Not enough. Not yet.

She opened her eyes, curious, when he pulled his fingers away, but they widened and she bit her lip when he pinched the pulsing nub at the center of her between his thumb and forefinger. When he rolled it there, increasing the pressure, squeezing, harder, rolling again, her mouth opened wide and she cried out. With his free fingers, he entered her slick, trembling passage again, working her as before. His teeth closed on her nipple pinching with gentle force.

She broke into a scream that was the sweetest music. She shook like a willow in a windstorm and convulsed around his fingers and fought to breathe.

And then she relaxed all at once. Lying back in the water, only his hand at the small of her back and her legs locked around him keeping her afloat. He groaned softly, looking down at her breasts, nipples still pebble hard, peeking out of the dark, cold water. Then he met her eyes and saw her gentle smile.

"You don't think you're going to get away with that, do you?" A teasing gleam lit her eyes.

"What—"

But she clasped his shoulders, loosened the hold her legs had on him just a little, and lowered herself. Her wet center slid down over his rigid core, and Ren closed his eyes in sweet ecstasy. Grating his teeth, he rasped, "But what about, ah . . . what about the baby?" He was damned close to losing the power to think, let alone speak.

"Same rules as the horses, Ren," she whispered. "Slow and easy." She lowered herself further, took more of him. "Actually, that's what I called about in the first place. I didn't give a damn about the horses or the swimming. Just . . ." She took him to the hilt, closing her eyes and tilting her head back. "Just this."

Her hands at his nape, she lifted herself to kiss him, and Ren gave up. There was no resisting her. Siren. Lake fairy. Enchantress. No, he heard himself whisper. None of those. *Just Annie. Just my wife.*

He began to move with her, so carefully and slowly that his need doubled in his loins. It burned in him, and he trembled a little, and then more, as he forced the gentle pace to continue. His hands at her buttocks, he lifted her, lowered her. Again and again, and the silken sheath of Annie caressed him and pulled away. Encompassed him and released him. And slowly, agonizingly, his mind spiraled upward, his body reached for the heavens. And because of the slowness, he savored it when it finally came, washing over him as completely as the waves. Flooding him, and going on and on and on. He heard her cry his name, felt her climax joining his, becoming a part of his.

He held her tight, closed his eyes, and with everything in him wished he would never have to leave her again.

Chapter Twelve

∽ When she woke in the morning, they were inside, bundled together in the big bed beneath a mound of covers. Vaguely she remembered the trip. Laughing, kissing, stumbling naked and wet and leaving dollops of water through the cabin on their way to the bed. She remembered the goose bumps from the chilly air, and the other ones Ren gave her. And she knew she loved him as much now as before. More than before. And she always would, even if he did have to leave her in the end.

Annie bit her lip at the pain that swelled inside her at that thought. She knew what life would be without him. A dark, empty, barren place. A place she'd been stranded in for the last eight months. One to which she had no desire to return. But she would. And maybe this time she'd be a little more able to deal with the loneliness, the ache in her heart. Or maybe this time it would destroy her. She thought she was stronger now than she'd been before. Coming here with him had given her a new layer of steel. Maybe because she'd discovered the woman she'd once been and had found a way to draw on her strength. Or maybe it was her child, so close to being born now, making her strong again. Or maybe it was having her husband back with her for this precious time. Whatever it was, she had to find a way to hold on to it.

But would it last? Would it see her through the dark times to come?

God, she hoped so. Otherwise she'd sink into depression and despair once more, perhaps this time never to emerge into sunlight again. And she was finding she liked the sunlight, liked living without the blackness of despair weighing her down. She'd never realized how precious true happiness was when she'd had it. Now that it had reappeared, she cherished it all the more.

A tiny foot thumped her from within, and she automatically put her hand on the spot, smiling down at it. "I know, I know. I can't let that happen, can I?" She closed her eyes, found and clung to that strength within. "All right, then, little one. I won't. I'll be strong for you, no matter what happens. No more drowning in sorrow. Not for you and me." It was a whisper. A secret promise between her and her child. One she vowed to keep, some-how, some way.

But not now. Right now she had no desire to waste precious time feeling sad about the future or wondering how she'd manage to bear living without him again. God knew she'd have enough time to miss him later. If Ren still insisted on leaving her again. Maybe he wouldn't. Maybe now he'd understand . . . and want to stay. And if he decided he wanted to stay with her after all, she'd find a way to make that happen. She'd fight to the end for him. And she had a feeling that was exactly what she was going to have to do if she hoped to win this battle.

She sat up and just looked at him, sleeping so close to her. With a secret smile she whispered her thanks to the universe for this time with him. She'd cherish it always, no matter what else might happen.

Ren stirred. He always did within a few minutes of her waking. Always had. She waited, watched. The sheet only clung to his hips and a portion of his thighs. His broad, tanned shoulders and toned back enticed her, made her fingers itch to touch him. His golden hair caressed his shoulders, and as she devoured it with her eyes, Annie decided she liked it this way. Long and untamed. She'd ask him to keep it this way—if he stayed.

He said he couldn't stay. Not wouldn't but couldn't. He said that breaking his oath to this Sir George character was punishable by death.

Annie blocked out the voice in her mind that warned her against getting her hopes up. It couldn't be true. It couldn't! She wouldn't let it be! She'd find the strength to fight the forces that would take him from her again, and this time she would win.

Ren opened his sleepy blue eyes and sent her the lazy, crooked smile she adored. A little knot formed in her stomach at the sight of it. Just the way it always had. How could things be so much the same and yet so very different? So very strange and distorted?

"Hi, beautiful." His hand rose to cup the back of her head. He pulled her down to him and thoroughly kissed her mouth. "Breakfast ready?"

She shook her head. "Afraid not." She should ask him what would happen if he tried to stay. They should talk this through, make a plan. They should plot and strategize until they knew how to beat this thing.

Not now, though.

Part of her knew it was cowardice to put it off. She was afraid to hear him tell her it was impossible for him to remain here. She didn't want to know that. Until she knew that, she could hold on to hope. She could convince herself that there must be a way. There had to be a way. As long as there was a shred of hope, she could bask in his closeness, relish his nearness, revel in his love the way she'd always done.

"I *do* vaguely remember offering to fix it, though," she put in, shaking her hair with her fingers in hopes of shaking the disturbing, depressing thoughts from her mind. "I'll get busy right away." She sent him a wink. "I have an inkling you're very hungry this morning. You were rather . . . busy last night."

She saw the flare of desire in his blue eyes as she moved to get up, and she wasn't surprised when he caught her arm and kept her still.

He sat up on his elbow, gazed at her, pushed the hair off her face, and cupped her cheek. "You're an incredible woman, Annie. And you're gorgeous in the morning." He kissed her once again, this time drawing her back down into the bed and holding her against him. "Sorry, Annie-girl, but I can't let you get up just yet."

Annie knew she was in heaven. And she didn't want to ruin it by talking about his eventually leaving her again. There would be plenty of time to discuss that later. Not now, not here in their special place.

"French toast," he whispered against her

lips, making the words sound erotic. "With maple syrup. I'll make you a plateful of it too delicious to resist."

"I thought I was responsible for cooking breakfast." She spoke around his kisses.

He nuzzled her neck, nibbled it. "I lied. I'm cooking. Later. Quite a little bit later, actually. But I don't want you lifting a finger, Annie. I want to pamper you while—"

She kissed his mouth to keep him from finishing the sentence. She didn't want to think about the future. It hurt too much.

An hour later, after some delicious experiments in lovemaking, Annie found herself relaxing in the little rowboat, amid a decadent nest of cushions and pillows pilfered from the cabin. They moved quickly through the still waters, beneath an orange ball of a sun as big as the world. Mists rose from the surface of the lake as if the water were steaming hot. Long, twisting tendrils of pale gray, reaching upward, ghosts trying to get to heaven. They danced in slow motion, changing shape again and again until the little boat pierced their cloud of illusion, and the ghostly curtains parted to let them pass.

The cool breeze that touched her face smelled of pine and fresh, sweet water. As it gained force, the mists dissipated a bit more. And Annie was glad. She didn't like the creepy feeling the fogginess stirred in her. That sensation was chased away even more thoroughly when first a few and then a thousand morning birds lifted their voices in a raucous opera that seemed designed to welcome the sun.

Ren stopped rowing when he judged them to be in a suitable spot. He pulled in the oars, took a covered dish from the basket he'd brought along, and set it in her lap.

Annie took off the lid and eyed the steaming stack. "Oh, this smells heavenly."

"Powdered milk, powdered eggs, and God knows how long that loaf of bread has been in the freezer," he informed her. "But the spices might make it edible."

She dug in while Ren poured coffee from a thermos. "Here," he said, handing her a cup. "Decaf. It's better for the baby."

She smiled and took the warm mug. True to his word, Ren was pampering her. He'd flexed his culinary muscle while she'd showered and dressed this morning, refusing to let her lift a finger to help.

"French toast was always your specialty," she told him as she leaned over to inhale the luscious scent.

"No wonder it came so easily. So I was a great cook, was I?"

She grinned at him. "It was your specialty

because it was the one and only dish you could prepare with any kind of success."

He looked sheepish. "So you were stuck doing all the cooking for us? That hardly seems fair."

"Oh no. You cooked." She grimaced. "Or you tried to."

"It was that bad?"

"I always smiled and told you it was wonderful."

"And I'd see right through you and call for pizza," he said.

Annie went still, her smile dying. "Ren . . . ?" He closed his eyes, biting his lip as if he wanted to take back his words. But she knew. "You remember," she whispered.

He looked into her eyes. "Only bits and pieces. Things . . . come back to me at odd moments. I just . . . I just thought it would be easier on you if you didn't know."

She reached out to stroke his hair. "Like you thought it would be easier on me if I didn't know you still wanted me," she said softly.

He only nodded. "I held out as long as I could." Then his eyes glittered as they probed hers, and his hand covered hers in his hair. "I should have known better, though. I didn't stand a chance." He smiled at her—devilishly handsome, that smile. And it chased away the sadness the thought of his leaving her had evoked. "Eat your French toast," he told her. "It's good for you. Besides, I want you to keep your strength up." And he winked.

She smiled at him. It was the first time they'd talked about their life together. And suddenly it felt as if he'd never left her. Annie sipped her coffee and ate some more of the food. "God knows there's little nutritional value to French toast," she told him, "but it tastes heavenly." She slapped her forehead as that thought prompted another. "Oh, great. I forgot my vitamins this morning, Ren. Remind me when we get—"

He pulled the little bottle out of the picnic basket with a flourish. "I thought of everything."

"I guess you did." She took the pills from him, twisted off the cap, then paused in mid-motion, her head coming up, eyes scanning the fog-shrouded waters in the distance.

The wind had changed. It came more briskly than before, rippling the water, making the rowboat turn and bounce harder in time with the waves.

Frowning, she glanced at Ren, a question in her eyes. Something seemed . . . odd. It had grown so quiet all at once, except for the wind. The fish had stopped jumping, and the birds no longer chirped their boisterous chorus from the surrounding forest. Ren's brows bent to touch one another. He, too, seemed concerned.

"Well, that's odd. It was so placid up until a second ago." She shook one of her vitamins into her hand.

Before her eyes the fluffy white clouds dotting the pale sky picked up their pace, first skittering, then stampeding. The sky had the look of some experiment in time-lapse photography. Wind whipped her hair, snapped the hem of her blouse. Waves swelled from water that had been still as glass only moments before. The rowboat rose suddenly, as if in the grip of a huge hand, then sank rapidly, dropped into the deep trough the wave left in its wake. Again and again they were tossed and shaken. The pill bottle flew from Annie's hand as she gripped the sides of the rowboat. She reached for it, only to see it land in the bottom of the boat, its contents spilling helter-skelter.

"Hold on, Annie!" Ren's hand pressed hers back onto the boat's side. "Just hold on!"

He was yelling at her, she realized, because she wouldn't have heard him otherwise. The wind howled and moaned now, and the water was churning in response. She did as she was told, gripping the sides for dear life as the sudden windstorm whipped and twisted around them. Ren fought the storm, struggling to row the boat toward shore. The waves grew angrier, greedier. They rose right up over the sides now, slapping him, soaking him. One hit Annie full in the face, so hard it nearly knocked her backward. She held on tighter. She could barely see for the wet hair plastered to her face, but she didn't dare let go even long enough to push it away. She only shook her head hard and blinked the lake water out of her eyes. Vaguely she noted that their picnic basket had been swept overboard. Their dishes, their Thermos. She just caught a glimpse of her pill bottle before it was sucked under by the hungry waves.

Whatever it was, it was over fast. The sudden windstorm's fury passed over them. She could see it move away, see the trees bowing with it as it swept through them. The lake calmed, gentled, until the little boat settled down into its embrace once again. The sun seemed to shine more brightly than before, and the clouds fled from its golden rays as if burned by them.

Ren's gaze met Annie's, and she saw the perplexity it held. He was puzzled. Warily she eased her grip on the sides, swiped the dripping stragglers from her face, looked down at her soaking-wet clothes, and shook her head. "What the hell *was* that?"

"I don't know. But I don't like it."

He bent to the oars, his powerful arms rippling with effort. The boat skimmed the blue surface, and in a few moments they were at the dock and Ren was jumping up onto it, tying the little craft securely at the far end. Then he reached for her, and the frown lines she saw marring his beautiful face worried her. Something was wrong. She felt it down deep in her bones.

"Ren, what is it?"

He took her hand, drew her to her feet, and steadied her as she stepped up onto the solid wooden dock. "I don't know. That windstorm, it worries me. It just didn't seem . . ." He shook his head.

"Didn't seem what?"

"Natural." With his arm tightening around her shoulders to draw her close to him, he tipped his head skyward as if searching for something.

She fought the shudder that raced up her spine and glanced down at her tightly clenched fist. Slowly she opened her hand to see the green-blue capsule beginning to disintegrate in her palm. "Well, at least I didn't lose all of my vitamins." As an attempt at levity, it was weak. Still, she popped the bitter-tasting pill into her mouth before any more of it could dissolve, and hurried into the cabin for a drink to wash it down.

*   *   *

Blackheart saw her swallow the drug and smiled slowly. At last he'd made some head-way.

Odd how that windstorm had come from nowhere, dumping the poisoned pills into the lake. Not Ren's magic. Couldn't be—the man didn't have that kind of power. Sir George's, perhaps? But if the good George had known about the pills, he'd simply have told Ren, wouldn't he? And the White Knight certainly wouldn't have given them to her, encouraged her to take them, had he known the clever way Blackheart had switched them that night in her house. The way he'd replaced them with new ones, specially designed just for her. Besides, Blackheart was fairly certain that Sir George's magic could no more influence that sort of reaction in the lake than Ren's could have. There was something else at work here. Something that worried Blackheart only briefly.

Then again, it might have been mere coin-cidence. Whatever. It no longer mattered over-ly much. Annie had taken the drug. A single capsule, yes, but one was enough. He'd made them very potent. He only wished he'd thought of this ploy sooner, for he had to won-der if it was even too late for premature labor to kill the child. Blackheart knew the baby's chances for survival would be far lower this way, but he would have preferred a sure bet. Still, he figured his odds for success were fairly good. Born here, no one to help it, no medical facilities nearby, the baby would have few advantages.

That was the key, he realized. To keep them here. Alone. Completely cut off from outside assistance.

Blackheart rubbed his hands together in delicious anticipation. He would doubly relish his victory this time, because this time it was going to hurt. His adversary was *really* going to hurt.

Ren followed Annie inside, his every instinct urging him to pick her up and carry her. Only knowing how strongly she'd object to the suggestion that she might need that kind of help kept him from giving it. It did not, however, keep him from acting once they were inside and she'd sipped her glass of water. He headed into the bathroom for towels and, on the way back through the bedroom, snatched the comforter from the bed.

"Get the wet clothes off, Annie. It's freezing in here. The last thing you need is to catch cold at this late date."

She set her water glass down and rubbed her arms. "You're right. It is chilly. I think I'm wet clear to the bone." She peeled the soaked blouse over her head.

Ren rubbed her down with a towel, ignoring the signals his body sent him and focusing instead on getting her warm and dry before she was thoroughly chilled. He wrapped the blanket around her shoulders and eased her onto the sofa.

"Pants, too, Annie," he warned. "I want you warm and dry. Double pneumonia wouldn't do you or the baby any good."

Annie saluted as if he were her commanding officer giving orders, but she did it with a smile. One he couldn't return. He was worried, first and foremost about her and the child she carried. But there was something else bothering him, too, something he couldn't quite identify.

Poor Annie. She'd been tossed like a leaf in that little boat, soaked to the skin, shaken, scared half to death, no doubt. He turned to the fireplace and knelt, carefully arranging some kindling and a small pair of logs atop the nearly dead embers from last night's fire. Bending low, he blew gently until flames licked to life.

Satisfied with that, he hurried to the kitchen to set a kettle on the burner, then back to the bedroom again for some dry, warm clothing for Annie.

Then he was with her again, kneeling in front of her, rubbing her hair with a towel. She smiled at him from within the voluminous folds of the comforter. She seemed fine, calm. Ren was the only one feeling the touch of panic's flame licking at his tinder-dry nerves. But why?

She wriggled under the blanket, and a second later her shoes plunked to the floorboards. Her socks joined them, and finally her pants. She sank back onto the sofa and closed her eyes.

"Are you all right, Annie? You didn't get hurt out there, did you?" He studied her, wondering why she wasn't filled with questions, worries, the way he was. She seemed fine, though.

"No, Ren, I'm okay. I promise. I'd tell you if I wasn't. Stop clucking around me like a mother hen." He heard the kettle whistling. Her brows shot up. "What's that?"

"Hot cocoa. I thought it might help chase the chill away."

She smiled again, that sexy smile reserved only for him. He knew that, though he wasn't sure how. Another bit of knowledge from his life before, he supposed. She'd never bestow that particular look on anyone else. Not even if he was forced to leave her forever this time.

"Well," she said with a mischievous gleam

in her eyes. "I guess you can continue clucking, at least until I get a mugful of that cocoa.
But that's all I'll tolerate, you understand?"

He couldn't help smiling back, despite his
sense of foreboding.

"And, Ren, I'm not going to touch that cocoa until you get into some dry clothes yourself," she gently admonished. "You could get
sick, too, you know."

She shook her finger at him. He caught it,
drew it to his lips, and saw passion spark in
her eyes. Then he left her, returning a few moments later with a mug of steaming hot cocoa
in each hand and dry clothes covering his
chilled skin. His sword was once again belted
at his side. He handed a cup to her. "Be careful. It's hot."

"You're spoiling me."

"That's my privilege."

She sat up, sipped, then leaned back again,
cupping the warm mug between her palms.
Ren sat beside her. "You're sure you're all
right?"

"Yes."

"Good. Because as soon as you've had a
minute to recover from that ordeal, I want you
to get dressed. I think we ought to leave."

The look in her eyes was one of utter surprise and terrible disappointment. "But we

just got here! Ren, I like it here. I haven't felt
this happy and content since . . ."

She didn't finish. She didn't have to. And
God, it killed him to take away the first peace
she'd found in such a long time. But Ren
couldn't let himself be swayed by nostalgia or
romance. "Annie, something just feels . . .
wrong. It didn't before, but now I sense . . ."
His voice trailed off as the dark threat he felt
loomed even nearer.

Like a wolf scenting the air, he lifted his face
to the changing light pouring in through the
window. But he couldn't identify the threat.
He only knew it was there. Waiting. Drawing
closer even as he sat there. The brilliant yellow
sunlight began taking on a darker hue and
painted the room in odd sepia tones. His every
instinct pricked with awareness of the danger
closing in—danger to Annie and their child.

Apparently oblivious to it, Annie parted the
blanket she wore. "Come in here with me.
You're shivering."

He looked at her, saw her there beneath the
covers. Her breasts full and swelling, her
graceful neck and slender, strong arms. Her
legs, so shapely he wanted to trace them with
his lips. And her delicate torso struggling to
contain and nurture his child.

"Annie . . ."

"Please," she said. "Just for a minute or two."

Sighing, he slid closer and let her fold the blanket around him. She snuggled into the crook of his arm, resting her head on his shoulder. "You worry too much, you know that, Ren?"

Her lips feathered his neck as she spoke, and he nearly forgot what it was he'd been so worried about.

Then thunder rumbled, a deep growl of it, rolling ever nearer. Frowning, he pulled free of her gentle embrace and rose, hurrying to the door. He opened it, searching the sky, and his heart tripped to a stop.

It began as small black spot in the middle of the sky, but rapidly, in the space of a heartbeat, the unnatural dark cloud spiraled outward, growing, expanding, blotting out the sun.

Oh God, he thought in anguish. The final confrontation. It was at hand. Just after he'd broken his last remaining vows. First he'd made love to Annie, and then he'd declared in his soul that he wanted to be free of his vows. He'd longed with everything in him to remain here with her. And he'd prefer death to living on without her.

His days as a White Knight were numbered. Perhaps even over, right now. He couldn't believe Sir George would take his powers away so soon, especially not with the importance of this mission. His child—Ren's chest swelled with pride when he thought of it—*his* child, and Annie's, must be born. It must be, for the hope of the entire world rested in the still oblivious baby. No, he couldn't believe Sir George would allow his own anger—or even his precious rules—to interfere with the birth of such a vital leader. And even if he did, Ren would find a way to protect Annie and the child. Somehow, he'd find a way.

Deep inside him, though, Ren knew that even if Sir George's wrath might be put off, it could not be avoided. He certainly wouldn't allow Ren to stay in his service. Not now. And there was only one alternative.

Death.

As if in response to Ren's morbid train of thought, the sun seemed to extinguish itself. Those black clouds must have finally obliterated its light, plunging the cabin into swift and unexpected darkness. The change drew Annie's attention, too. She came up behind him as he stood there, her hands going to his shoulders to rub him gently. When he turned to face her, he didn't need light to know that there was real worry clouding her emerald eyes. Ren put his arm around her shoulders as the clouds roiled angrily and the wind answered their summons, springing to life with bitter breath.

Ill wind, Ren thought. Something evil, something dark.

He held Annie tight and drew her inside, closing the door on the evil without. He drew her to the sofa, felt for the clothing he'd brought out earlier, pressed it into her hands. "Get dressed, Annie. Quickly."

It was black as night in the cabin now. He moved away from her only long enough to flick on every light.

"What's happening, Ren?"

He shook his head. He didn't know exactly what was happening. He couldn't tell her anything to ease her mind. He only knew it was bad. "Hurry."

He heard her hasty movements as she pulled on the pants and the oversize knit sweater he'd brought for her. He glanced at her and saw Annie tug big socks up over the legs of the pants and reach for the white running shoes that lay near the door. As she put them on, Ren reached for the CB radio, turned on the power, and lifted the microphone.

A roar of thunder rang louder than an erupting volcano, splitting his nerves. It was accompanied by a blinding explosion of white heat so close that the hairs on Ren's nape bristled in reaction, so potent that the microphone sizzled in his grip, burning his palm, and he dropped it to the floor, jumping back.

The lights flickered and died just as Annie yelped and came to him, grabbing his arm. He smelled the burning of shorted wiring, the acrid melting of its plastic coat. "You dressed?" he whispered.

"Yeah. What should we do?"

He squeezed her closer. "That lightning took out the radio. He's up to something, Annie. I can feel it. And the last place I want you to be is out here." He cursed himself inwardly for acting on what had seemed a good idea at the time. "I never should have brought you here in the first place."

"Yes, you should." Her palm slid up one side of his face, turning it, pulling it downward. She stood on tiptoe to press her lips to his, and kissed him softly, sweetly. So sweetly, his arms crept around her and his senses spun for a moment. "No matter what happens, Ren, I won't regret the time we spent here. Not ever, I swear it to you, darling."

He closed his eyes as pain lanced his heart. "I might. If anything happens to you or the baby . . ." He fought past the lump that formed in his throat. "Come on. We're getting back to civilization. We need to be closer to help, just in case . . ."

"In this?"

He nodded. Already he heard the rain pummelling the roof. Heard the thunder's vicious battle cry. Heard the wind escalate to hurricane proportions. He felt his way to the front door, gripping her hand and drawing her with him. He felt for the rain slicker that still hung there, determined to protect Annie in every way he could. He detested the very thought of taking her out into the violence of the storm. But he sensed there was little choice. Blackheart obviously wanted them here. So there was no doubt they had to get out.

Ren shook the slicker hard, then put it over her head. "Pull the hood up."

She obeyed, then took his hand once more. Holding to her tightly, Ren ducked out the door and moved quickly to the small corral. Rain poured down in torrents, and his clothes were soaked through by the time he'd opened the gate and made it to the small shed. The horses huddled inside, skittish and wide-eyed.

Speaking softly, Ren approached them. He coaxed and soothed with his words, stroking their muzzles. Annie was counting on him. This was going to be Blackheart's strongest attempt so far, and Ren couldn't let his lady down. His last battle would be, ironically, the most important one he'd ever waged. And he'd win it, dammit, or die trying.

Carefully he readied the horses for travel.

When he finished, he reached for the door. But Annie's hand stilled his in midair. She gripped it, and he felt the way she trembled.

"It's him, isn't it? This storm and . . . and the power going out. It's him. He's out there . . . somewhere . . . isn't he?"

Ren swallowed the lump in his throat. The fear in her voice stabbed through him, but not for his life would he lie to her. She'd be far better off knowing what they faced. She'd be more prepared for the nightmare that might await them.

"Yes, Annie. I'm afraid he probably is."

"He's going to . . . he's come to try to kill our baby. Just like before, with the gas. Only this time we're all alone up here. Out of touch, and—"

"I won't let him succeed."

"God, Ren, I'm so afraid!" She flung herself into his arms, her face buried against his chest, sobs racking her small frame.

Ren held her. His hands found their way up under the rain slicker so he could rub her back, stroke her shoulders. "Annie, Annie, it's all right. I promise you, it's going to be all right. I won't let anything happen to you or to our baby. I'll protect you both with my life; I swear it to you."

Her trembling hand curled into a fist that thudded impotently against his shoulder where before she'd clung to him. "Dammit, Ren, I know you will. That's what I'm so afraid of."

He held her harder, unable, unwilling to tell her that he, too, was afraid. Afraid of losing her when he'd only just found her again. Afraid that this might be the last time he'd have the chance to hold her in his arms this way. For this battle, Ren had no doubt, was going to be the end of him, one way or another. Win or lose.

He only hoped Annie, remarkable, wonderful Annie, would be strong enough to go on without him. To raise his child, their child, to be the leader this world so desperately needed. To love it enough to make up for his not being there to do the same.

Chapter Thirteen

જ Annie bowed over the patient mare, clinging to a handful of her wet mane and clamping her jaw tight. Even through the rain slicker, she felt the cold. It had come suddenly, the drastic drop in temperature seemingly accompanying the furious storm. The wind was brutal, and Annie realized now that the sudden windstorm she'd experienced on the lake had been mild in comparison. It had tossed and shaken her, soaked and chilled her, but she'd never felt as if she'd been in any real danger.

This, on the other hand, was cruel. The sheets of rain stung her face, making mere droplets into razors. The vicious wind turned gentle fragrant pine boughs into lashing whips. The rain slashed so violently that she couldn't see the trail they followed. The cold was so intense that even the horse shivered and shook its head in protest with every few steps it took.

Or maybe the mare simply sensed the evil presence as clearly as Annie did.

And it was dark. Such thick, murky darkness that it was like a living thing. She felt as if it were pushing out the air around her, replacing it with its putrid presence. The darkness wasn't night. Not this time. According to the clock it should be broad daylight here now. No, this darkness was made of evil.

And then Annie felt something, and a new terror swept through her. Her trembling intensified. She was wet and cold, but the shaking came more from fear than from the chill that had settled into her bones. Brilliant, blinding terror clutched Annie's soul. And its source wasn't the one Ren might guess. It wasn't the storm that so frightened her. It wasn't Ren's certainty that his nemesis was about to make a move against them. It wasn't just the isolation and the darkness and the feeling that they were utterly alone here to face this powerful enemy without any hope of assistance.

No.

Her fear was based solely on the sudden cramping pain that banded her lower torso like an iron girdle. It crushed around her abdomen and lower back, drawing ever tighter, chasing the breath from her body, taking her so fiercely, she couldn't even cry out in response, couldn't even utter a single word.

Instead she bent lower over the mare's back, one arm hugging her middle instinctively beneath the tentlike poncho. With her other hand, she grasped the slippery wet pommel. For once she was glad Ren held the reins. She closed her eyes tightly and focused on the warmth and the scent rising from her mount's wet coat. She closed her ears to the high-pitched keen of the wind as it ravaged the pines overhead, violating their purity with its filth. She even avoided inhaling that bad air when it swept down and up again, filling the hood she wore like a balloon and sending it backward, exposing her head to the rain.

Unnatural rain! Impure! Polluted!

The thoughts racing through her mind were insane, but she jerked the hood up again, feeling contaminated by the water in her hair.

She clenched her teeth as the pain intensified, and dropped her chin to her chest, keeping her face hidden within the folds of the yellow hood. If Ren should look her way at the moment a flash of lightning split the black sky, she didn't want him seeing her face contorted in agony. No sense alarming him. Not yet. There was nothing he could do. It was a mere thirty-minute ride down off the mountain and to her parents' ranch. There would be help for her there.

She envisioned her parents' cozy home to

distract herself from the pain. A warm, dry place to lie down. Her mother's efficient bustling and the I-told-you-so tone in her voice. Her father's solid presence. He hadn't changed in years, and she realized now that his constant presence in her life was as important to her as that of this place. Her father had always been there when she'd needed him. Always. He'd be there when she arrived. He'd be strong and stoic and calm.

And Ren would be there with her as well. She visualized him stroking her brow, kissing her face, easing her mind as she gave birth to his child. Ren's soothing voice would make the pain easier to bear. His touch, his pride in her, would get her through anything.

Sweet María would be there, too, holding her hand and telling old, familiar stories.

A telephone. An ambulance. Paramedics on the way to take her to a nice safe hospital. Reassuring thoughts. Surely all of those things and more were only a few minutes away. All she had to do was sit on the gentle mare and hold on. Even in this storm the horse could find her way down to the ranch. It would be just a few more minutes. Labor lasted far longer than that. In a few more minutes, she'd get help.

Unless the phones are out. What if the phones

*are out and we still can't call an ambulance or get
any help? What then?*

She chided herself. The phones would not
be out. And even if they were, Annie assured
herself that María could probably do a better
job delivering a child than most obstetricians
with twenty-twenty vision. She'd know what
to do. María would know.

When she got to the house, María would
probably comfort her while calmly explaining
that this was just a false alarm. It wasn't true
labor. It couldn't be. It was too early. She had
a month to go.

The giant fist that had been squeezing
Annie's middle relaxed just slightly, and
she lifted her head. Immediately the wind
whipped her hood back and rain slashed at
her face. She drew her first full breath in what
felt like a long time, and she blinked the hot
moisture from her eyes, grateful for the darkness that shielded her tearstained face from
Ren's watchful gaze.

But before the first wave of pain had fully
receded, a second, even stronger one slammed
into her, the force and unexpectedness of it
pushing a strangled cry from her throat. She
felt the horses come to an abrupt halt, sensed
the way Ren's head snapped around toward
her. Felt his eyes piercing through the darkness.

"Annie, what is it?"

She tried to answer and found it impossible. Her jaw seemed to have locked itself into a painfully tight clench. Her teeth grated and she could barely draw a breath, let alone answer his urgent question.

"Annie?"

She heard the creak of wet leather, then his feet as they slapped the muddied ground. She wanted to straighten, to look at him, to reassure him. But for the life of her she couldn't unbend. If anything, her body wanted to fold itself in half, only her protruding belly made that impossible.

His hand covered hers on the pommel, and before she understood his intent, he was mounted behind her. Bending close to her, his face pressed to the wet yellow vinyl of the hood, he spoke to her, and she heard the concern in his deep voice. "Annie, tell me. What's the matter?" As he spoke, his arms came around her waist, slipping beneath the poncho. His strong hands opened and his palms flattened against her belly.

The pain clutched tighter, and she felt her abdominal muscles contract so hard and fast and brutally that it seemed she was being torn apart. She screamed. Her cry echoed into the storm, joining its ghostly wail and finally becoming lost in it. Annie's spine felt as if it would snap in two. The pain didn't ease. She stopped screaming only because she'd run out of breath and she couldn't draw another.

Ren swore loud and long. "God, not now! Not here!"

His protests, she knew, were directed at fate, not at Annie. And then he kicked the mare's sides and the horse moved ahead at a brisk walk. As they passed the stallion, Ren leaned over and caught his reins, leading him along beside them.

"Lean back against me, Annie. Try to relax. We'll be at the house soon. Your mother will be there. I'll get help for you. You'll be all right; I swear it. And so will the baby."

She answered him quickly when the tide of pain began to recede, knowing too well how soon she'd be flooded again. "Ren, this isn't right. It's . . ." She paused, panting, dizzy from lack of oxygen, barely able to find the strength to speak as loudly as she must in order to make herself heard above the storm. "It's too intense. Too sudden. It can't be—"

The next contraction cut her off midsentence, attacking with no buildup, no warning. Just a sudden, wrenching pain that had no mercy. And as she clutched herself, she tilted sideways in the saddle, only realizing how close she came to tumbling from the horse when Ren pulled her upright again and held her to him.

"My God." It seemed to be all he could say.

He held her, rubbing her belly with his soothing hand, kissing her face as they moved onward—until the mare blew angrily and stomped her forefoot, coming to a stop and refusing to take another step.

Ren went very still, not saying another word. Annie felt the tension in his firm body double, and she knew something was happening.

She didn't ask what was wrong. She couldn't. She managed to pry her eyes open, and she blinked away enough moisture to see the giant pine lying at a cockeyed angle down across the bridge. Or rather, what was left of the bridge. Even in this unrelieved darkness, she could see that there wasn't a hell of a lot.

It was too dark to eye the steep incline of the washed-out hollow the bridge had spanned, but Annie didn't need to see it. She'd practically grown up here. Without the bridge, that gully would have been difficult to cross under any circumstances. Especially for her, in this condition. Now, with all this rain, its raw banks would be mud-slicked and treacherous.

"We can't go on," Ren said. "I'm sorry, Annie. Is there a way around?"

She bit her lip, lifted her gaze to his, shook

her head. "T-too . . . far," she croaked.

"We'll have to go back."

The horse obeyed Ren's hands, turning in the path to face the way they'd come. But it didn't move forward. And before Annie could start to wonder why, she heard her answer.

"Well, White Knight. We meet again. And fate seems to be working against you this time."

Annie's head snapped up fast, and she saw the villainous bastard there. Blackheart, still anonymous within the folds of his black-hooded garment. He sat astride one of Satan's own stallions, a beast as black and menacing as its rider. It pranced and pawed at the muddy ground.

"Ah, the lady's still conscious. Well, what a little trouper she must be."

"Go back to hell where you came from," Annie shouted. The force of her pain gave the words strength and venom.

"Not just yet, fair lady. When I go, I'll be taking your handsome knight with me. He's broken his vows, you know. Taking physical pleasure with a mortal woman." He shook his head slowly. "Penalty for that is death. But he knew that. Didn't you, Ren?"

"No," Annie whispered as her blood slowly drained to her feet. A new pain overshadowed even that of her unnatural labor for an instant:

the knowledge that by seducing her husband, she could have sentenced him to death. By trying so hard to hold on to him, she may have lost him.

"Oh, yes," Blackheart all but hissed.

"Don't listen to him, Annie." Ren held her, spoke close to her ear.

"A crying shame, really, that it's against the rules for me to kill you, too, dear Annie. You'd probably rather I did, wouldn't you? Are you really going to want to live once I've taken your knight and your child?"

"Don't answer him! If you consent, he'll be free to murder you. Don't—"

"You aren't going to kill either of them, you filthy bastard!" Annie put all of her remaining strength into that proud declaration.

Blackheart's laughter was dark and menacing. And in it Annie heard the gloat of certain victory. Then the pain hit her again, and she heard nothing at all. She bent over and tried to breathe.

"Why, lady, you seem to be in a bit of distress," Blackheart mocked. "Whatever could be wrong? Ren, attentive Hero that you are, you haven't been neglecting her, have you? And of course you've made certain she's been taking her vitamins, those modern wonders of this day and age. Haven't you?"

Annie's eyes flashed wider, but she couldn't

look at him. Oh, God, the vitamins. It all came back to her now. The way she'd questioned her own mind when they seemed to become so bitter-tasting overnight. He'd switched them, given her some powerful labor-inducing chemical. He'd drugged her!

Then why hadn't she had the baby before this? Oh, but as her mind fought for clarity, she knew the answer. She hadn't taken a pill before this. That morning at home, as she'd tried to do so, the glass had seemingly leaped off the sink of its own accord. And this morning when she'd tried, a wind-driven wave had swept the whole bottle right out of the tiny boat.

Almost as if the lake itself and the sky above it had been trying to protect her. If such a thing were possible. God, she'd thought herself so clever, managing to save one small capsule from the lake's greedy hands. She should have known better.

The lake is pure.

For some reason, María's tales about Mystic Lake came back to haunt Annie. Someone—some*thing*—had been trying to keep her from taking those pills. María used to say the lake had a magic all its own.

Annie shivered as she thought maybe it was true.

Whatever it was, she prayed the benevolent

force would return and help her just once more. She needed it now, more than ever.

"Dammit, Blackheart, this goes beyond even your code of conduct!" Ren searched the storm-tossed forests in every direction, seeking help, finding none. Knowing he wouldn't, even during the battle. Having broken his vows, he could hope for no support from the powers of goodness. And there would likely be no assistance or guidance from Sir George. Ren suspected he was on his own this time.

He knew he had to fight the bastard, but he detested leaving Annie alone in this condition. Her pain tore at Ren's heart.

Blackheart stopped laughing and eyed Annie. "She'll probably pass out soon from the force of the pain. There's only so much a woman can take, you know. The baby will be forced partway, but with her unable to push . . ." Blackheart shrugged. "Poor thing will likely suffocate."

Annie shuddered violently in his arms, and Ren tasted bile. "This woman," he stated, "is stronger than you can imagine. And she won't faint from the pain, Blackheart. But you might, before I'm through with you." Ren wanted nothing more at that moment than to see the forest floor run red with Blackheart's lifeblood.

The bastard only grinned, a white smile

glowing from within the folds of the black hood he wore for anonymity. He seemed oblivious to the slashing rain, the driving wind, the bansheelike scream of it whistling through the needled boughs.

And still he wore that hood, Ren noted. To keep Ren from recognizing his human form in case he failed this time and needed to try yet again. Perhaps he wasn't quite as confident as he seemed after all.

"I'll destroy you for this," Ren said in a voice that shook with rage.

"Nothing besides absolute purity can destroy me, Ren. You know that. And you're far from pure. Especially now, having broken every vow you've taken."

"Then I'll hurt you—enough that you'll wish for the second death. Enough to make you beg for it, Blackheart."

"Threats bore me, Ren of the White Knights. If you think you can hurt me, then by all means let's dispense with the discussion and get on with it."

Ren shook his head. Annie's pains must have eased for a moment, since she leaned back against him, panting. Stroking her hair, Ren prayed she'd be strong enough to survive this.

"No," he said to Blackheart. "I won't fight you here."

"No?"

"No. We take her back to the cabin. I'll have her inside, warm and dry. Only then will we finish this between us."

Blackheart smiled, shaking his head. "That would give her child a slightly better chance of survival, Ren. Why on earth would I agree to it? Besides, the way I see it is that I am here, astride this horse, blocking your path. You could get around me, I suppose. But then you'd have to outrun me. Now, can you really see your lady withstanding a good hard gallop?" Blackheart leaned forward and added, "And if I get close enough to drive my blade into your spineless back, Ren, believe me, I will delight in doing so."

Ren felt his lips thin and his fists clench so tightly, his hands shook.

"And if the lady should fall, perhaps get her big belly trampled under thundering hooves, then that wouldn't be my fault, would it?"

"Damn you, Blackheart."

"I'm already damned, Ren. But the way you've been acting lately, I believe you might be, too."

"How the hell would you know *what* way I've been acting?"

"I've been watching. I, too, have access to magic, Ren. But you knew that."

"Black magic," Ren clarified. "The devil's own brand."

"It gets the job done. Are you ready, then? This fascinating discussion will soon put me to sleep in the saddle."

Ren looked around, at least wanting a sheltered spot for Annie to lie down. He spotted a copse of huge pines, their boughs so dense and interwoven that they formed a canopy, and the ground beneath them appeared dry. He slid from the horse, pulling Annie into his arms, kissing her gently, hating the way she trembled in fear, the clamminess of her skin, the pain he knew she suffered.

"I'll be all right, Ren. Don't . . ." She grunted against the pain, and forced herself to go on. "Don't think of me. Don't be distracted. You have to beat him, Ren. You can't die, the way he said you would. You can't—" she broke off.

"Annie?"

She grated her teeth, drew a breath, and forced herself to speak. "Is it true, what he said? That you broke your vows by making love to me?"

He didn't want to answer her, but she deserved nothing less than the truth. He nodded, the hairs on his nape prickling with the knowledge that Blackheart grew tired of waiting.

"So, if he kills you . . . if Blackheart kills you, Sir George might not—"

"Blackheart isn't going to kill me, Annie."

"But . . ." Her words were choked off by a strangled cry. Tears rolled silently down her face, and despite the darkness, he saw her expression, saw the paleness of her skin and the way she grimaced in agony.

God, the pain she must be in. "I'd take it on myself if I could," he whispered, his words for her alone, not for the evil Blackheart to hear. "I love you. I want you to know that, in case . . . I just want you to know. I love you, Annie." He bent to kiss her again, long and lingeringly, memorizing the shape and texture of her mouth, its flavor, its heat. He'd take her memory with him, he vowed. Even into death, if that was indeed where he was bound.

He ought to tell her to go deep into the forest and hide. Because if Blackheart defeated Ren, Annie would be at his mercy. And if he could, the cold-blooded bastard would kill the child before it was born. But Ren knew Annie couldn't do it. She couldn't walk, let alone run and hide. It was up to him to protect her.

He turned to carry her toward the sheltering trees and sensed Blackheart's approach.

"That's right," he called without so much as glancing behind him. "Come on, attack while my back is turned and my arms filled. God knows you're too much a coward to fight me fairly. Maybe this way you'll stand a chance of beating me, Blackheart. But it's the only way. I think you already know that, though, don't you?"

The Dark Knight went still. Ren could feel Blackheart's hatred, but he no longer sensed imminent attack. He lowered Annie to the blessedly dry forest floor, wishing he had blankets to cover her. She rolled onto her side, clutching her middle, panting, sweating, shuddering. Completely at the mercy of the pain the bastard Blackheart had caused in her.

Ren couldn't turn away from her at a time like this. God help him, but he couldn't. Let Blackheart attack from behind if he would.

"Go."

The soft young voice was somehow gentle and commanding at the same time. Ren looked up to see Sara, mounted on a pure white stallion whose mane hung halfway to the ground, curly and pristine. The horse pawed, blew. As if it could sense the rot of evil standing so nearby.

"I'll take care of her," Sara told him. She urged her mount into the shelter of the trees and pushed back the white hood that had covered her. Her raven hair was dry and her eyes bright, even in the darkness, as she swung off the horse and hurried to lead it up beside Ren.

She pressed the reins into his hands.

"Take him," she said softly. "Neither of the others is trained in battle. This one knows what is expected. He's very good."

"How—"

"It's better not to ask, Ren. There's not time enough to explain anyway. Not now."

Ren knew she was right, but he marveled when she glanced back to the trail where he'd left the Appaloosa pair and both horses came to her at no more than a crook of her finger.

Trusting them not to wander, it seemed, Sara crouched beside Annie.

Still, Ren hesitated.

"Go on," Sara said. "You have to, Ren; it's what you came here for. It's your destiny to fight him. You know that. Now go. I'll stay with her for as long as I can, I promise you. I'll take her to the lake. She'll be safe there."

Ren frowned, puzzled.

"I was conceived there," Sara said, sending a loving look down at Annie. "It's a special place with a magic all its own, Ren. She'll be safe."

As Sara took Annie's hands, Annie sent Ren a loving look and gave him a nod. "Go, darling. But come back to me. Whatever you do, Ren, you come back to me!"

Ren turned to face what awaited him.

*   *   *

"Sara . . ."

"Shh. You have to save your strength now, Annie. It won't be much longer."

Annie was so glad to see the girl, so comforted by her presence. But Sara's words and the certainty in her voice were startling. "But . . . there's still a month. . . ."

"No, Annie. This is it. Today's the day. Can you walk? Stand, even?"

Annie shook her head. "I don't think so."

Sara chewed her lip as if worried. But Annie barely noticed. She struggled to push herself into a sitting position, despite the bolts of pain snapping through her with every movement. She braced her back against the stringy, sticky trunk of the pine and managed to raise herself. She scanned the trail, looking for Ren. And as she squinted through the darkness and rain, the storm suddenly began to dissipate.

The pouring rain stopped all at once, just as if someone had turned off a spigot. The ripping, brutal wind died to an impatient sigh, and then utter stillness. The roiling black clouds didn't so much blow away as dissolve, and within minutes the entire forest was bathed in golden sunlight. Like magic.

And she could see them there, on the trail. Ren mounted on Sara's white horse, Blackheart still sitting on the evil black one with the red eyes that made Annie wonder if it was truly a dragon in disguise. Or perhaps one of the devil's own demons.

They faced each other, Ren and his enemy, but neither moved. Not yet.

Annie looked skyward once more, then sought Sara's unfailing wisdom. "What—?"

"Blackheart needs all his power to fight Ren. He couldn't keep the storm going. It saps his strength."

Annie frowned, beginning to wonder if her life would ever be normal again. If she'd ever have a conversation that didn't include magic and fantasy. Only it wasn't fantasy, was it? It was real.

And deadly.

Another pain came. She hadn't been expecting it, and didn't bite her lip in time to prevent herself crying out. She knew Ren's head snapped toward her. She cursed herself inwardly for distracting him with her weakness. God, if he was killed just because he'd been looking toward her . . .

For a time, while her body twisted and clenched in on itself, her vision was red-hazed and unfocused. She braced her back against the fragrant trunk and pressed her feet flat in the pine-needle carpet. And though the pain threatened to tear her into pieces, she didn't close her eyes. She forcibly kept them open, and she forcibly made them follow the terrible scene being played out before her. She had to remain alert, had to know what was happening. She couldn't take her eyes off Ren for a moment.

And she wouldn't pass out from pain and let her baby die, as Blackheart had grimly predicted. She'd be as strong as Ren had claimed she was. She'd do this, no matter the pain, for her child.

As Ren sat astride the white horse facing Blackheart on his hellish demon, he slowly drew his sword and lifted it skyward. The very air around him began to glisten and shimmer, and for an instant it was as if the two men became liquid, then thinned to a gas. Only colors remained. Their shapes disintegrated before taking solid form again. Only this time Ren was in his white-gold armor, and his horse pranced and nickered. The horse wore white armor, too, and a mask over its face, and a shield of sorts strapped to its broad chest. On the back of that magnificent beast, Ren looked like an avenging angel, ready to unleash the wrath of God on an unrepentant sinner.

But Blackheart looked his part, too, covered in his dark raiment. Helmet, visor, sword, and shield. His mount snorted and pawed at the ground like an infuriated bull about to charge.

Annie struggled against the pain, wanting

to see everything that happened, afraid for Ren as she'd never been afraid in her life. He'd broken his vows. By sleeping with her and perhaps, she imagined, by slowly becoming Richard again. Becoming the man he supposedly no longer knew.

Oh, God, what if Sir George was as angry as Annie feared he'd be? What if Ren was killed and that ancient knight refused to bring him back? Or what if he *couldn't* bring Ren back, whether he wanted to or not? What then? Annie knew only that she couldn't bear to lose him twice in one lifetime.

But Sir George would take Ren from her, even if death didn't. She'd been warned, hadn't she? The old man had told her so himself.

She panted against the pain, let her own moans come freely now, no longer having the strength to hold them in. And she kept her eyes open despite the ever growing urge to close them tight. She watched as the men kicked their horses into action. They leaned low, both drawing their swords and brandishing them dangerously. Madly. They surged forward and met. The swords clashed, ringing clearly through the forest and sending brilliant showers of sparks into the sky. She heard the ring of steel on steel and the pounding of those tireless hooves again and again, almost feeling each impact herself.

Then Blackheart was thrown from the saddle when Ren caught him full in the breastplate with a swipe of his sword.

By the time Blackheart hit the ground, Ren was leaping from his horse. He ran forward and stood over his enemy, the tip of his sword at Blackheart's throat. But the dark knight lashed out with his feet and Ren tripped, falling facedown as Blackheart surged to his feet.

"At last," he crowed.

He plunged his blade downward and Annie screamed. But Ren rolled to the side, avoiding what would surely have been a deadly strike. Ren sent a worried glance in Annie's direction, and their eyes met as she shouted her warning. Too late, for Blackheart's sword found flesh, drew blood. And Annie suspected he'd struck Ren's old wound, reopening it. The bastard.

Ren never stopped moving, even when the sword cut him. He rolled to his feet, panting, and lifted his sword once more.

"This isn't looking good, Annie," Sara whispered. "And I'm not going to be able to stay with you much longer."

Annie was shaking her head, eyes fixed on Ren, tears flowing freely. Between her own pain and his, she paid little attention to the girl.

"Annie, listen. Look at me. Now, Annie!"

Annie looked. She focused on Sara's beautiful dark eyes and then on that crescent-moon birthmark on the girl's pale-skinned neck.

"You have to get to the lake," Sara told her. "Do you understand? In case Ren can't beat him—"

"He *has* to, Sara!"

"I know. I know, but Annie..." She bent, pulled Annie's arm around her shoulders, and urged her to her feet. "Come on. I'll have to leave soon, but not until I get you to the lake. Can you make it to the horse?"

"I can't! I can't just leave him!"

"He'll fight better if you do. He's so busy checking to be sure you're still all right that he isn't focusing on the battle. Honestly, Annie, you'd be doing him a favor. Come on."

She had a point. "But Sara, what if he's hurt again? What if he needs me?"

"You couldn't help him in your condition anyway. You're in labor, Annie!" Sara sighed in frustration when Annie turned once more to watch the raging battle. "Annie, listen to me. Your baby needs you right now, do you hear? You have to get to the lake if you want to save your baby. It's up to you, Annie."

Her words, so earnest, so intense, caught

Annie's attention at last. She looked into Sara's eyes and knew the girl wasn't lying or exaggerating. Sara had shown the depth of her wisdom again and again. Now was no time to doubt her.

"All right," Annie whispered. "If you're sure, Sara. I'll . . . I'll try."

"I am. Now, come on. Lift one foot; put it in the stirrup."

She obeyed as Sara steadied her. The pain was intense, but she tried. And it was difficult when every instinct in her was telling her to turn her head, view the battle, check on Ren each time she heard the metal impact sing out. Find some way to help him.

She summoned all her strength and pulled herself up into the saddle, Sara pushing for all she was worth. Then the girl jumped up behind Annie and took the reins. She clicked her tongue and the horse was off, obeying her instantly and giving the combatants a wide berth before regaining the trail.

Annie moaned in agony. Sara was showing no mercy. She kicked the horse into a gallop, and each fall of the horse's hooves sent jarring blasts of additional agony through Annie's trembling body.

Sara kept one arm around Annie, her strength surprising in one so young. "I'm sorry, Annie," she said close to her ear, "but we're running out of time."

On and on they flew, back along the trail that led to the cabin. The impacts rattled Annie's teeth, and she shuddered to think what this mad race must be doing to the baby.

She was about to protest when she heard the other hoofbeats, and looked back.

Dark as death itself, the black horseman rode after them, no longer in armor but in that hooded monk's robe, his face concealed. And in one hand he held that deadly black sword. Something thick and red was dripping from the blade.

"No!" Annie screamed, craning her neck, eyes straining. She shook her head in frantic denial, searching the trail for a sign of Ren and not finding one.

Blackheart's armor was gone. Did that mean the battle was over? Was Ren lying back there in the mud? Dead? Dying? She cried his name, her voice ringing straight to the heavens, she thought, and echoing endlessly in the forest. But there was no answer.

And then the pain clamped so hard, she thought she'd be torn in half. The pressure between her legs was so intense, she screamed again and again as she felt the rush of the fluids her body released.

"That's it," Sara said, and her voice sounded

uncertain. Frightened and sad. It was the first time Annie had heard it sound that way. "I can't stay with you any longer. My time is up." Sara was pressing the reins into Annie's hand. "The lake, Annie. Get to the lake."

Annie nodded. "Yes, I know. The cabin is there, and I can—"

"Not the cabin! The lake!" Sara cried as if it was the most important thing in the world. "Don't let me down, Annie. I need you."

At that moment she seemed more like a frightened young girl than an oracle of wisdom. She took her hands away from Annie's, leaving the reins there. Then she leaned forward and brushed a feather-light kiss over Annie's cheek.

Annie felt the cramps increasing, changing, felt the pressure, wanted to push the pain away. She restrained the urge. Not yet. She couldn't give birth on the back of a horse!

"I can't stay with you any longer, Annie. I have to leave. But I'll be back. If you just get to the lake, Annie, I promise you, I'll be back."

The horse was still galloping, and Annie could see the lake now, glimmering like a precious sapphire in the sunlight. Glittering like Ren's eyes. She could see the cabin, too.

"You can't leave," she whispered. "We're almost there. See? Sara?"

"I'll be with you again," the girl whispered,

even as her shape thinned, becoming transparent. "Soon. Be strong for me."

Annie turned her head to beg Sara not to leave her.

Before her eyes, Sara vanished like a wisp of smoke caught by the wind. What was the girl? An angel? A spirit sent to help her through her time of need? But if that was the case, why had she left just when Annie needed her most? Annie's tears came faster, harder than before. She was alone now. Utterly alone, except for the madman pursuing her, intent on murdering the child whose head was beginning to stretch her body, even now.

Chapter Fourteen

᪐ Ren didn't think he'd have regained consciousness at all if he hadn't heard Annie screaming his name. It was her voice, choked with pain and grief and fear, echoing through the forest and reaching him somehow. It shouldn't have. She was too far away for him to hear her—he knew it as well as he knew he'd heard her all the same. Though he'd been unconscious, her cries had reached him. As if by magic. And it was those cries that gave him the strength to fight his way back to consciousness.

When he had, the pain that seared every part of his body nearly made him wish he'd remained oblivious. He was coated in blood from a dozen or more wounds. Apparently Blackheart had used him for a pincushion. Simply defeating him hadn't been enough.

But he wasn't defeated yet, was he? No. Not as long as he drew a breath. He'd never give up trying to save his wife and his baby from the touch of evil.

He forced himself to his feet, not bothering to take stock. There was no time. Instead, he discovered his wounds as he staggered toward the magnificent white horse. He knew there was a sizable gash in his neck. The bastard's blade must have missed the jugular or he'd have bled out already. He felt the hot sting of the cut and the sticky warmth of the blood that coated his neck and shoulder, and soaked his shirt.

The armor was gone. It would have vanished as soon as Blackheart turned away. But his sword remained, devoid of magic now, but there all the same, lying bloodstained in the mud. Ren bent to close his hand around its wet, sticky hilt, then rose again, though it cost him, and slid the blade into its sheath.

He leaned against the horse for an instant, gathered his strength, and reached up to pull himself into the saddle. His grip slid from the pommel, and that's when he discovered another wound, this one in his forearm. The cut went to the bone, he was certain, leaving his hand and fingers blood-slicked and numb. Tough to grip the pommel that way.

Using his good hand more than his bad, he managed to drag himself up into the saddle, but when he did, he felt a hot pull in his side and then wet heat as blood pulsed anew from that reopened wound. Of course, the flow from all of his injuries increased as he moved, but he didn't care about that. His wife was about to give birth to his child. And without his protection, the bastard who'd cut him would do the same to his baby before it had the chance to draw its first breath.

Ren would die trying to prevent that. He'd fight Blackheart to the very last breath of life in him. And beyond, he vowed.

He dug his heels into the horse's flanks and clung to the pommel with his all but useless bloody hand. He drew his sword again with the good one. When he caught up to Blackheart, he'd be ready. He'd reach Annie in time. He would, though he sensed it would be the last act he ever committed.

Annie slapped the horse's backside with the reins, steering it right up to the cabin door before hauling it to a stop.

The black horse was thundering toward her as she slid to the ground. God, the baby was coming. Right here, right now! But she knew that if she stopped running, if she lay down to give birth to her child, the animal behind her would kill it before it ever opened its eyes. God, what could she do?

She staggered forward, instinctively going

toward the cabin. But Sara's words floated into her mind like a healing breeze. The lake, Sara had told her. *Go to the lake.*

God, but why the lake?

She shook her head, unable to see any sense in the girl's advice. But then, Sara's words had proved true often enough to make Annie loath to doubt her this time. And something inside was telling her to trust the girl. Sara wouldn't steer her wrong. Sending a frantic glance over her shoulder, she hobbled around the cabin and started down the grassy slope to the gentle shore. She saw the dock, the rowboat bobbing serenely at the far end. Maybe Sara's idea wasn't so bad after all. If she could make it to the boat and manage to row out far enough, Blackheart wouldn't be able to follow. Would he?

She stumbled over the grassy hill with her baby fighting to emerge into the world, its mother fighting to hold it back. Her face contorted in agony. She ran, but knew she was clumsy and awkward, as likely to trip and roll into the water as to reach the dock upright. Running wasn't easy when one was in the process of giving birth. She poured everything she had into reaching the dock before that dark-robed beast could overtake her.

The Dark Knight pursued her. She heard the pounding feet of his horse as he came after her, down the hillside, gaining on her. God, she couldn't outrun a horse! Her feet touched the wood of the dock. The rowboat at the far end seemed a hundred miles away. And yet, so close. Even as she hurled herself toward it, she heard the clatter of hooves on the wood.

And she whirled defensively, only to feel that wet, black muzzle pressed to her face. The horse's breath was fetid; its flesh, hot. She tried to turn away, but the horse stepped forward, simultaneously lifting its big head. The beast butted her chin so hard, she was lifted off her feet and hurled backward.

She fell flat to the dock, her back hitting the wood so hard that it made her dizzy. Every trace of air burst from her lungs at the force of the impact. For a time she didn't think she'd be able to inhale again. And when she was finally able to speak, she heard herself sobbing hysterically, begging, her words incoherent pleas for mercy to a man she knew had none to give.

The baby was coming.

Blackheart got off the horse and grinned down at her. He placed the tip of his sword at her throat, so she didn't dare to move.

"Now," he said softly, "we end this." He pushed the black hood away from his face, and Annie was shocked to see Bartholomew

Cassius standing there, staring down at her with murder in his eyes.

"Bartholomew?"

God, Ren had been right in telling her to trust no one. She'd thought Bartholomew was her friend. She'd trusted him. But he'd been an agent of evil all along. Plotting the murder of her firstborn while pretending to be her friend. The beast!

"You can have other babies, Annie. But this one is just too important to my master. You understand, don't you? I can't let it see life."

He frowned, his gaze riveted to the spot where his sword pressed into her throat, instead of on her face. "But I can't kill you. It's not allowed. Hmm." Then he brightened. "Ah, I have it. You lie still like a good girl, all right?"

And, still grinning, still holding the sword to her neck, he gripped the demonic horse's bridle and drew it forward.

"He's well trained, my horse. He'll take care of this little matter for me." He frowned again. "I'm afraid this is going to hurt." And he snapped his fingers.

The black horse's eyes dilated wildly, and it reared up on its hind legs, forelegs pumping in the air, right above her swollen belly.

"Tell me, Annie," Blackheart said softly as the horse danced on its hind legs, its deadly forelegs flailing in the air and poised above her, "have you ever seen a stallion dance?"

She scrambled backward but knew it was useless. She wasn't fast enough. Those deadly hooves were going to crush her baby, and her along with it. She rolled to her side, shielding her belly with both arms.

And that's when she saw Ren, his face smeared with a dark mingling of blood and sweat and dirt—mostly blood, she feared. He emerged from the water just beyond the dock, on the grassy shore. His face contorting with the effort, he sprang up and forward, hurling himself beneath the legs of that mad beast. And with what had to be all of his strength, he pushed her right off into the water on the other side. He shoved her so hard, she cleared the edges of the dock and splashed into the water, and just before she did, she saw him landing in the spot she'd left behind, rolling defensively onto his back. Lifting his arms to shield himself. Then she felt herself swallowed up, the chilly lake water closing over her head as she sank.

The pains in her abdomen were constant now, and the baby was determined to be born. And still her thoughts were of Ren. What was happening to him right now? Had the horse trampled him?

She struggled to the surface. When her head

broke through, she inhaled deeply, swept the hair from her eyes, and swung her head around, trying to get her bearings and find Ren. When she did, she nearly vomited. He lay on the dock, curled into an unmoving ball as those horrible hooves trampled down on his motionless, armorless body, over and over again.

"No!" She screamed the words at the top of her voice. "I'm here. Here, dammit! Leave him alone! I'm the one you want!"

As if by magic, the horse stopped with its feet pawing the air. Blackheart cocked his head toward her. "It's not you I want, sweet Annie. It's them. Both of them. Your child *and* its father. The enmity between Ren and me goes back a long way, you see."

"You don't have time for both," she said as she grimaced, praying she was doing the right thing, "because by the time you finish with him, the baby will be here." As she spoke, she edged along the dock, ever closer to the rowboat at the end. She had no plan and little hope. She only knew she had to lure him away from her husband or he'd be dead. If he wasn't already. He still wasn't moving. His body was twisted and broken and bleeding.

"Kind of you to let me know, Annie. All right, then. I'll kill the child first, since you insist."

He flicked his forefinger, and the horse came down one last time, hooves punishing Ren's tortured body still further. Annie stopped edging. She lunged and swam for the boat.

Smiling wickedly, Blackheart walked toward it, leaving his suddenly calm horse to wander off the wooden platform in favor of the grassy bank.

She swallowed water when the sharp pains stabbed harder, and the baby pressed nearer, stretching her, tearing her. She grated her teeth and groped. There. She had the side of the boat in her hands. Now to pull herself up into it. She was weak with grief, mindless with pain. But she managed to grip the sides of the tiny rowboat and hauled herself up . . .

. . . only to see Blackheart standing in the boat, smiling at her. "Join me, Annie?" He had one fisted hand anchored on his hip, and his weapon in the other. He twisted his sword this way and that, studying its bloodied tip, and she knew he was thinking of ways to use it on her child.

It was the smile that did it, the suggestion that he'd very much enjoy what he was about to do to her baby. That, and the sight of Ren's bruised, blood-coated body lying so still in the bright sunlight on that dock. Rage took over, blotting out everything else.

There was a sound, a deep-throated growl,

like that of a killer wolf closing in on its prey. Only it was no wolf. The sound came from Annie. Her adrenaline surged and she levered herself up, putting all her weight on the side of the boat, tipping it up so high and so fast that Blackheart tumbled right over her head and into the lake.

There was a splash, a gurgle, and then, when his head broke the surface close beside her, a terrible blood-chilling scream. He tipped his chin heavenward, his mouth working, eyes rolling as he wailed like a banshee. His arms flailed frantically, and the veins stood out in his neck as if they would surely burst.

"Pure! The water's pure! It burns! Lucifer help me; it burns! It . . ."

The skin of his face collapsed on itself like melting plastic, dripping, then running down in rivulets away from eyes that turned to black smoldering bits of soot. Like a Popsicle in the sun, he shrank at high speed, until there was simply nothing left. Only a hissing sound and a black mist rising from the surface of the water in the spot where he'd been.

María had been right so long ago. And so had Sara, Annie realized. The lake was pure and contained a magic all its own. And for the second time, that magic had saved her.

And then the baby's head pressed through, and there was no time to marvel. She was giving birth.

Chapter Fifteen

❦ Ren moved his eyes. They seemed the only part of him he was able to move at all, and even they didn't seem to be operating at full power. His vision was blurred. His reactions slowed to a crawl. He had to think about changing his focus for long moments before his brain seemed to get the message to his muscles, before his eyes would actually move. So it took him a long time to find what he sought. Annie.

She'd pulled herself halfway out of the water and lay panting on the edge of the dock. With everything in him, he wanted to reach out to her, touch her, help her. But he couldn't move. Couldn't make a sound, lift a finger. Couldn't touch her or hold her or help her.

Ren knew he was dying. There was little doubt. And he knew that Sir George had no intention of pulling him from the jaws of death. Not this time. He'd broken his vows. He'd fallen in love with the woman all over again. He'd thought of nothing but her since he'd come here, and he'd been longing with every fiber of his being to find a way to stay with her. He'd put her first in his mind, his heart, his soul. Ahead of goodness, ahead of service, ahead of his word. And if given the chance, he knew he'd do the same all over again. Nothing worse than an unrepentant sinner.

Sir George wouldn't forgive that kind of disloyalty, even if he could. As he so often said, rules were rules. So Ren would die. Even now he felt himself fading.

God, please let Annie be all right. Please. And the baby. Let the baby survive!

She seemed to gather her strength as she lay there. Then she pulled herself more fully onto the dock. Moving as if every effort caused pain, she lay on her back, bare-legged. Her soaking-wet sweater reached to her thighs. She struggled free of her panties, gasping, panting, but with such a look of determination on her face that he marveled at it. So strong, his Annie. She braced her feet on the wet wood and bent her knees. Her face contorted as she groaned low and harshly.

And Ren saw the miracle happen before his eyes. His child, small and slick and misshapen, emerged from Annie's womb. From the haven of her body into the reality of the world it came. The savior of humanity. The greatest leader this nation would ever know. The one who would change the course of history.

A tiny, wrinkled baby girl.

Ren blinked. Yes. A girl.

The child lay still between Annie's legs. Unmoving. And Ren's chest filled with icy dread.

But Annie was too determined for that. She sat up a little, gripped the baby, and brought it up to lie upon her belly. Annie cleared the little mouth, smacked the tiny soles of miniature feet.

The sound was like the congested bleat of a newborn lamb—weak, tremulous, but getting stronger all the time—punctuated by strong gasps between each wail.

Annie's arms closed around the child. "You're all right," Annie whispered. "We did it, baby . . . sweetheart . . . you're really all right." She stroked the child, her very touch seeming to impart strength. "But Ren," Annie whispered, turning her head toward him. Her eyes found his. When she saw that they were open, she sighed her relief and smiled at him. "It's a girl, Ren. A little girl. Our daughter."

He tried to smile, unsure whether his facial muscles were responding. He couldn't feel much of anything now. Numbness settled like a shroud. He tried to part his lips, to tell her he loved her. But his voice seemed soundless.

And then he realized that the baby's cries had faded, too. And Annie's lips were moving, but he couldn't hear her words.

This was it, then. He was at the threshold of death. He'd been here before, but this time Ren knew of nothing that would stop him from passing over.

His eyesight blurred, and he blinked it clear again. Just a little longer, he prayed. Just a moment of joy with his wife and his daughter. Just one. He saw Annie crying, saw her hand holding his, but felt as if it were no longer attached. Only vaguely did he sense the barriers between the realms thinning. That shimmer that came into everything, even the air itself, while the invisible barriers between the worlds dissolved as if to let someone pass through. Was he about to be taken back to the other side, then? About to face Sir George and the results of his own disloyalty? Or was Sir George coming to him, perhaps to say goodbye?

And then he saw the little mark on the baby's neck, and he was stunned, even in the throes of death.

He looked at Annie. She hadn't noticed. She didn't understand. He had to tell her. Ren tried to summon the will to utter just a few more words before he left her forever.

* * *

"Ren..."

Annie turned to face him, reaching toward him with one arm while cradling her baby with the other. She could feel him slipping away, leaving her again. And she wanted to touch him, cling to him. She couldn't let him go. She wouldn't.

"Ren, don't! Don't leave us, darling. We need you, your daughter and I. Please, Ren, don't go!" Bracing her shoulder blades and flattening her feet, she inched closer to him, carefully holding the baby on her stomach. She reached out a hand, touched his face.

His still eyes parted, but only slightly. "Annie?"

Rolling a little toward him, Annie brought his hand closer and laid it over the child. "Your daughter, Ren."

He could see her, and he understood. Annie knew because his eyes had regained a tiny hint of their old sparkle when his hand touched the baby. It was the first sign of life she'd seen in them. Was there a chance? There had to be.

"My daughter," he whispered. He strained, the muscles in his corded neck standing out, the vein in his temple pulsing. Annie wasn't certain what he was trying to do. Then she saw. One of his arms had been dangling over the edge of the dock, his hand in the water.

The pure water, she recalled now. Sara had known about it. Sara had known, somehow, that Blackheart couldn't bear the touch of purity.

Ren strained to lift his hand, palm cupped full of the crystalline water. Slowly, agonizingly, he brought it closer and drizzled it over the wriggling baby's head, pouring it on her neck. The baby closed her eyes tight, scrunching her face up comically.

"My . . . daughter," Ren intoned, his voice holding only a modicum of its former vigor. "She is . . . Sara, Annie. Sara Dawn Nelson."

Annie frowned at his words. She knew Ren was fond of Sara, even though he'd met her only once. But fond enough to name his daughter after her?

There was something in his eyes. He didn't speak, only sent her a silent message. Annie looked down at the baby again, noting the pink skin on her face and neck, rinsed clean by the lake water Ren had drizzled there. She caught her breath. The birthmark was there, a perfect berry-colored crescent moon, high on the left side of the baby's neck. Just below her ear.

Sara Dawson . . . Sara Dawn . . . Nelson?

I was conceived here.

Yes, Sara had said that, hadn't she? And this baby had been conceived here as well.

"My God, could it be . . . ?"

She stared in wonder down at her daughter's face, the deep dark eyes and thick ebony swirls of hair. The serious expression. She wasn't crying. Just staring, taking in the faces of her parents as if she were filled with questions she couldn't yet ask.

"Sara?" Annie whispered.

"Yes, Annie," said a deep, gravelly voice. "It's her. I don't know how, but she saved you. And herself. She couldn't save Ren, though."

Annie's gaze snapped upward, and she saw Sir George, standing over her, staring down at Ren with the saddest expression on his face. His old eyes were dull, his lips downturned. He even seemed pale.

Half afraid to look, Annie turned to see Ren, so still, barely alive. It was obvious. She could almost see the life draining from him as he lay there. His eyes remained open, but the light in them faded rapidly, until they resembled worn denim more than the sapphires they'd once been.

His lips moved, but his voice was little more than a whisper. "I . . . love you . . . Annie. S-Sara . . . my Sara . . ." His fingertips flexed as if he wanted to reach out to touch Annie and the baby. But that was all he managed to move. His eyes fell closed.

"No!" Annie shook her head frantically. "Sir George, you can't let this happen! You can't!"

The old man bowed his head, and she swore his back stooped, as if bearing a great burden. "I'm sorry, Annie. I love him, too, you know. But he broke his vows. There's nothing I can do now. Believe me, I would if I could. He was my most beloved knight. . . ."

"You don't love him," Annie said, getting up to her knees, clutching her newborn daughter in her arms. "If you did, you wouldn't let him die! You couldn't."

"I'm sorry," he said softly. "But there's nothing I can do. He already died, you see." Sir George's voice was glum. Low. Toneless. "This is painful enough for me without your accusations, lady, though I understand your pain. Believe me, if I could save him, I would."

"He can't die," Annie whispered.

Sir George came forward, and she thought she saw a gleam of unshed tears in his eyes. He bent over Annie, touched the baby's face, and spoke in a voice as soft as the deep wind on a winter night. The baby gurgled and sang in reply. Impossible. She was only a few seconds old.

"Yes, you did well. You did well, little one. I don't know how, but you did. You're a special girl, you know. And I'm so glad my knight

... your father ... managed to save you. Despite the rest. I knew he would."

He looked at Annie again. "She has magic in her, this child of yours," he explained. "A will to live, stronger than anything I knew could exist. Somehow, she sent her spirit ahead of her, sent it to help you and Ren get through this."

Annie shook her head in wonder and bent to press a kiss to the top of her daughter's silky head.

Sir George touched the baby again, and little Sara shimmered like a heat wave. When the shimmers cleared, Sara was clean, and the cord that had attached her to her mother had vanished. The baby lay snugly wrapped in a downy blanket of purest white. When Annie gave her head a shake, she realized that she, too, was clean. And dry. And clothed in a white dressing gown that felt like silk.

"My God ..."

"I only wish I could do more for the two of you," the old man whispered. "And more for Ren. My finest knight."

"But he isn't your knight, is he, Sir George?" Annie said. "Not anymore. He broke those vows he swore to you, and that means he can't be your knight any longer."

Sir George nodded slowly. "Alas, it's true. If he were still my knight, I'd be using my heavenly magic to heal him." Sir George looked at Ren and closed his eyes. "I'm powerless to help him now." The man sounded ashamed of his impotence.

"So now he's just an ordinary man again," Annie said softly, leaning closer to her husband, brushing a hand over his forehead.

"An ordinary man who is dying," Sir George said softly. "He was killed eight months ago, Annie. When he gave his life to save a busload of children because he couldn't do otherwise."

"Please," Annie cried, tears flooding her eyes. "Please, there has to be a way. Think, Sir George, there must be something. . . ." Then she lowered her head as a sob tore from her chest. Her vision blurred, and her arms trembled with the weight of her daughter.

Immediately a cradle appeared beside her. Some antique work of art, all intricate carvings and obscure symbols. Sir George took Sara from Annie's arms and tucked the baby into the bed as gently as if he were handling a china doll. Then he turned to stare sadly down at Ren again.

"His mortal life ended. His mortal body died, Annie. I wish it were different, but—"

"No." Annie turned her head sharply, meeting George's eyes. "No, wait. His body . . . We never found his body. Sir George, why didn't we find him if he was truly killed back then?"

George blinked slowly. His brows lifted, and his eyes widened. "You're right," he said. "By almighty God, you're right, Annie. I broke my own rules back then. I couldn't wait to bring my most favored mortal into service as my first and most worthy knight." He licked his lips, a gleam of excitement lighting his eyes. "So I used my magic to pull him from the truck before it exploded on the banks of that river. His body was never found, his family never given the comfort of burying him . . . because . . . because, Annie, *he never actually died.*"

Though he spoke quickly, even while kneeling to move his gnarled hands over Ren's broken body, Annie found herself running out of patience with the man. But those ancient eyes met hers, and they were filled with hope—a hope that hadn't been there a moment ago.

"I . . ."

With the baby safely in the cradle, Annie turned her attention back to Ren. She crept closer to him, to cling to his hand as if she could keep him with her by holding on tightly enough.

"Don't leave me, darling," she whispered. "Please, Ren, hold on."

"He's an ordinary mortal man," Sir George was saying. "A man who never died in the first place, and so there's nothing stopping him from resuming his life with his beautiful wife and extraordinary daughter. Nothing stopping him," Sir George said softly, "except for mortal wounds that are even now drawing his life from his body. And I can't help him, Annie. The power to heal . . . it isn't mine to bestow."

Annie looked up, tears filling her eyes. "Maybe you don't need to bestow it," she whispered. "Maybe . . . the lake . . ." She bit her lip, glancing out over the clear blue water. "His mother always said there was magic in this water. That it was pure."

"Of course," Sir George muttered. "Of course! There are times when the magic of Mother Earth is what's needed. And this, perhaps, is one of those times." He shook his head. "I can't be sure it will work, Annie. Earth's magic only works for those most deserving. But it's the only chance he has."

He straightened then, and held his hands out over Ren's body. Annie felt her husband's all but lifeless form begin to vibrate, and she sat up, gasping.

Sir George knelt beside Ren, touched him, and began to push him toward the dock's edge . . . but then he stopped and closed his eyes. "I can't," he whispered. "I haven't the strength to risk it."

Annie stared down at the pallor of Ren's face. "I have," she said. And before she could change her mind, she pushed Ren's lifeless body with all her might. He rolled into the water with a splash and immediately sank beneath the deep blue surface.

And then nothing.

The lake stilled as if nothing had happened, as if a hero did not lie in its cold embrace. Annie stared into the depths, hands over trembling lips. "What if I was wrong?" she whispered. "Oh, God! I have to go in after him!" But Sir George's old fingers caught her gently by the wrist and held her utterly motionless.

"Wait, sweet Annie. If the lake's magic can heal him, it will be but a moment. And if it can't . . . if it can't, then this lake will be his grave."

Annie shook her head. "But . . . but . . ."

Sir George stared into the water where Ren had vanished. Annie sobbed, hunched on hands and knees, staring down at the ripples on the surface. Aching, dying inside with every second that passed. It was too long. Too long. He'd drown!

There was an explosion of water then, droplets surging upward and soaking Annie's face as Ren emerged. His head broke the surface first, chin down, and then he straightened, flinging it upward. Water flew from his golden hair, and Annie cried harder as she heard him draw a deep, gasping breath.

He stood there beside the dock and slowly opened his eyes. Bare-chested, water lapping low around his hips, he met her gaze. "Annie?"

"Ren?" His name was little more than an exhalation. She couldn't take many more surprises. But God, this was a good one. "Oh, God, Ren!"

He looked down at his flawless skin as if expecting to see the wounds and blood that had covered him only moments ago. Then he gazed back at Annie again and shook his head, lifting his hands palm up as if in wonder.

"It worked," Sir George said in a relieved sigh. Then he laughed aloud. "By heavens, it worked!"

As Ren stared at him, blinking in shock, Sir George stopped laughing. He bent slowly to pick Ren's sword up from where it lay on the dock. Then he straightened again. "Your wife's wisdom, or perhaps the strength of her love, seems to be stronger than even my magic, Ren. You're no longer a knight in my service. You're free of your vows to me. Free to live out your days as a mortal man." He lowered his head. "I'll miss you, Ren. But perhaps you'll return to me one day." George glanced at the sword. "I'll keep this for you until then."

Ren opened his mouth, a question in his eyes, but before he could speak, Sir George shimmered and then vanished, taking Ren's sword with him.

Ren blinked at the spot where Sir George had been, shaking himself. "I don't . . . I don't understand any of this," he said, and he pulled himself up out of the water and onto the dock. He pressed his palms to his temples, closed his eyes. "I'm no longer a White Knight. But I'm not dead either. And . . ."

"It's the lake," she whispered. "It's magic, Ren."

He nodded, met her eyes. "Just like Mother always used to say back when . . ." His eyes widened, and he gave his head a shake, then just stared at her. "My God, Annie, I remember. I remember everything! It's as if I'd never been gone!"

Annie slowly shook her head and tried to stifle the tears, without success. She had Ren's hands in hers. She was drawing him closer to her. He was helping her to her feet, pulling her near. She felt those strong arms come around her, felt her head cradled against his solid chest.

"It's going to be all right now, Annie. I know it is."

"Yes." She nodded, sobbing so hard she could barely breathe. "I have you back, Ren, and I'm never letting you go again! Not ever!"

His hands cupped her face, tipping it up, and he kissed her, hard and long and deep and endlessly. Then Sara cried, and they parted a little guiltily.

"Your daughter wants her daddy," Annie whispered.

Ren turned. A robe like the one Annie wore, only bigger, lay over the foot of the cradle. More of Sir George's magic, she guessed. One last gift from a man who hadn't lied when he'd claimed to love her husband as she did. She picked the robe up and handed it to her husband. He put it on. Then he bent and scooped little Sara up into his arms.

"An important little lady," he said softly. "Hard to believe such a mite of a thing will change the world someday." He lowered his head, kissing the tiny face. "I'll cherish and protect you always, little Sara." He lifted his gaze to Annie's. "And your mommy, too."

He pressed the baby into Annie's arms, then scooped her up into his. "Come on, my ladies. You both need rest and a nice warm fire and some major coddling. Mommy's been through hell today." He dropped a tender kiss on Annie's forehead. "Are you okay?"

"I hurt like you wouldn't believe, I'm exhausted, and I..." She smiled up at him. "And I feel better than I ever have in my life. I have you back. I really have you back."

"Damn right, you do."

"Oh, Ren, your mother is going to be so happy. But, God, how are we going to explain this?"

He shrugged, carrying her up the steps, crossing the porch. "You told me once that my body—God, it feels odd to say that—was never found. We'll have to say I was thrown clear and that I've been in a hospital somewhere, slowly recovering. And naturally, the second I was able to remember who I was, I made my way right back to my wonderful, beautiful, sexy wife." He kissed her once more.

"Now that Sir George and his magic are gone..."

"I suspect everyone will see me just the way you do," he confirmed.

Annie sighed in relief.

He opened the cabin door and carried her inside. But before putting her down, he strode right to the back and looked out the window. Annie followed his gaze out to the gentle waters of Mystic Lake.

"Thank you," she whispered.

Ren squeezed her.

"I love you, Ren," she told him.

"I love you, too," he said, and his voice was a bit coarse. "Just one thing, Annie."

"What?" She looked up, worried at his serious tone, only to see a hint of the old mischief in his eyes.

"Call me Richard."

Richard eased his wife, baby daughter in her arms, down from the gentle mare's dappled back, and carried them up to the glass-enclosed porch of his in-laws' home. Before he was halfway there, Georgette and Ira were gaping at him from the doorway, blinking in disbelief, both at the man they saw, a man they'd believed to be dead, and at the baby, safe and healthy in their daughter's arms.

"R-Richard?"

"It can't be. . . ."

He only smiled at them and kept to his path. They stepped aside to let him through, and he carried Annie inside, straight through to the bedroom, knowing exactly where it was. He regretted that he didn't see his mother, María, in her rocker on the porch as he passed. But maybe it would be better to see her later, break it to her gently.

When he pushed open the bedroom door, however, it was to see her sitting in a chair beside the turned-down bed, looking toward the open door as if expecting him.

"Richard?" she asked.

"Yes, Mother," he said very gently, and his throat tightened so much he couldn't say more. He stepped inside to ease Annie and the baby into the bed, then turned. "It's me."

Her fragile arms encircled his neck when he knelt before her. "I knew you'd come back to us," she said, and her voice was choked and coarse. "I knew."

He held the frail woman close, kissed her tear-dampened cheeks, and thought he was the luckiest man alive.

"I don't understand," Annie's mother, Georgette, said, bustling into the room. "How is this possible?"

"I was thrown clear when the truck went through the rails," Richard explained. "But I was still badly injured. Wandered off in shock and wound up in a hospital with no memory of who I was or what had happened." He turned to Annie. "But that's over now. Isn't it, Annie?"

"It's all over," she said. "And he's never getting away from me again."

"But where's Ren?" Ira asked.

Richard met Annie's sparkling eyes, and they exchanged a secret smile. "He had to leave. Look, you two," Richard told them, "it's a long story, and we'll have all the time in the world later. Right now, why don't you come and meet your new granddaughter?"

Georgette beamed, hugged Richard's neck, squashing María between them, then turned to gather Sara into her arms and fuss over the baby while Ira stepped up to the telephone to call for an ambulance. Eventually Georgette brought the baby to María and gently gave her over to the older woman's trembling hands.

"Hello, little one," María cooed. She cuddled the baby close. Georgette stood nearby, so Richard stepped away from them to sit on the edge of the bed and pull his wife, whose eyes were still brimming, into his arms.

"I love you, Annie-girl. I never thought I could love you more than I did, but being without you . . . well, it just showed me I could."

"I know," she whispered. "I know. We're so lucky, Richard. To have been given a second chance—and a daughter like Sara in the bargain."

Richard wrapped his arms around her, his precious Annie, the woman who'd refused to let him go. "Thank you, my love," he whispered. "Thank you."

Epilogue

ॐ It was that magical time between light and darkness. That twilight time when each breeze is a brush stroke that paints the sky a shade darker, when fireflies begin flitting like miniature animated stars, and when fairies are said to scamper through the forest.

The little girl dipped her toes into the edge of the crystalline water, touching the liquid moonlight, rippling its perfection. Then she raced away, ebony pigtails flying, four-year-old giggles ringing through the air. Her parents lounged in the new swing on the back lawn, their watchful eyes always on their daughter. She reached them, crawled up into her daddy's lap, breathless, still grinning. And though her smile was beautiful, they both saw the depth in her dark eyes. The underlying seriousness. She was called a genius by the experts who'd tested her. But to her parents, she was more than that. She was their little girl. She was their most miraculous blessing. The fruit of their boundless, limitless love.

Richard stroked the length of one silken pig-tail lovingly. "What's making my girl giggle so much?"

"I love it here, Daddy."

Tiny, chubby arms clung tight to his neck, and he bent to kiss her cherubic cheek. Then she squirmed from his lap to Annie's, which was not a long trip since their thighs were pressed together. "I don't want to go home in the morning. Can we stay a little longer, Mommy?"

"Well . . ."

"Please?" Sara batted dark lashes at her mother, and Annie found it just as hard to say no to her as it had always been.

"We'll see," she said, knowing already she would probably give in. Sara didn't enjoy crowds of other children overly much. Instead, she seemed to prefer the solitude of Mystic Lake.

"Okay." Sara jumped down, satisfied with that answer for now.

"Hey, slow down a minute," Richard said, stopping the imp in midflight by catching her tiny hand in his. And for a moment he paused, remembering a time when he'd wondered if he'd ever hold this little hand nestled in his larger one this way. He blinked a few times and cleared his throat.

Annie smiled, knowing exactly the kind of wonder he was feeling. It hit at odd moments. The awe. The gratitude. The overwhelming joy. She'd felt them often.

"What is it, Daddy?" There was an edge of impatience to Sara's voice. Just a hint.

Richard gave himself a slight shake. "I . . . just want to know where you're going in such a hurry."

Sara looked up at him, bit her lower lip, and dug the toe of one sneaker into the lush grass. "I . . ."

"You what?"

She drew a breath and lifted her dimpled chin. "I just want to play near the water. It's . . . different . . . from other water."

Richard lifted his brows. "How is it different?"

"You'll think it's silly," she said.

"I won't, Sara. I promise. You can tell me."

She looked up at him, dark eyes searching, probing his, and then warming with the love and trust she felt for her father. Her voice dropping to a conspiratorial whisper, she said, "I think it's magic."

Those dark eyes watched her father's face, awaiting his reaction. Richard didn't laugh, or even grin.

His eyes intent, he glanced around. "Really? What makes you think so?"

Assured he believed her, Sara grew more excited. She seemed to consider her answer, her small brows bunching up as she thought about it. "I guess it's just a feeling I have," she said slowly.

"Sounds just like the feelings your mommy always had about this place," he told her, glancing at Annie.

"Mommy thinks so, too?" Sara breathed.

"Sure I do," Annie said. "You'll have to ask Gramma María to tell you all the stories she told me when I was little, Sara. She knows everything about this lake, you know."

"Yeah," Richard said. "And I can tell you a story or two about it myself."

"Wow," Sara whispered, eyes round and wide with wonder.

"C'mon," Richard said, and he held that tiny hand a little tighter. "Let's go together."

Sara smiled from ear to ear. And ran off at his side, beaming adoringly at her father as he walked beside her, down to the shore.

Annie watched them go. She stared out toward the water's edge and dashed a tear from her eyes as she whispered a silent thank-you to Sir George, to the lake, to the universe itself.

The wind hissed through the pines, and she almost thought she heard an ancient voice ringing like a deep bell, breathing a gentle "You're welcome."